Switch Hitter

Roz Lee

DEDICATION

To all those who are afraid to be themselves.

ACKNOWLEDGMENTS

There are many people standing behind and alongside me who make it possible to bring my stories to light. First and foremost is my husband of thirty-five years. Never once has he complained about a late meal or voiced a doubt about my ability to succeed in the crazy world of romance fiction. His unwavering support is a gift beyond measure.

Standing with him are my children who are the light in my life. They've grown into the beautiful people I knew they could from the very beginning. They inspire me daily.

I am a storyteller at heart, but not much of a grammarian. This is no fault of the excellent teachers who gave it their all in an effort to make their lessons stick. The lesson I did learn was, if you can't do it yourself, hire someone who can. Many thanks to Laura Garland, my excellent editor, who must have been an English teacher's dream student. For her, the lessons stuck, and I couldn't be more grateful.

CHAPTER ONE

Bentley slipped on his shoes and straightened the hems on his dress slacks. He'd played a decent game, no errors, fielded two outs, and contributed a single, a double, plus two RBI's to the Mustangs' win. Not bad for a day's work. All he wanted to do now was go home, kick back a few brews then go to bed. With a little luck, Ashley wouldn't have to work late tonight, and he'd have someone to cuddle up to. He smiled to himself thinking of all the ways he'd like to snuggle with her, but she'd been working insane hours the last few weeks. The chances of getting to do anything with her tonight were slim to none.

A ripple of excited chatter near the door caught his attention. *Another reporter, most likely.* With one last check to make sure nothing was hanging out that shouldn't be, he slid his cell phone, car keys, and wallet into their respective pockets. Turning the corner at the end of his bank of lockers, he stopped. A group of players in various stages of dress clustered around a central figure. His heart stuttered. When it found its rhythm again, it took off like it had been zapped with a cattle prod.

Sean fuckin' Flannery. In the Mustangs' Clubhouse.

Stripping him in his mind, his memory filled in every detail hidden by the man's designer duds. The interloper looked up, those laser blue eyes meeting his. The air between them seemed charged with electricity. Bentley realized time and distance hadn't done a goddamn thing except maybe make him want the man more. Blood rushed south. His dick stood at attention.

I don't need him. I'm a man, not a fucking pervert.

He moved, intending to get the hell out, but Sean pushed his way through the group of players surrounding him. The bastard looked like a fuckin' cover model. An artful scruff of beard screamed testosterone overload, setting off his perfect facial features, making him look perpetually ready for bed. At just over six feet tall, he moved with the grace of a natural athlete.

I don't want him.

From the corner of his eye, he caught movement. The next thing he knew, a fist headed right at his face. Bentley ducked, causing the bastard's rock of a hand to connect with his eye instead of square in the middle of his face.

What the fuck?

Five years of fear, self-hatred, denial, and disgust bubbled to the surface. *I want him. I want to fuck his brains out—right here, right now.* He retaliated in a more appropriate way, given they were surrounded by people—he smashed the man's too perfect nose. Blood spurted like he'd smashed one of those little ketchup packets from a fast-food place.

Take that, you fucking asshole.

The man went down. Bent followed him to the floor where they rolled around, punching and cursing at each other like a couple of hotheaded adolescents. The bastard landed his share of blows to Bentley's ribs and stomach. Bent got in a few jabs of his own before someone shouted, "Whoa!"

"Hey!" Strong fingers closed over his forearm, yanking it back before he could slam his fist into the man's face one last time. "Break it up!"

Doyle Walker's voice felt like a bucket of ice water dumped over his head. Panting, he allowed his teammates to haul him to his feet. He stepped back a respectable distance. Someone handed Flannery a towel that he pressed to his nose.

I hope I fucking broke it.

"What's going on here?" Doyle demanded.

"Nothing," they answered in unison.

"It sure as hell didn't look like nothing to me." The Mustangs' manager looked around at the gathering. "Get out of here, all of you." No one moved. He pointed his index finger at the man who started the altercation. "My office. Tomorrow. Ten-thirty."

Bent smirked then Doyle turned to him. "You. My office, tomorrow. Eleven o'clock."

Well, shit.

Sean headed off in the direction of the restroom, the towel still pressed to his nose. Bent shrugged off the hands still holding him. Ignoring his teammates' curious looks and amused grins, he left.

Bentley gulped the beer, placed the empty bottle on the kitchen counter, and grabbed another from the still open refrigerator. The chilled air raised gooseflesh on his bare arms, but did nothing to cool his raging temper. Using his forearm to wipe the sweat from his brow, he slumped against the counter and raised the bottle to his lips. The frosty liquid went down smooth, providing a momentary distraction.

His eye socket throbbed where the son of a bitch hit him.

Unbelievable.

Closing his eyes, he brought the cold bottle to his temple, gently rolling it over the tender flesh around his right eye. The bruising was going to be epic in a few hours. *Just fuckin' fantastic.* With a little luck, he'd messed up Sean's face, too. The asshole was too damn pretty for his own good.

An image formed in his pounding head. His cock sprang to attention. His stomach churned. Why Sean Flannery? He'd never had any reaction to a man before, and he damn sure didn't want it now any more than he'd wanted it five years ago.

He rubbed his aching cock through his trousers. *Shit.* He'd hoped the intervening years along with the move to Dallas would have cured him of his perverse desires, but apparently, that wasn't the case. All Sean needed to do was look at him and he got hard. It was those damn blue eyes of his. They did something to Bent, made him crazy because they saw too much. Saw things no one else did, things that shouldn't be there in the first place.

Five fuckin' years since he'd left the Pioneers, and he still remembered the kick to the gut that sent him running as clear as if it happened yesterday.

The circumstances hadn't been unusual. Naked men in showers and locker rooms were a part of baseball, but they'd both been late leaving. He had no idea what Sean's excuse had been, but he'd spent too much time with the trainers after the game. The locker room was empty when, naked, he'd headed to the shower.

He always remembered the moment in slow motion as if it had been over too soon, when in reality it seemed like forever. The hiss of water spraying, the plop-splatter of large soapy drops hitting the tile floor, beckoning his tired muscles. As soon as he breached the curtain of heat and humidity, he stopped dead in his tracks.

Sean Flannery stood there with his back to the open doorway. Desire hit Bentley like a wrecking ball to his gut. Blood rushed to his groin, short-circuiting his central nervous system and robbing him of good sense. He couldn't move. His cock throbbed, demanding attention. He automatically fisted the heavy flesh, seeking relief he had no right wanting.

He watched, transfixed as Sean slicked his too-long black hair back from his face. Water sluiced over his muscled back forming a wide river running along the deep valley created by his shoulder blades. Bentley's gaze followed the stream down, down…down to the first baseman's tight ass. He couldn't look away, could only stroke himself, imagining what it would be like to touch his perfect skin, to slide his cock between those taut cheeks, to command and possess such a glorious creature.

He had no idea how long he stood there holding himself…staring, creating fantasy after fantasy in his mind of them together, fucking, kissing—doing every perverted thing he could dream up. But then the object of his desire noticed. Bent felt like a deer in headlights, the car speeding right at him a hundred miles an hour. He knew he needed to get out of its way or die, but he couldn't. The bright lights blinded him to the danger, held him enthralled, so deep down his fear became need.

When Sean twisted his torso, his chin skimming his shoulder like some fucking porn star, those goddamn blue headlights locked on him, he welcomed the head-on collision—anything to put him out of his misery, to end the sick, perverted thoughts running through his mind before he acted on them.

Sean took advantage of Bentley's paralysis, looking his fill, his gaze pausing on his fisted erection, which just made the damn thing grow harder. Without a word, Sean turned so the shower beat against his back.

Bentley's brain screamed, "Don't look," but the message from his cerebral cortex never made it to his eyes. His gaze traveled south. Water drops glistened on Sean's bronzed chest, clung to whirls of dark hair matted over flat copper nipples. A smattering of hair arrowed downward, drawing his attention to an impressive erection.

His mouth went dry. His cock throbbed in his fist. Warning bells clanged in his head. *What the fuck are you doing? Get out! Now!* His gut twisted. Forbidden yearnings heated his blood, tightening his scrotum. Sweat stung his eyes. He was one dying brain cell away from dropping to his knees and sucking Sean's enormous appendage into his mouth when the harsh clank of a door slamming nearby jolted him out of his stupor.

Fear of discovery doused his ardor faster than a cold shower. Breathing like a racehorse on the backstretch, he locked gazes with Sean who didn't seem in the least disturbed by the encounter. The bastard pursed his lips in a mock kiss then turned around to resume his shower as if nothing out of the ordinary had happened.

Bent's stomach heaved. Panic released a flood of adrenaline, loosening the shackles of desire binding his feet. Turning, he fled to the restroom where he bowed to the porcelain god until his abdominal muscles cramped and his head felt like it might burst.

Five years later, the memory still made him harder than cured lumber, striking fear in his heart. He'd asked to be traded the next day. Within a week, he'd landed in Dallas. He'd faced Sean on the field over the years but managed to keep his distance. Until today.

In an instant, everything he'd felt in the Pioneers locker room rushed back in a tidal wave of wretched need and sickening desire. He had no idea why the fucker swung at him today, but he had. The instant Sean's fist made contact with his face, something inside him burst loose.

Bent used the back of his hand to swipe at the tears streaming down his cheeks. Damn it. Fuck yeah. He'd wanted to hit Sean for years. Had *dreamed* of beating the shit out of the man. And, goddamn, it had felt so fucking good to touch him at last—to feel those muscles beneath him, the solid weight of Sean pressing into him as they rolled around on the floor.

After all the intervening years, not a goddamn thing had changed. He still wanted Sean Flannery.

He drained the bottle in his hand then opened another, slinking down to the floor, his back to the cabinets. Toeing off his shoes, he released his belt buckle with his free hand then fumbled with the zipper. His head hit the cupboard with a thump.

"Shit!"

Another long drag from the beer bottle then he gave in to his need. He worked his zipper down, sighing at the sheer relief of releasing his cock from its imprisonment. Drowning his desire with alcohol was useless. He'd tried it countless times since that day in the showers, to no avail. Desperate, he'd endeavored to bury his unholy need for Sean under a slew of women. One after another paraded through his life, until one, with her honesty and devotion, captured his heart.

Ashley made him forget about Sean. He'd even begun to think about marrying her, but hadn't yet gotten up the nerve to pop the question. Thank God, she wasn't home to see his sorry state or everything he'd built with her would be over.

Taking his dick in hand, he pumped, savoring the languid push and pull that couldn't make him forget, but would at least give him a few seconds of peace. He worked his cock, while at the same time he tried to numb his brain with legal depressants. Watching the purple head rhythmically peek through the ring formed by his thumb and index finger, he thought about the fight. God, Sean was in great physical shape. His abs were sculpted marble, his arms, solid muscle. Those thighs! Oh man. He'd imagined how they would feel five years ago, but now he knew. There was strength there.

Bentley spit on his palm. Moments later, he gave up on saliva as a lubricant and poured the last of his beer into his lap, the cold brew was no match for the flame burning inside him. Scrunching his eyes tight, he pulled is knees up, letting them fall wide. He increased the tempo. With every slap against his pubic bone, he imagined it was the sound of Sean's thighs slamming against his ass. The groans escaping his lips became his lover's. When he came, spewing cum over his dress shirt, the name on his lips was one he hated.

Ashley got home late—again. She'd been putting in longer hours at the office than Bentley put in at the ballpark the last few weeks, but she wouldn't have it any other way. She loved her job as the News Director for a major sports network. She was the first woman, as well as the youngest to hold the position. One day she hoped to marry and have a family, but she wasn't in a big hurry. For the moment, she was happy enough with the way things were. Bentley Randolph was everything she wanted in a man—smart, focused, and sexy as hell. What wasn't there to love about a professional athlete in his prime?

The Mustangs game had taken place earlier in the day. From what she'd heard, Bentley had played well, so when she walked in to find him sulking in his favorite easy chair with an ice pack pressed to the right side of his face, she panicked.

"What happened? Did you get hit by a pitch?" She dropped to her knees beside his chair, covering his hand on the pack with hers as if her touch could make him better.

"Nothing. It's nothing."

His sullen tone rocked her back on her heels. She dropped her hand to the arm of the chair. "Bentley. What happened to you?"

"It's none of your concern. Just a disagreement in the clubhouse. I'm fine."

She stood. "You don't look fine." She pried the ice pack away long enough to see the damage. His eye looked like someone had taken a purple felt-tipped marker to it. "You look like hell."

"Go to bed, Ashley. Okay? I want to be alone."

It hurt to think he didn't want her help, but then again, she had no experience with this side of her boyfriend. He wasn't the kind of man to get in fights. "I take it there's someone else out there in equally as bad shape?"

"I fuckin' hope so," he said.

"What's gotten into you?"

"Just leave me alone." Standing, he headed toward the kitchen.

She followed him, pouring herself a glass of wine while he refilled his ice pack with short, angry movements. She wasn't too happy herself. His rejection stung, but she wasn't ready to give up just yet. She sensed there was something more at stake here than him fighting in the clubhouse, but she didn't have a clue what it could be.

"Why can't you tell me what's going on?" Crossing her arms over her breasts, she propped her hip against the countertop to watch him.

"Because there's nothing to tell." He helped himself to a beer from the refrigerator then stalked back to the family room and his well-worn chair.

Leaning against the doorjamb where she could see the top of his head over the back of his chair, she sipped her wine and weighed her options. There was more to the story than he was telling, but if he wouldn't let her in, let her help, there wasn't much else she could do but let him work it out on his own.

"I love you," she said to the back of his head. "I'm here for you, Bentley, no matter what." When he didn't respond, she returned to the kitchen, emptied her glass into the sink, then headed upstairs to bed.

Let him sulk. But the fact he wouldn't confide in her hurt more than she could bear to think about.

The next morning, his side of the bed looked as if he'd been there, but she had no idea what time he'd come to bed or how long he'd slept. Glancing at the clock, she groaned. It was too early to be up on her day off, but Bentley had a game later. She wanted to see him before they went their separate ways for the day. Maybe he would be in a better mood this morning, more willing to talk.

Or not. She found him in the backyard, water hose in hand, tending his precious rose bushes. She liked roses as well as the next female, but Bentley babied these, especially when he had something on his mind. Having been raised on a farm, he said growing things relaxed him. It didn't appear to be helping today. His shoulders were tense, and in profile, his jaw was clenched tight.

"You keep working your jaw, you're going to grind your molars to dust," she said, approaching with caution.

"You're up early," he said, not looking up from his task.

"I have things to do. How's your eye?"

"I'll live."

She moved closer to look for herself, but he turned his face away. "Look, I'm just trying to help. Don't shut me out."

He twisted the sprayer nozzle to the off position before he faced her. His eye was swollen, the bruising was more colorful than it had been the night before. She'd seen worse, but not on him.

"I'm sorry," he said. "I know you want to help, but trust me, there isn't a thing you can do. It's over and done."

"You aren't going to tell me who you fought with?"

"No, I'm not. Can we just forget about it, please?"

She wasn't ready to forgive him completely, not yet anyway. "You aren't going to fight anymore, are you?"

"I didn't start the fight," he said. "I'll do my best to keep my distance. That's all I'm willing to promise."

"I feel like I'm trying to reason with a child. This is insane, Bentley. Grown men do not settle their differences with their fists."

"I'll be sure to bring your point up the next time someone takes a swing at me."

She groaned at his absurd remark. "Okay. Have it your way. I'm out of here. I have a million things to do today. I don't have time for pointless arguments."

"I've got a meeting in a couple of hours," he called after her. "I probably won't be here when you get back."

"Whatever," she mumbled, leaving him to work out his problems on his own.

The summons to appear in Doyle Walker's office wasn't unexpected. Management couldn't ignore violence. Hell, he'd been in the Mustangs' clubhouse all of ten seconds before he started a fistfight with another player. But damn it all to hell, why did the first person he laid eyes on have to be Bentley Randolph?

It was almost too much to bear, seeing him again in a locker room and remembering how Bent had walked out all those years ago. He'd asked to be traded! Hadn't even given them a chance, just walked away...no, make that *ran* away. As fast as his chicken shit legs would carry him.

God, the memory still hurt. Seeing him periodically throughout the years hadn't been near enough, but at the same time, it had been too much. How many times had he willed the Mustangs' left fielder to come find him after a game, but the damned stubborn son of a bitch never did. He'd known he wouldn't.

Bentley was a twisted fucker. He screwed every female who came within a half-mile radius, but the idea of being with a man he desired scared the shit out of him.

Fuck you, Bentley.

Sean hadn't asked to be traded to the Mustangs, had tried his damndest to keep it from happening, but he was here, and he'd be goddamned if he was going to pretend nothing happened between them in the Pioneers' shower. Even if it hadn't, the erection pressing into his thigh when they rolled around on the clubhouse floor the day before told him the man wanted him. That was something. If nothing else, Bent would acknowledge his part in the debacle. No way was he going to suffer alone. Not anymore.

Bentley had always made him a bit crazy with want and need, but he'd managed to keep it under control until one day five years ago. He'd thought everyone had already left, so he was taking his time in the shower when he'd sensed someone watching him. When he saw who it was, his knees almost buckled. Damn, the Pioneers' left fielder was built. That he'd stood there letting him get an eye full, stunned him, but he wouldn't pass on the opportunity of a lifetime. He'd seen bits and pieces around the locker room, but a guy had to be discreet. Ogling another player just wasn't done—unless of course he allowed it. Bentley more than allowed it. He'd all but begged Sean to satisfy his curiosity.

The guy hadn't tried to hide his erection or his open perusal of Sean's body, so he'd turned—let him see he felt the same way. It was risky, but Bent's openness had given him courage. Then the bastard ran, chicken feathers flying, he was out of there so fast. Out of the shower. Out of the clubhouse. Out of town.

Talk about fucked up. Classic denial. Lots of gay guys slept with women—himself included on occasion—but it didn't make them straight. Or maybe Bent really was bent. Could be he desired both sexes equally. He could live with him being bisexual as long as he could find a chick who didn't mind her guy having a man on the side. He liked watching hetero sex. Hell, he'd fuck Bent while his lover fucked a woman. He couldn't think of anything hotter.

But at the moment, there were other things to worry about—like explaining to Doyle Walker why he'd felt compelled to punch the left fielder's lights out, while managing to keep his ass off the bench in the process. Even more difficult, he had to accomplish the task without telling the team manager he would rather fuck the man than fight with him. It might be the twenty-first century, but when it came to sexual issues, professional team sports were pretty much stuck in the dark ages.

He couldn't tell the truth. *I took one look at those kissable lips of his, and all I could think about was five years of jacking off while imagining coming down his throat. I snapped. I was trying to rearrange his mouth, but the chicken-shit bastard moved so I clipped his eye instead. 'My bad?*

Yeah, that would go over well. He'd be playing single A ball on the Mexican border in a matter of hours. He needed to come up with a different excuse, one that made a shred of sense. Bentley would need to tell the same story. He might have gotten them into their present predicament, but it went back to the beginning, and that was all on the other guy. If only Bentley had just kept on walking back then. He never would have had the nerve to approach a guy on the team, much less one as heterosexual as Bentley appeared to be—not unless he was given encouragement. He smiled to himself, remembering. He'd had more inches of encouragement than most men could truthfully boast of.

They were in this together. They would get out of it together.

CHAPTER TWO

Sean rang the doorbell then took a step back. If Bentley wanted to try breaking his nose again, he would to have to come get him. He was through making it easy on the fucker.

Well before noon, the day was already hot. Heat shimmered off the curved driveway where he'd left his car behind another one. Probably belonged to some bimbo Bent was screwing. He didn't care as long as he didn't keep him waiting out in the heat forever. Hell, the place probably had security cameras, and Bent had no intention of letting him inside. It wasn't the end of the world. He'd find another way in.

He was about to go looking for a side gate when the front door opened. A woman with flowing brown hair, large, beguiling brown eyes, and long legs made longer by the short shorts she wore, stood in the doorway. No doubt Bent's flavor of the day.

"Yes?" she asked.

"Is Bentley here? I'm Sean Flannery from the Pioneers. I mean, the Mustangs." He smiled. "Just got traded the other day. I'm not used to the new situation yet."

"He's here." She scowled then waved her hand toward the back of the house. Grabbing a purse from the table in the foyer, she gestured for him to enter. "He's all yours, but I warn you, he's lousy company."

She donned sunglasses that almost covered her face then sashayed past him, leaving it to him to close the door behind her.

Lousy company. He smirked. "Ain't gonna get any better, sugar. I can guarantee you that."

For a moment, he stood still, listened, looked around. Why a single man had such a huge house, he had no idea. *Because he can afford it.* Bentley's financial status wasn't in question. He had buckets of money, thanks to the recent contract extension he'd signed with the Mustangs—ten years plus a figure with more zeroes on the end than he could count. He guessed it made sense to invest some of it in real estate.

The place was nice. It looked as if an actual human might have selected the furnishings as opposed to an interior decorator. A person could be comfortable here. He wouldn't have to worry about knocking something over every time he turned around. It was nice stuff, but it didn't look museum caliber. He'd give the owner points for that, at least.

There were a few paintings on the walls, but most of the frames held enlarged photographs—artful renditions of ballparks and outdoorsy places—rivers and such. He gave them a cursory glance as he moved past, deeper into the house. Every step he took, he was aware of the silence surrounding him. No television blaring. No stereo.

The woman who'd let him in had seemed to indicate Bentley was downstairs, so Sean ignored the staircase continuing on. Turning a corner, he stepped into the kitchen.

Damn. What looked like acres of granite countertops gleamed—not from polishing, but from lack of use, he guessed. The place was spotless, a gourmet cook's heaven. A bank of floor-to-ceiling windows looked out on the backyard. A low fountain trickled into a large swimming pool on one side of the enormous yard. The other side was grass edged with neat flowerbeds. Well-placed trees provided shade to that side, while a canvas cabana did the job for the pool. At the back of the property, sitting at an angle, was another structure mirroring the main house like a miniature reflection off the shimmering swimming pool.

Bentley was halfway down the grassy side of the yard, water hose in hand, irrigating a bed of rose bushes. Sean watched, taking the unguarded moment to enjoy the man's shirtless back. Tan cargo shorts hung low on his hips, revealing two dimples just above his ass. Hair a shade or two darker than the light brown on his head covered his calves. One of the fastest base runners in the league, his legs were sculpted and toned. His fingers itched to touch them, to feel the strong bones in his ankles, to suck his toes into his mouth so he could watch Bent's eyes roll back in his head.

Oh fuck! Get a grip, man. You're here to talk to him. Nothing else. Come to some sort of understanding, save your career then get the fuck out.

He wrestled his libido under control then stepped out into the yard.

Guilt nearly choked Bentley as Ashley walked away. She just wanted to help, but there wasn't a thing she could do. Telling her who he'd fought with would lead to why, and he loved her too much to put her through that kind of pain. He didn't understand his insane desire for Sean, so how could she?

You're better off not knowing, babe.

He made a mental note to adjust the automatic timer on the sprinkler system before his rose bushes dried up in the Texas sun. He'd spent too much time and effort on them to let them die He didn't know squat about landscape or interior design, but he knew what he liked. Roses. If doing so made him a pansy, well, so be it.

He aimed the hose at the last bush in the bed, frowning as the stream died to a trickle. Spinning around, he was prepared to yell at his meddling girlfriend, but the words died on his lips when he saw the man standing next to the outdoor spigot.

"What the fuck are you doing here?" he asked, crossing the yard in long, angry strides. He had to get him out of here. This was his home. His sanctuary. The last person on earth he wanted there was Sean Flannery. "How did you get in?"

He narrowed his eyes, looking for Ashley behind the glare of the glass partition. He hoped to God she wasn't there or he'd have to find some plausible explanation for the man's visit, and there wasn't one.

"Some cute thing in a hurry to leave let me in." He held his hand up about shoulder high. "About so big. Brown hair. Short shorts."

"She had no right." He pointed the hose in the direction of the kitchen. "Get out."

"Not until we talk, asshole."

"Asshole?" Maybe it was the heat. Or perhaps it was seeing this particular man in his backyard, on his turf, but he lost it. Dropping the water hose, he launched himself at his unwanted guest.

His abs still hurt from the punches he'd taken from the man the day before, but it didn't stop him. He swung with his right, connected with a wall of solid muscle in Sean's mid-section with enough force to garner a grunt.

"Son of a bitch." Sean swung his left fist.

Bent dodged just like he did the day before, his attacker's knuckles scraping along his jaw. He retaliated, aiming his fist at the purple bruise on the bridge of Sean's nose. His opponent ducked, came at him shoulder first, connecting with his solar plexus. Bent crumpled to his knees, clutching his stomach.

"Get up."

He fought for air, held up a hand signaling for a time out.

"I haven't got all day. Get u—"

Bent lunged, catching Sean at his center of gravity, toppling him to the ground. His victory was short lived. The first baseman grabbed for him, dragging him down to the grass with him.

They rolled around, two combatants with no skills for warfare. Punches missed their mark more often than they connected. Nevertheless, Bent did his best to defeat his opponent who was taller by a few inches—plus, he had a slight weight advantage. He punched, dodged then punched again and again, managing to elicit a few satisfactory grunts from the man when his fists found flesh. But it wasn't long before Bent found himself in an untenable position.

He spit grass out of his mouth while he struggled to buck Sean off his back. The larger man had him pinned face down, the full length of his body pressing him into the soft earth. A massive erection dug into the cleft of his ass through layers of clothing. His cock stirred. *Shit.*

"Get off me, you fucker."

"Not yet."

Bent struggled to breathe beneath Sean's weight. His sudden awareness of how close they were to doing something so foreign, so forbidden, yet so exciting, scared the living shit out of him.

"Don't," Sean whispered, his lips brushing the shell of Bentley's ear, sending a shiver down his spine.

Bent curled his fingers into the grass. He closed his eyes, surrendering to the inevitable. He was exhausted, had nothing left to fight with, physically or mentally. Whatever Sean wanted to do, he just hoped to hell he got it over with quick.

Gentle fingers traced his jaw, along his neck to his shoulder then down one arm. "I won't hurt you. Just let me touch you."

The anguish in Sean's voice mirrored what Bent felt inside, though somehow, he'd thought their situation was easier for the other man. Maybe not. Maybe Sean was as lost with what was going on between them as he was. He tried to even out his breathing, but each touch of the man's fingers on his skin stole oxygen from his lungs. Every movement was a reminder of the physical strength of the man atop him.

I can't do this. Oh, God, please. No. His mind screamed, but anticipation stilled his body.

"I've wanted to touch you for so long." Sean's left hand closed over Bentley's where he clutched the lawn while the other trailed over his shoulder, down his ribcage to his waist.

Holy shit. What they were doing was so wrong, but yet it felt good. Too good. His head buzzed with the pleasurable sensations.

Sean's fingertips slid into the no-touch zone. Panic warred with excitement. He wanted Sean to caress him there almost as much as he wanted his next breath, but at the same time, the idea of a man knowing him so intimately made him sick.

"Let me see you. I promise I won't do anything."

No. Yes. "No!"

Pressing him into the grass with one big hand in the center of his back, Sean sat up. Gut wrenching fear immobilized Bent more effectively than the knees bracketing his hips or the solid weight pinning his thighs.

He squeezed his eyes shut as long fingers curled beneath the waistband of his shorts and tugged. Warm summer air brushed across his clenched ass cheeks.

He forgot to breathe. Other men had seen his ass. Modesty had little place in a locker room. Locker room shenanigans never turned him on, but God help him, Sean looking at his ass in this forbidden way did. It excited him more than he would ever admit. Mortified at the need to grind his hips into the lawn to find release, he squeezed his eyes shut and ground his molars instead, silently willing his lower half to keep still. Heaven help him if Sean realized what was going on in his head.

Rogue tears irrigated the lawn. "Don't. Please." The words

came out as feeble admonition as well as unwilling encouragement.

"I've dreamed of your ass so many times."

Oh God. This can't be happening. Please, God. No.

"One touch. That's all. I'm sorry, Bent. I can't help it. I have to."

"No." His protest was moot.

"Shh."

Sean covered both cheeks with his hands. He squeezed—not a gentle squeeze, but less than bruising. Bent clenched his ass even tighter and prayed the earth would open up to swallow him. No man had ever touched him. He'd never wanted a man to, but dear God, Sean's hands on him felt good. His cock twitched, painfully erect, pinned between him and the ground.

"Please. Don't."

"Your ass is perfect, just like the rest of you."

He squeezed again. Bent's dick tried to dig a hole in the yard.

"I won't take what you aren't offering. I promise. I know you're thinking I'm taking something from you now, but I'm not. If you wanted me off, you have the strength to move me. Believe it or not, I didn't come here to rape you or to seduce you." While he talked, his fingers massaged and stroked, sparking equal parts of desire and fear. "I came because we need a story to tell Doyle. We need to be consistent. I don't think it's in our best interest to tell the truth."

He pried Bent's ass cheeks open, groaned, and let him clench them tight again. "So fucking beautiful," he said, running his fingers over the small of Bent's back, up to his shoulders then down again. "I'm going to tell him I owed you one because you stole my girl back in St. Louis. That's why I punched you yesterday. I'll say I got it out of my system, and it won't happen again."

While he talked, his hands roamed Bent's back down to his ass. His touch was firm, nothing like a woman's touch, but just as exciting. He was hard enough to drill for oil, but all he could think about was drilling Sean, and to his everlasting shame, letting Sean drill him.

"I'm going to leave now." After hefting Bent's shorts back into place, he leaned down, pressing their bodies together again. "I won't come back here unless you invite me. I won't make another move toward you unless you ask me. Think about what you want. You want the same things I do. I knew you did five years ago. But go on denying your true nature if you want to. I won't try to change your mind."

He lay there until the front door slammed followed by the rumble of a car engine in the distance. He rolled over, shielding his eyes from the sun with his forearm. His other hand lay across his chest, inches from his aching cock. Beneath his palm, his heart hammered and his lungs heaved with each labored breath.

He's wrong. I don't fuckin' want him. It's all some kind of aberration. I don't want a man. Not now. Not ever.

But he still felt Sean's hands on him. No matter how much he tried, he couldn't quit imagining how the man's massive cock would feel buried in his ass.

"Don't you have someplace to be?"

Bent jerked upright at the sound of Ashley's voice. "What?" he snapped.

"I said, don't you have someplace to be? I thought you had a meeting."

He squinted, shading his eyes with his hand. "What time is it?"

"Almost eleven. Are you okay? Why are you laying in the yard?"

Good question. Better yet, why am I lying here alone? "Come here."

He reached for her. She allowed him to roll her beneath him in the soft grass.

"Bent."

There was a question in her voice, but desire in her eyes. She had every right to question his motives after the way he'd treated her the night before and this morning, but he'd make her forget it all. Before she could question him or point out all the reasons they shouldn't have sex in the backyard, he crushed her mouth with his. He loved the way she was all hot, wet, combustible desire beneath him.

She's what I need. I want her.

Their tongues sparred. Her small hands on his shoulders were soft and arousing. So different from *his* he wanted to cry with relief.

I want her—not him. This is real. This is me.

He worked the fastenings on her shorts loose. In seconds, she lay exposed to him. Cupping her with his palm, he savored the feel of her soft mound. His fingers played between her legs, found her wet and ready for him. Love for her filled his heart. He swallowed hard to keep from drowning in the feeling.

"I love you, babe. I want you. Now."

Her legs spread, inviting him to take what he wanted. She

arched up, kissing his shoulder, his neck, anywhere she could reach. "I love you, too, Bent. Please…."

He plunged into her with an urgency he'd never known before. She gasped at the bold intrusion, but her hips soon found his rhythm. She moved with him, meeting his strokes with matching fervor.

Have to have her. Fuck her. Her. Her. Her. Mine. Mine. Mine.

She felt like Heaven, so fucking wet and hot. Nothing else could feel as good. Nothing. No one. No asshole could steal his breath or his sanity the way her pussy did. She was what he wanted, needed. What he *craved*.

He rode her hard. Each time he drove into her, the soft cries of pleasure she made erased a little bit of the memory of Sean's hands on him, of wanting to fuck and be fucked by him. Ashley was his. His future. The love of his life. He'd be damned if he was going to fuck it up because of some perversion from out of the blue.

He focused everything he had on her pleasure, reading her body movements, listening to the sounds she made for clues. She was always so responsive it made him feel as if he ruled her body, when in truth, it was she who ruled him. He'd do anything to see the look of wonder on her face when she came, to hear her articulate her pleasure with breathless gasps. He lived to feel her pussy tighten around him.

Reaching between them, he wet his fingers with her juices then found her clit, rubbing it in slow, firm circles the way she liked it. Ashley stiffened beneath him then, bucking wildly, she shattered. Her pussy clenched around his dick, urging him to come inside her. A ball of fire shot from the small of his back, rocketed through his groin then burst like flames from his cock. Grinding against her in short, hard thrusts, he claimed her.

He'd never been more grateful for the pill or a monogamous relationship in his life. Nothing else felt as good as coming inside Ashley. The thought of his seed swimming inside her filled him with pure male pride and satisfaction.

Wrung dry, he buried his face in the crook of her neck, drinking in her scent mingled with the smell of fresh cut grass and moist earth. Those scents, grass, earth…and another—Sean's—flashed through his brain. He jerked upright, rolling to Ashley's side, coming to his feet instantly.

He righted his clothes then looked at the woman sprawled at

his feet. Naked except for the red tank top hitched up on one side where he'd groped her breast in his fervor, she looked like a sexy pinup. She'd closed her legs, but her skin was still flushed from the sun and their exertions. One hand lay palm up in the grass above her head, the other lay on low on her stomach as if protecting the love he'd planted inside her.

"I want to have a kid." The words were out of his mouth before his brain had a chance to process the implications.

Her eyes popped open in shock, her mouth gaped. She looked at him as if she'd just woken up in the bed of a stranger and didn't know what to say or do.

"I want to make you pregnant." His cock stood to salute the idea. *See. I'm a red-blooded male. I found my woman, and I'm going to make damn sure everyone knows she's mine.* "Marry me."

"Bentley." She reached for her panties, pulled them over her calves then, rising to her knees, pulled them all the way on.

He clasped her raised hand, assisting her to her feet.

"What's going on?" She stood toe to toe with him. Her eyes were still soft from her orgasm. Crooking her index finger beneath his leather necklace he always wore, she drew him closer. "I enjoyed what we just did, but sex in the backyard in the middle of the day isn't like you. You aren't impulsive." She dipped her head to one side, studying him. "Does your sudden desire to go all caveman on me have anything to do with you fighting? Did the guy who came to see you say or do anything?"

"What we just did has nothing to do with anything else except our love. I love you, Ashley. I want to marry you." He shuffled closer, looped his arms around her waist. Tilting his head, he kissed the pulse point on the side of her neck. She melted against him, as he knew she would.

"I'm sorry about the way I asked. I should have given you flowers and sweet words, but there was something about the way you looked, lying there all rumpled and satisfied in my backyard. I knew I had to have you, forever. You won't deny me the pleasure of your company and your body for the next fifty years or so, will you?"

"Oh, Bentley. You know it's what I want, too, but kids? Pregnant? Those are words I never expected to hear from you. Marriage, yes. I figured someday you would come around on that one. But the others?" She shook her head. "I hoped, but I never thought I'd hear them."

He dropped his forehead to hers then bowed his hips away from hers leaving room to place his hand on her stomach. "I want to make a baby with you. Now."

She splayed her hand over the thick ridge behind his fly. "I see," she teased. "I don't know if I'm ready for kids, but I know I want them with you."

He was hanging onto the proverbial rope, grasping with both hands for something, anything to keep him from falling.

"You'll marry me?"

"Can we wait a while on the babies? My career...."

"As long as you want, but not too long, okay?"

"Not too long." Her smile lit her eyes. "Yes. I'll marry you."

Relief swamped him. He grasped the lifeline she'd thrown him, clinging to it with all his might. Pulling her close, he took her lips in a savage kiss of possession. Moments later, they were on the ground. Clothes were unwanted barriers discarded without a care.

"Mine," he growled. He held her legs wide, her hips on his thighs, her hair spread across the grass with abandon, her arms tossed above her head. She was so damned beautiful, she took his breath away.

"Mine." She opened herself to him, gave him everything, and she'd consented to take all he offered. She was *his*. She was going to have his kids.

Her scream rent the air, set the neighbor's dog to barking. He couldn't have cared less. With one last powerful thrust, he claimed her and the future he felt sure would save him from himself.

"Mine," he whispered, letting her legs fall from his grasp. "Mine."

They lay side-by-side on the grass until the neighborhood dogs quieted. His mind was clearer. He'd done what he had to do to make sure Sean Flannery left him the hell alone. He'd never regret marrying Ashley. She was everything a man could want in a woman, beautiful, smart, a match for him in bed, or the backyard.

"Why did you come back?" he asked. "I thought you were going to be gone most of the day."

"I forgot the clothes I was going to drop off at the dry cleaners."

Her doing his errands today confirmed how close they'd become in the last year. In truth, a signed marriage license wouldn't change much between them. Just the moving in part. She still had her own apartment, but she spent more time at his place than her own.

He grunted his acknowledgment.

"What did Sean want? It was Sean Flannery who came to see you, wasn't it?"

His mind flashed back to what Sean had done to him less than two hours ago on the very spot he'd asked Ashley to marry him and bear his children. Two mind-blowing orgasms with the woman he loved, but the mention of Sean's name still made his cock twitch.

"Yeah, that was Flannery. He came by to say hi. We played on the Pioneers together."

"That's nice," she said, dreamily. "You should invite him over sometime for dinner or something."

When hell freezes over. After pushing to his feet, he began gathering their clothes. "I've got to go. I'm going to be late for the meeting."

The drive to the stadium turned out to be a nightmare due to construction and impatient drivers. As he predicted, he arrived half an hour late. Cynthia, the team manager's secretary waved him in.

"He's waiting for you," she said.

Bentley wiped his palms on his pants, just then considering he should have worn something nicer than jeans. He was in enough trouble already. Looking as if he didn't take his career seriously wouldn't help his case.

"Thanks." After taking a deep, cleansing breath, he knocked then let himself in.

"It's about time you got here." Doyle made no attempt to be polite, remaining seated behind his desk.

"I'm sorry. I got a late start, and the traffic was bad." He crossed the room, not daring to sit until he was told. He felt like a kid called to the principal's office, sweating palms and all.

"Have a seat." He gestured to one of the chairs facing his desk. Bentley chose the one to his left. "What the hell happened yesterday?"

Wasn't that the sixty-four thousand dollar question? Swallowing, he launched into the lie Sean provided—the one he'd practiced on the drive over. "It's old news." He shrugged, hoping he appeared relaxed when every muscle in his body felt like it was attached to an electrode and the controls were in the hands of a madman. It was all he could do not to twitch.

"I may have dated someone Sean was interested in, back when I was with the Pioneers. I don't remember, but it seems he does."

Doyle leaned back in his chair, the tip of his pen between his lips while he studied Bentley. If only he was facing detention instead of a possible suspension or worse. If he'd been smart, he would have let Sean hit him and walked away. His own stupidity had gotten him here.

"I'm sorry. I shouldn't have hit him back, but he hit me first." Christ. He sounded like a snot-nosed teenager. *Keep your mouth shut. Don't offer anything. Just answer his questions.*

"That's pretty much what Sean said." The older man sat up, bracing his elbows on the desk. "What was her name?"

"Uhh…." Damn. He racked his brain for a name. Sean hadn't mentioned one, he was sure. "I don't know." He shook his head. "As I said, I don't recall anyone in particular."

Doyle nodded. "I imagined as much. You have quite a reputation, Randolph. I knew it when we bought your contract from the Pioneers, and I've looked the other way since you've kept your personal life out of the papers since you joined our organization."

There was a *but* coming….

"But I can't ignore your behavior yesterday. Brawling in the locker room will not be tolerated. I know you didn't start the fight, but you didn't stop it either. In my opinion, and mine is the only one that counts here, you're as guilty as Flannery."

A chill raced down his spine. *Fuck.* A suspension loomed over his head.

"Two things are going to happen here," the manager continued. "First, you're going to assure me there will be no more fighting in the clubhouse, or anywhere else. Second, you're going to sit on the bench for the next series."

Detention, adult style. He nodded, accepting what he considered light punishment. *It could have been far worse.* "I can promise you it won't happen again. I shouldn't have hit him back. If he leaves me alone, I'll do the same."

He stood, sensing he'd been dismissed. Pausing at the door, he turned. "I appreciate your faith in me. I'm not the man I was when I came to the Mustangs. I've been with the same woman for over a year. Just so you know, we're going to get married."

Doyle smiled. "I'm glad to hear it. Congratulations. When's the big day?"

"We haven't decided. Hell, I haven't even bought her a ring yet, but you'll be one of the first to know."

CHAPTER THREE

Sean took the long way around to his new locker. He'd hoped for a better start with the Mustangs than sitting on the bench for the first series, but as punishments went, he'd gotten off easy. After greeting the owners of the lockers flanking his, he put on his practice uniform, then headed for the dugout and his first batting practice with his new team. At least Doyle hadn't taken pregame activities away from him.

The summer Texas sun was unrelenting as he began his stretching routine. His ribs hurt from two rounds with Bentley, and his nose throbbed with every heartbeat. Both were constant, unnecessary reminders. Memories were all he had, and they never left.

Working by rote, he completed his routine despite the physical discomfort. He couldn't let anyone know just how bad the pain was or he'd be out on his ass before he ever played a single game. Playing hurt was something he was used to—hell, every athlete was, but he, more than most, made a career out of it.

Rolling to his right hip, he leveraged his body using a two-armed push to stand. His left hip felt like it was on fire. With hands raised above his head, he leaned to the right, stretching the muscles along his left side. He closed his eyes against the pain knifing from his hip, down his thigh then upward to his aching ribs. The injury he'd suffered sliding into second base four years ago had healed, but it didn't take much to aggravate it, and fisticuffs with Bentley amounted to a lot more than not much.

"You okay?"

Releasing the stretch, Sean straightened. Jason Holder stood before him, his brows knit with concern.

"Yeah, I'm fine. Just a little sore."

"You had quite a row in the locker room. I take it you don't get along with Bentley?"

Placing his right hand on his hip, Sean leaned into it—an easy stretch he could do without it pulling on his hip too much. "I owed him one," he explained, keeping with their fabricated story. "It's over now."

"Well, I hope so. We can sure use your bat in the lineup." Jason slapped him on the shoulder with his catcher's mitt. "Welcome to the team."

"Thanks," he called to the starting catcher's retreating back. At least someone on the team was glad to see him.

He waited for his turn to swing at a few pitches, managed to hit some without collapsing in pain, then headed for the locker room. Being one of the first back in, he showered then put on his uniform before most of the team finished batting practice. Since he would be warming the bench, he'd done enough. Maybe by the time his sentence was over, he'd be in good enough shape to play.

Wandering out to the dugout, he sat on the wooden bench. Damn. He hadn't considered how sitting on a hard surface for hours would feel. Standing, he leaned against the rail, letting his right leg take most of his weight. After the home series, the team would be on an extended road-trip—three cities within ten days. He had to be better by then because traveling was difficult enough when you weren't a physical wreck.

"Flannery," Doyle greeted him.

"Hey." Sean lifted his chin. "How's it look?" he asked, referring to today's match-up against the Angler's.

"We should win today. Rodgers has been pitching well for us, and he has a good record against the Anglers."

Nodding, he moved to a shadier spot. "Yeah, he has. I sure as hell can't hit against him."

"Well, thank goodness you don't have to anymore. I wish I could put you in. We could use your bat. They're pitching Roebuck today."

"I think half my homeruns have been off him."

Doyle laughed at Sean's statement. "You've had your share." His smile died. "You sure you and Randolph can get along on the same team?"

"Positive."

"News to my ears." The team manager hung the clipboard containing today's lineup on the back wall then returned to the clubhouse.

Sean folded his arms over the top rail of the dugout fence then rested his chin on top. No one had to tell him the Mustangs were his last chance. Since leaving the Pioneers four years ago, he'd been traded two times. If he blew it here, his career was over.

Several more players entered the dugout. Resuming his seat on the bench, he fell into the general camaraderie. Most of them had been in his shoes, new guy on the team in the middle of the season, so they made him feel welcome. He laughed off a comment about restricting his swinging to the batter's box then looked up to see Bentley Randolph step out of the tunnel leading to the clubhouse.

The object of all his fantasies accepted good-natured ribbing from their teammates, then as if to prove all was well, or maybe because they were the only two in time-out, he walked over to where Sean had staked out a place on the bench, and sat.

"See?" he announced to the dugout, "no problem. We're pals now." He half turned to face Sean. "Right?"

"Right. Pals," he confirmed. He flashed a smile Bent's direction then focused on the pregame activities taking place on the field.

Shit. He had to concentrate on something other than the way the man sitting beside him smelled—like fresh soap with an earthy scent unique to him. He especially needed to think about something besides the way the shadows in the dugout made Bent's eyes look like dark lakes and his full lips appear a deeper rose than usual. So damned kissable. He ached with the need to taste him, right here, right now—the whole world be damned if he did.

The team took the field for the national anthem. Afterward, Sean chose to stand at the fence, hoping being close to the action would help, but all he could think about was Bent sitting on the bench behind him. They were trying too hard to make it look like everything was all right between them when nothing ever would be. Bentley wasn't going to acknowledge his feelings, and he'd promised his teammate he wouldn't push him to. Shifting his weight to his right leg again, he forced his brain to focus on the game in front of him.

After seven innings, the Mustangs were up by three runs and the atmosphere in the dugout was guarded joviality. Spirits were high. When Jason Holder added a two-run homer in the bottom of the eighth inning and his brother Jeff came out of the bullpen to seal the deal, Sean found himself caught up in the moment. For the first time since he heard he'd been traded to the Mustangs, he felt as if it might work out. All he needed to do was focus on his job, shove his personal life back into the closet where it had been until Bentley walked in, opening the door, and everything would be okay.

Simple.

He'd spent three days looking at Sean's ass while his own squirming backside rode the dugout bench. With a smile pasted on his face, he congratulated his teammates on their successful three game sweep against the Anglers, all the while he seethed inside. In a profession where there was always someone younger, someone eager to make his mark, a player couldn't afford to sit out a single game, much less an entire series. Over the three game home stand, it was obvious Rick Powers was capable of playing left field with the big boys, and he would smile while he did it for millions less than Bentley's contract.

Bentley kept his morose thoughts to himself as he packed for the road trip. No need worrying Ashley. She'd bought the same story he'd told team management to explain what happened in the clubhouse, and as far as she knew, a three game suspension would be the end of it.

He knew better. The media was having a field day with the unexplained benching, speculating on what had caused the Mustangs to discipline two seasoned veterans. Bruising on both their faces led to mostly accurate speculation about some kind of physical altercation, leaving the reporters shaking their heads as to a reason behind it.

"You'll be back on the field tomorrow, won't you?" Ashley handed him a stack of folded briefs to add to his suitcase.

"Yeah, I will. Doyle said three games."

"That's good." She returned to the dresser, pulling a drawer open. She counted out the number of socks he would need. Juggling them across the room, she dumped them unceremoniously on the bed.

"Thanks."

"No problem."

She was doing it again—that thing she did when she was pissed at him. It was far from yelling and screaming, yet it wasn't the silent treatment either. She talked to him, but in clipped, coldly formal sentences. It drove him nuts.

"Just say what you want to say," he said, halting his packing to confront her.

She folded her arms across her breasts and glared at him. Brittle silence descended on the room, broken only by the distant hum of the air conditioning unit straining to keep the Texas heat at bay. Cold sweat formed on his nape but he refused to look away.

"I want to know what's going on with you."

"I'm going on the road." He gestured at his half-packed bag. "That's what's going on."

She sighed then, like a popped balloon, dropped to the edge of the bed. "Bent," she implored, "I know something is wrong. I've known you long enough to know when you aren't telling me everything. Something happened with Sean Flannery, and I want to know what it was."

"Nothing happened. He's new in town. He came by to get some advice on where to look for houses."

"He's been traded enough to know the relocation service can help him find a place. Even if he did come here for help, why you?"

Bent shrugged. "I don't know. We played on the Pioneers together for a while. I guess he thought he could trust my judgment."

"So, he comes over to ask advice then, as soon as he leaves, you decide you want to get married and have kids."

One of the reasons he loved Ashley was because she wasn't stupid, but right at the moment he would give almost anything for her to be at least a little oblivious.

"He'd been gone for a long time when you came home. It might have seemed sudden to you, but it wasn't to me. I've been thinking about marrying you for a few months.

"But you hadn't bought a ring, or planned something romantic for your proposal?" She held one hand up, her high ponytail swishing over her shoulders as she shook her head. "I'm not buying it. Impulsive is not your style."

"Maybe I'd been out in the sun too long. I don't know, Ashley. I'm sorry I wasn't eloquent or romantic, but none of it changes the facts. I do want to marry you and have kids. I was being honest with you."

"I know it is. I wouldn't have said yes if I thought otherwise, but ever since you came home with a black eye, you've been keeping something from me. You won't tell me how you got it, or why you were fighting. I love you, but I feel like you're keeping secrets from me. I don't like it."

"The black eye was nothing. I told you it was just a clubhouse disagreement."

"That got you benched for three games! You and Sean Flannery."

Bent pressed his lips together, refusing to acknowledge the truth of her statement.

"Go on. Pack." She waved her hand at the gaping luggage. "Go on the road. Leave the ignorant little girlfriend behind to worry about you."

Tears welled in her eyes. Her lower lip trembled. *Shit.* He walked around the bed, holding his arms open for her. She walked into his embrace, wrapping her arms around his waist, then proceeded to sob against his shoulder.

He hated her tears. He never knew what to do to make them stop.

"Babe. I'll be fine. No more fighting. I promise." He hoped to God he was saying what she wanted to hear.

"Use your words, not your fists?" She snuffled into his shirt.

That's more like it. Smiling, he kissed the top of her head. "You know, you're going to make a wonderful mom."

"You think so?"

She hugged him tighter, her feminine frame feeling good pressed against his length. He stroked her back with one hand while he held her close with the other.

"I know so. You're intuitive, loving, wise, and protective."

"I don't want you to get hurt. I hate seeing your face bruised up. I wanted to hit someone myself."

He chuckled, imagining her fighting off bullies for him. "It won't happen again," he promised.

Her hands slipped down his back then inside the waistband of his shorts. His cock, half-alert already came to full attention as her hands played over his bare skin, kneading, exploring. So different from the way Sean had touched him, but just as arousing.

He pushed thoughts of big, callused palms and blunt fingers out of his mind to focus on the woman in his arms. He wanted her and no one else.

Leaning forward, he brought his face even with hers. "I want you."

Her lips opened, invited him in. He accepted the invitation, covering her mouth with his, plunging his tongue deep to taste her.

She intoxicated him, made his cock swell and throb with need. Her fingers found his cleft, played there a bit though her arms weren't long enough to allow her better access. He flexed those muscles, startling a groan from her.

He held her close with a hand pressed between her shoulder blades while his other one snuck between their bodies to stroke the satin skin of her stomach. Inching lower, his fingers found her soft mound, then lower, her moist slit. She writhed against him, encouraging him to explore deeper. Blood rushed to his groin, making him lightheaded, desperate.

"I need you. Now," he said. Pulling his hand free, he created enough space between them so he could work the fastenings on her clothes.

Her fingers were as eager as his until just his T-shirt remained. Reaching over his shoulder, he fisted the fabric and yanked it over his head.

Fusing their bodies tight, he kissed her. Her lips were pliant, responsive. She might be furious with him, but she wasn't resisting. Lifting her, he laid her on the bed beside his open valise. God, she was beautiful. How could any man ask for more? She spread her legs, inviting him into her heat. He drove into her again and again, cherishing everything she was to him—lover, friend, a piece of his heart.

Sweet heaven. His mouth feasted on every part of her he could reach, his hands memorizing every place they touched, startling muted gasps from her lips. Bracing himself, he rose above her, changing the angle of entry. She adjusted, rocking her hips up to meet his thrusts, her neck arched. Gasps turned to moans that were like gasoline thrown on the flames of his desire.

She reached for his hips, grasping for purchase as he rocked between her soft thighs. Digging her fingernails into his flesh, she held him fast. Answering her demand, he thrust harder, faster. He recognized the signs of her impending release—the tensing of muscles, the moment of stillness when it overtook her.

"Yes," he growled. "Give it to me, babe."

Panting, she bucked beneath him. Her hot sheath clamped down on his cock, blinding him to everything but the feel of her surrounding him, drawing on his flesh, stealing his sanity and his control.

As her orgasm eased, tension ebbed from her and, seemingly, into him. Collapsing on top of her, he reached under her, angling her hips to take all of him. Her hands fell away from his ass to lie limp at her sides. Her breasts pillowed his chest, her thighs cradled him as her contented sighs urged him to his own release.

Fire consumed his insides, licking along his spine all the way to his groin. With short, hard thrusts, he ground against her. He spilled his seed inside her in great, wrenching spurts. He'd never loved her more.

"Mind if I sit here?" Sean indicated the last empty aisle seat on the plane.

"Help yourself." Tanner Haversford, the single occupant of the row of seats said, turning back to peer out the window.

After folding himself into the seat, Sean fished around for the ends of the seatbelt. Tanner didn't appear to want company, and truth be told, he wasn't feeling too sociable himself. His hip hurt like a son of a bitch, thus the reason he wanted an aisle seat—more room to stretch his leg out. He couldn't tell anyone or he'd go straight to the Fourteen Day Disabled List before he'd played a single inning in a Mustangs uniform.

A short time later, the plane lifted into the air. Reclining his seat, he stretched his leg into the aisle then closed his eyes.

How had his life gotten so fucked up? One day he had a promising career in the Major's, and the next, he was moving from team to team faster than a tournament ping-pong ball, doing his best to forget the one man he thought might be his soul mate if not for the man's homophobic tendencies.

His professional fortunes had turned on one bad slide intended to break up a double play then his personal life had slid down the drain of a locker room shower—all in the span of a few months.

Pathetic.

He'd held it all together for the last five years, but he could feel it slipping away since his trade to the Mustangs.

This is your last chance. Gotta get it right here or your career is over.

A sharp pain shot from his hip to his ankle. Shifting his weight, he prayed no one had noticed the grimace he was sure made it to his face. He opened his eyes, scanning the rows around him. Everyone was wrapped up in their own little worlds. He noted a few reading books and magazines. Others tuned out the engine noise with headphones connected to iPods. No one was paying any attention to his discomfort. Even if they did, he could blame it on the seating.

They aren't any more comfortable than I am. Damned cramped rows. Just once, I'd like to play for a team with their own plane. I bet the Yankees don't have to put up with this shit.

He squirmed some more, found a better position then relaxed again. A couple more hours and they'd be in Los Angeles. Tomorrow he'd be on the field for the first time as a Mustang. Closing his eyes once more, he tried to visualize a positive outcome. It wasn't as if he was totally washed up. He was damn good at first base, and his batting stats were decent. He wouldn't be hitting in the top of the order, but he was okay where he was. He'd never hit leadoff or clean up—had never wanted to. Too much pressure.

Middle of the lineup is fine. I know what's expected of me there. Move runners over. Get on base if you can. Make the pitcher work to get you out. All doable. Even banged up. Piece of cake.

If only he knew what to do about his personal life.

Nothing you can do. It's his play now. He knows how you feel.

No. He knows you want to fuck him, but that's all he knows.

You should have told him.

I couldn't tell him. Just touching him scared him out of his mind. Imagine if I told him the rest.

You still have to work with him.

I know. If there was any other way…. But there isn't. I made him a promise, and I'm going to keep it. I just hope to God he stays the fuck away from me.

CHAPTER FOUR

Bentley shrugged, gave his neck a good twist left, then right, to release the tension. Lifting the bat, he stepped into the batter's box and dug his cleats into the dirt. It took every bit of his self-control to keep from looking over his shoulder at the man standing in the on-deck circle. Why, God, did Sean Flannery have to bat next in the order? Wasn't it enough he was on the field nine innings every fucking day?

It was a long way from left field to first base, but as far as he was concerned, it was too damn close. Fucking first base saw a lot of action during a game. He couldn't just ignore it, or the man whose job it was to defend the square rubber milestone—no matter how much he wanted to.

They were three games into the road trip, with six more to go in two more cities. Which meant Sean was everywhere. Their rooms were on the same floor of the hotel, and if he didn't know better, he'd swear the man was stalking him. He always managed to show up at the bank of elevators at the same time Bent did—as if the guy had inside information about when he was leaving his room. Some of it was to be expected. The team had arranged catered meals for everyone in one of the hotel banquet rooms. Players could take it or leave it, go out on their own, but more times than not if a person wanted to eat, it was better done in the private room where fans and the press weren't allowed.

This morning, out of desperation, he'd ordered room service. Eating alone in his room was better than being in the same room with Sean. Today's breakfast was the first decent meal he'd had since they arrived, because his stomach tied itself in knots whenever Sean was around.

Like now.

Fuck.

The first pitch came in fast and perfect, breaking inside just as he swung. The bat sliced the air, too high.

Hearing the stinging slap of the ball hitting the leather catcher's mitt then the umpire's inevitable call, "Strike!" brought a curse to Bent's lips.

Outside the box, he wiped sweat out of his eyes with his sleeve.

Focus. Runners on. Bring 'em in.

He went through his batting ritual before stepping into the box again. His shoulders felt like they were caught in a vise.

Relax.

Forcing his shoulders to loosen, he concentrated on the next pitch, watched it follow the same trajectory as the previous one— only there was something different. Disbelief paralyzed him for a nanosecond. Adrenaline shot through his system. He swung.

Thwack!

Vibrations shimmied through his hands, along his arms to the rest of his body. Time slowed. Dropping the bat, he took the first step toward first base—in no hurry as the ball sailed high and long. Deafening silence cloaked the stadium, the crowd holding their collective breath.

The ball cleared the right field fence, dropping into the grasping hands of some lucky spectator.

Yes!

Bentley smiled as he circled the bases, vaguely aware of the jeering crowd, save for a few Mustangs fans who celebrated with him. Rounding third base, he jogged toward the small clutch of players waiting for him at home plate—Todd Stevens and Jason Holder who had been on third and second, respectively. There was one more waiting for him. Sean Flannery had come over from the on-deck circle to take part in the celebration.

A jolt of elation at seeing him there, a big smile on his face, made Bent shit-faced happy for a split second before he squashed the feeling.

As soon as his foot touched home plate, he raised his hand to accept the round of high-fives from his teammates. He would have looked like a total ass if he hadn't slapped palms with Sean, too. Their hands met in mid-air, but instead of a quick slap, Sean wrapped his fingers around Bentley's hand, turning the celebratory smack into a masculine caress.

To everyone watching it appeared normal, but there was nothing normal about the sizzle of lust the first baseman's touch incited. Bent looked from their clasped hands to the other man's face. Their gazes met, held for a second before Sean looked away, Bent saw something that rocked him to the core. Not just lust, but something more—a depth of understanding beyond the physical. Yeah, the other guys understood the elation, the excitement, the pride in what he'd done, but they had their own agendas. Ashley, too, would be proud of him, but her understanding was limited. She didn't play the game. She couldn't know what it meant to him to achieve his level of success.

Sean did. He'd seen it in the other man's eyes. The man had been genuinely happy for him. No professional jealousy. No envy. Just pride and a wealth of understanding with no hidden agendas.

As much as the knowledge frightened him, it warmed him, too. He'd never had such a connection with another person. Maybe if he'd had a brother like Jeff and Jason Holder had each other. They both played, and he'd never gotten a whiff of any jealousy between them. But he'd grown up with one pesky little sister who did nothing but complain about having to go to his games.

He accepted congratulations from his teammates in the dugout, racked his helmet and batting gloves before taking a seat on the far end of the bench. Dispensing himself a cup of water from the cooler next to him, he drank it down.

A gap between players standing along the dugout fence allowed him to see Sean in the batter's box. The count was already one ball, one strike on the batter. A lefty facing a left-handed pitcher. Too bad Sean wasn't a switch hitter like himself. Didn't matter if the pitcher was right or left-handed, Bent could switch sides of the batter's box without skipping a beat.

"Strike two," the umpire called.

An invisible cord pulled Bent from the bench to the fence. He curled his fingers over the top rail. Sean appeared relaxed going through his pre-batting ritual.

One foot in the box, one out, Sean adjusted his grip on the bat then looked toward the dugout. His gaze landed on Bentley. Time stood still for the space of a heartbeat. The noise of the crowd faded away. There was no one else, just the two of them locked in silent communication.

Come on, Flannery. You can do it.

Sean stepped into the box and turned his attention to the pitcher, breaking the spell or whatever it was passing between them.

Bent's head spun. He clutched the rail with a white-knuckled grip to keep from tumbling off the low wall supporting the fence.

What the hell just happened?

Shaken, he focused on the field.

Nothing. It was nothing.

The pitcher wound up, threw the ball. Bent recognized the instant Sean made the decision to swing. His gut clenched. He knew a moment of terror, understood the exact feeling his teammate experienced as they both realized he'd swung too high.

Smack! The ball landed smack in the center of the catcher's mitt.

"Steeerrrriiiike Three!" The ump, emphasizing his words with a fist jab.

Sean's chest rose then fell. Raising his chin high, he strode to the dugout.

Dignity in the face of defeat.

Pride swelled in him as he watched the conquered batter retreat. Had he ever shown as much grace after striking out? No, he didn't think so. He was more prone to curse under his breath, shake his head, or glare at the umpire. Sean, doing none of those things, appeared the epitome of the professional baseball player.

The railing cleared as players gathered their gear to take the field for the bottom of the inning. There was a lot of shuffling around as they found their caps and gloves. Sean trotted up the dugout steps to the field, stopping at first base. As Bent passed him on his way to his position in left field, he slapped the newest member of the team on the ass with his glove.

Sean froze. Ass slaps were commonplace in baseball and could mean anything from, "Cheer up, man," to, "Nice job." Under these circumstances, it could only mean one thing, "You're a screw-up."

But when he turned to see who had done the deed, he wasn't so sure.

Even if to chastise, the gesture was often in the spirit of camaraderie. Being chummy was the last thing he expected from the Mustangs left fielder. So what had Bentley meant by it?

The question puzzled him throughout the remainder of the game. As usual, the left fielder ignored him off the field, acknowledging him on the field only when necessary to a play, which was unusual between their two on-field positions.

For a split second before he'd stepped into the batter's box for the final pitch, he'd locked eyes with Bent. Something had passed between them—no doubt a hex to make him swing and miss, but it had felt like something more. Wishful thinking on his part. He was sure of it now. The butt swat had been a, "See. I made you do it," swat—nothing more.

But still. It felt like more. He couldn't explain it, it just *was*.

Following the game, the team went straight to the airport to board a plane for their next destination. Bent kept his distance, as he had ever since Sean had taunted him at his house. The behavior was to be expected, but after the two instances during their game today, the cold-shoulder treatment was somehow more brutal, more hurtful than before.

It seemed the tables were turned. Bent was taunting him, and there was nothing he could do about it. He'd told him he wouldn't pursue a relationship, any movement toward one would have to come from him. Even though Sean wanted to believe those moments during the game were overtures of sorts, they weren't the kind he could act upon. No, if the man wanted something more, he'd have to come right out and ask for it.

Hell will freeze over first.

Waiting, along with about half the team for an elevator at their new hotel, Sean watched as the first car to arrive filled. He hung back, preferring to wait for the next one rather than share a crowded cubicle with the one man he couldn't get out of his system.

The doors were closing when Todd Stevens stuck his arm out, forcing them open again.

"Flannery," he said. "Get in here."

"I'll wait," he said.

"It's late, and we have an early game tomorrow. Get your skinny ass in here."

The Mustangs third baseman wasn't going to take no for an

answer. Painfully aware he was still the new guy on the team, Sean wedged himself into the ornate box.

"Thirty-four," he said.

"Already punched."

The press of male bodies did nothing for him, save the one squashed in the back corner. Even if he hadn't seen him, he would have known he was there. He always knew when Bentley was nearby. The constant knowledge was his own private hell.

After a few stops, the crowd had thinned somewhat, and he breathed a little easier, able to move without bumping into someone. He watched the floor numbers light up as the car climbed upward. The car stopped at the thirty-fourth floor.

"This is me," he said, stepping out. "See you in the morning."

He paused, looking for the placard indicating in which direction he would find his room.

"This is me, too."

Bentley.

Shit.

Locating the sign, he prayed their rooms were on opposite ends of the corridor. He took off just as the elevator doors swished shut.

"Hey, Sean," Bentley called out.

He stopped, glanced at the ceiling, silently blaming the universe for conspiring against him. Taking a deep breath to steady his nerves, he turned to face the love of his life. "What?"

Bent checked the hallway before he spoke. "Can we talk?" He shifted on his feet. "I know it's late, but what I have to say won't take long. A minute."

"We can talk here."

He shook his head. "My room or yours?"

"I have a roommate."

"Mine then." Turning, he headed in the opposite direction.

Sean fell in step behind him even though every cell in his body knew it was a bad idea. Nothing good could come from a conversation between them.

Stopping at a door mid-way down, Bent inserted his key card. When the green light flashed, he pushed the door open. Like a starved puppy, Sean followed him inside. The door clanged shut behind him.

"How do you rate a single room?" he asked.

"It's in my contract."

Sean smirked, taking in the upgraded room complete with king-sized bed and a separate sitting area. An expensive looking piece of luggage waited for its owner on a rack in the open closet. "Of course it is. What do you want?"

Bent tossed his key card on the desk and faced him. "I wanted to tell you I think you did a good job out there today. You're an asset to the team."

Both eyebrows rose. "You brought me to your room to tell me I'm doing a good job?" His pulse raced. Every breath brought a subtle reminder of his tormenter's unique scent. Being alone with Bent played havoc with his libido, yet he couldn't help wondering what was behind the man's sudden goodwill. "You could have told me anywhere."

He nodded. "I could have, but I didn't want you to think I was saying it to appease management. I wanted you to know I mean it. The Mustangs are lucky to have you at first base. You're a damn sight better than that jackass, Wagner. He couldn't catch his own balls if they were falling off."

The words had the ring of sincerity about them. "I appreciate it. It means a lot coming from you."

Smiling, Bent slipped his suit coat off, hanging it on the back of the desk chair. His tie was askew, his dress shirt was travel rumpled. "Look, I know things aren't ever going to be easy between us—"

"How do you know?"

"What?"

"Things won't ever be easy between us?" Sean asked. "You sound as if you know something I don't. So, tell me. How do you know? You're going to have to convince me because I think things could be very good between us."

Bent's face turned red. A mask of stark terror replaced his smile. *There's a real emotion, at last.*

He pressed on, "I saw you from the dugout—when I was batting. You don't look at the other players on the team like you want to tear their clothes off and fuck them right there on home plate, do you? Or were you admiring my bat, wishing I would shove it up your ass?"

Bent's eyes narrowed, his complexion darkening to more of a plum shade. Sean hated himself for what he was doing, but the devil had a hold on him and wouldn't let him go.

"When you swatted my butt? You were thinking how you'd rather pull my pants down and squeeze my ass the way I did yours in your yard the other day. Or maybe you wanted to go down on your knees and suck my cock. Isn't that what happened today? Isn't that why you practically begged me to come to your room?"

A deafening silence followed his outburst, during which he knew what it was to hate himself. Bent didn't deserve to have his actions twisted and perverted in order for an asshole like himself to vent his frustrations. The source and recipient of all his angst stood like a monument. Sean knew Bent was alive because his chest rose and fell like a trapped animal staring into the eyes of the hunter who'd captured him.

Sean swallowed the giant lump in his throat. "I'm sorry, Bent. I...I shouldn't have said those things."

"No." He shook his head. "No, I deserved that. None of it is true, but after what happened with the Pioneers...you're entitled to believe them."

"Don't." He raised his hand to stop him. "Let's not go there. We both know what happened in the shower, and I, for one, won't ever forget it. But I understand you want to pretend it didn't happen. I can live with your denial, if you can. Just don't fu...toy with me, okay? Don't watch me bat. Don't touch me. Don't fucking speak to me. Most of all, don't invite me into your room again unless you want my bat up your ass, because that's what's going to happen if you do."

"I thought maybe we could be friends." His voice was almost pleading in its desperation.

"No. No way. I wish to God I hadn't been traded to the Mustangs, but I'm here, and there isn't a thing I can do about it. I want you so bad I can't stand it. Having to see you every day—not being able to touch you, not kiss you—is killing me. We can't be *friends*, Bent. Believe me, I hate you for that more than I hate myself for loving you."

Bent's hands were fisted at his sides, his face rigid. He looked like a cartoon character ready to explode except for the erection pressing against the fly of his dress slacks. *In denial much?*

Sean turned to leave, his hand on the doorknob.

"I'm getting married." Bent's words stopped him in his tracks. "I asked Ashley to marry me. She said yes."

Son of a bitch.

He clenched his jaw tight to keep from saying what he wanted to say. He gripped the doorknob hard enough to make his fingers hurt in order to keep from turning around and fucking some sense into the man's brains. His forehead dropped to the cool wood of the door. Taking a deep breath, he let the pain wash over him. It took every ounce of self-control he possessed to turn the knob, force his feet into the hall then to the elevator.

Bentley held onto the back of the desk chair, watching the door close. The sound of the lock engaging grated on his hearing then knocked his knees out from under him. He reached for the bed, stumbling to the mattress before he landed on the floor.

Oh, God.

He crawled to the center collapsing face first onto the down comforter. His stomach cramped, the dinner he'd managed to choke down threatening to come back up. Rolling to his side, he pulled his knees to his chest and squeezed his eyes shut to hold back the tears threatening to spill out. Hatred for Sean Flannery boiled inside him like lava beneath the surface of the earth, roiling and churning, looking for an outlet—an impossible outlet.

He couldn't tell anyone how much he loathed the man without having to explain why, and he could *never* explain why. To do so would destroy everything he loved—Ashley, his career. Everything would be in the debris field if he let the eruption happen.

"Ashley." Her name fell from numb lips. *I love you. Please, please, don't hate me. I won't let him come between us.*

But even as he thought it, the damning words came back to taunt him.

"I hate you for that more than I hate myself for loving you." The statement, condemning them both, was destined to follow him the rest of his life.

"I hate you, Sean Flannery. Why did you have to say it? *Why?* I hate you. I hate you. I fucking hate you!"

His trapped cock throbbed. He rolled to his back, fumbling with the fastenings on his pants. Fisting his cock in one hand, he flung the other over his eyes.

"I hate you," he groaned, sliding his fist along the length of his erection. He closed his eyes willing the unwanted image to go away. The truth he'd denied for so long had shown in the depth of Sean's gaze.

"I hate you. I hate you."

With each stroke, he repeated the mantra, his grip getting tighter, the tempo faster. His chest heaved with the exertion. Tears streamed down his temples.

"I hate you. I hate you. I hate you."

Lightning struck in the small of his back then seared his groin. He bucked his hips, fisting his throbbing flesh tighter. The climax soiled his shirt, wrenching a sob and another truth from his lips. "I love you, Sean. Oh, God. I fucking love you."

CHAPTER FIVE

Sean traversed the lobby at a fast clip. There was an unofficial curfew on game night, but it had been long past when they arrived. If any of his teammates saw him, they'd keep their mouth shut. Management, however, was another issue. They'd have something to say, but tonight, he didn't care.

Let them stop me. Do me a favor, cancel my contract.

No one stopped him. He hailed a cab, gave the name of a bar on the outskirts of town where he could find the two things he needed, booze and a good fuck. No questions asked. No denial. No hate.

Paying the driver, he exited the taxi in front of his destination. Muted music cloaked the sidewalk. The auditory aura froze his feet to the steaming concrete. He'd come all the way out here, why not go in, find the solace he needed?

The door opened. The beat of the music stirred him, but not as much as the couple that spilled out, too blind with lust to notice him. They paused a few storefronts down, unable to keep their hands off each other any longer. He watched for a few minutes, envying them their honesty. What would it be like to have the man you loved want you so bad he wouldn't care who saw you together?

The couple realized their circumstances then, after some

discussion Sean couldn't hear, crossed the street, arm-in-arm, to a parking lot on the other side. A few minutes later, he heard a car start. Still frozen on the walkway, he watched them drive away.

He glanced back at the door. With a resigned sigh, he stepped toward it.

The loud music assaulted his ears, but he wasn't there for conversation, so what did it matter? Even for a Friday night, going into Saturday morning, the place was crowded. A small dance floor in the center of the room was a mosh pit of writhing bodies he avoided, heading straight to the bar. Catching the bartender's attention, he raised an eyebrow in question. Without missing a beat, the man tilted his head in the direction of the far end of the bar. Nodding a thank you, Sean threaded his way to the one empty stool next to the wall and hidden behind the cash register.

Perfect.

He'd no more than pressed his ass to the cool leather seat than the bartender appeared, slapping a white square napkin down in front of him.

"What'll you have?" he asked.

After ordering a light beer in the bottle, he slid a twenty across the wood. "Keep 'em coming until the money runs out." As self-medicating went, he'd be safe enough if he stopped at a few beers.

The bartender nodded, anchored the bill with a bowl of pretzels then went off to fill the order. Moments later, Sean raised an ice-cold bottle to his lips.

Two rounds later, he looked up to see the bartender standing in front of him, waiting for…something.

"What, more money? How much are these things?"

"Nah, you're good. Just thought I'd see if you are looking for something other than a drink." He glanced over his shoulder then back at Sean. "A couple of people have been trying to get your attention."

Realizing he'd made the decision before he'd ever stepped in the bar, he shook his head. "Thanks—" He looked for a nametag. "—Roger, but you can tell them no. I just needed a drink tonight." He needed more, but not from anyone here.

Roger shrugged, collected the twenty, and put it in the register. "No problem. One more?"

Eyeing the empty bottle in front of him, he weighed his choices then stood. "No thanks. Keep the change."

"Thanks. If you change your mind, the guys asking are regulars. Come back any time. I'll hook you up."

"I appreciate it," he said, knowing he wouldn't be back. He only wanted one man, and though he'd come here thinking a quick hook up would help him forget Bentley's denial, time and introspection had brought him to his senses. No one else would do. Maybe in a few months, maybe never, but his loss was too fresh tonight.

He paused. "Hey, call me a cab?"

"No problem." Roger reached for the phone.

Smiling, Sean raised his hand in silent thanks as he moved toward the door.

The night was still. The low buzz of traffic on a nearby well-traveled thoroughfare along with the music still leaching from the bar swirled around him as he waited outside for his ride.

Bentley would never be his. He remembered the woman he'd met at his house. Was *that* Ashley? Probably. She seemed comfortable enough answering the door at his house. He tried to remember if she'd been wearing a ring, but for the life of him he couldn't recall. He'd assumed she was one of many who paraded through Bent's life, but in the last few years he'd made a point of not looking too close, so it was possible he'd known her long enough to make a serious commitment.

Hell. Did it make any difference if Bent had known her a week or a year? The fact was, he was going to marry her. It didn't matter when he'd asked her. She'd said yes, making Bentley off limits to other lovers, of either gender. Which was why he'd flung the information in Sean's face tonight—to warn him off.

You got it, buddy. Have a nice life. Just leave me the fuck alone.

Sean felt like hell. His body ached all over, and his head felt like a Little League team was using it for batting practice. By the time he'd dropped into his bed in the wee hours of the morning, exhausted and nowhere near drunk, he'd had four hours to sleep—which would have been enough if he'd actually slept. Instead, he'd listened to his roommate snore while he relived every second of the minutes he'd spent in Bentley's room.

Like game film, he analyzed every move, looking for ways he could have changed the outcome. What if he'd pressed him to say what he really wanted? What if he'd cut through the bullshit and kissed him? What if?

This scenario came down to one thing—the asshole was engaged to be married. To some bimbo named Ashley. Nothing he could have done would have changed the facts. One of the things he loved about the man was his honor. He wouldn't back out on his fiancée. He'd given his word, which meant, he would keep it.

Unless she backed out. No matter what he felt for Sean, he wouldn't want Ashley hurt. Finding out her fiancé has the hots for a man would devastate her. No, he couldn't imagine the news would go over well.

Unless she's an extraordinarily understanding woman with an open mind about sex. He didn't know shit about women, but he was certain the majority of them weren't into sharing—not their shoes or their beauty secrets, and for damn sure, not their men.

Hat over his heart for the national anthem, he focused all his lagging energy on the game ahead of him. As soon as he got back to the hotel, he could crash. Sleep was over rated anyway.

Bentley felt like hell.

What the fuck were you thinking? Just stay the hell away from him.

He didn't want to think about the night before, but there was no way around it. His brain wouldn't let the memory go. After Sean left, after what he now thought of as a mini nervous breakdown, he'd called Ashley. Hearing her voice, listening to her plans for their wedding had reassured him. He was a normal guy. He did normal things like tune out his fiancée when she rattled on about flowers and the color of bridesmaids' dresses.

But as soon as he hung up, the incident with Sean came flooding back in.

I love Ashley. I do. I want to marry her.

The national anthem ended. He ducked back into the dugout for his glove before jogging to left field. Wade Henning was already on the pitching mound, forcing Bentley to take a route closer to Sean on first base. As he passed by, his skin tingled with awareness.

Shit.

He kept going, didn't look back. He didn't need to. An image of Sean, standing inside his room the night before was forever etched on his memory. A person didn't have to be gay to notice Sean's height or his broad shoulders. Where some athletes looked like lumpy toads in a suit, Sean could be a cover model.

Once in his position in left field, Bent risked a glance toward first base. Flannery fielded a warm-up ground ball then threw it to Stevens at third base. The man could throw. There was power in his lean frame, but he wore it well. No bulging muscles, just thick, well-toned cords packed with efficient energy.

Whatever workout regime he used, it worked for his body type. Five years ago, there hadn't been an extra ounce of fat on the man. From what little he'd seen since Sean had joined the Mustangs, nothing had changed.

His mind flashed back to the two times they'd been in physical contact—the first day in the clubhouse then the next morning in his backyard. He could still feel Sean's body rolling with him on the floor and the following day, pressing him into the lawn. Solid muscle.

He shook his head to clear the images and dislodge the crazy thoughts running rampant through his brain. Standing near the warning track, all alone with nothing but time to think, he could admit one thing—he felt something for Sean. The night before he'd called it love, but probably because the asshole had said it first, put the idea in his head.

Lust. Yeah, that fit. It was crazy, but his body reacted to Sean the same way it reacted to Ashley. He wanted them both. There was just one difference—he could have Ashley. Nothing in the world compared to being inside her. She'd been different from the very beginning. She'd never been impressed with his job, his celebrity status, or his money. Employed at a local television station, she had worked her way up to News Director in charge of several syndicated shows. As such, she made a pretty good salary on her own.

He liked the way she wasn't gaga over him. Sometimes he was just the guy she wanted taking out her trash, but mostly, she was his friend. They liked the same movies, the same restaurants, and she took off her makeup before coming to bed, so when he took her, he was seeing the real woman, not a version of herself she put on for the rest of the world.

And, Lord, was she soft. Her skin smelled sunny and sweet, like a garden of flowers in bloom. He loved to wrap her silky hair around his fist then ride her from behind like a Mustang in heat. She liked it, too. She never shied away from trying new things in bed, which made for some rather memorable experiences.

He'd be a fool to screw things up with her over his ridiculous obsession with Sean Flannery.

The game seemed to fly by then, before he knew it, they were in the top of the ninth inning down by two runs. He came to bat with two outs, managed to draw a walk from the pitcher, which brought Sean up to bat.

Standing on first base, Bent's nerves hummed. The Mustangs needed Flannery to come through with a homerun to tie the game. Getting on base was the next best option, but with two outs and the bottom of the order batting behind him, the chances of Sean scoring from any base were slim.

The count stood at three balls, one strike. He cursed the struggling pitcher. "Come on. Come on. Give him something to hit."

The first base coach gave the sign to hit away, clearing the batter to swing if the pitch was good.

He inched down the line, crouched—ready to cut loose. With two outs, he was running if his teammate connected with the ball, no matter what. There was nothing to lose by doing so.

The pitch was low and maybe a little outside. Flannery swung, connected. Bent sprinted, rounded second before he saw the home plate umpire signal a foul ball.

"Damn," he muttered under his breath, retracing his steps back to second base.

Full count. Hit the damn ball, asshole.

Again, poised on the balls of his feet, ready to run, he watched, anticipated, planned for every possible scenario.

The next pitch was better, the batter swung, got more of the bat on the ball. There was no time to waste. He ran. Seeing the third base coach wave him on, he called on every ounce of power he could, sliding across home plate a fraction of a second before the catcher tagged him.

"Safe!" The umpire shouted.

He popped up, smiling. They were one run away from a tie game, with the tying run was on base. They might just pull off a win yet.

Wedging himself in along the dugout fence, he followed the action. When Sean stole second base, he pumped his fist in the air and cheered his teammate on. A solid base hit would get most runners across home plate from second base. Even Flannery, with his previous injuries, should be able to make it.

Next up to bat was the right fielder, Jake Riley. There was a reason he was batting eighth, one rung above the pitcher. He couldn't hit for shit. Crossing his fingers, Bent leaned over the railing in support of the second weakest batter on the team. Around him, he could feel the tension from his teammates. Everyone wanted to win, but they'd settle for getting the tying run across home plate.

Wade could hit. He just didn't do it very often, even less in clutch situations. You couldn't ask for a better right fielder though.

The count escalated to no balls, two strikes in a heartbeat. Leave it to the pitcher to find his control now, or maybe Riley was swinging at pitches he shouldn't be. It was hard to tell from where he stood.

The pitcher set. Bent held his breath. It looked like a good pitch. The batter thought so, too. He swung. Connected. The ball zipped past the short stop's glove. Sean was off and running, but he had to dodge the short stop who had stumbled in his effort to waylay the ball. Precious nanoseconds ticked by while the left fielder ran in, scooped up the ball then threw it to third base.

The result was a cluster fuck. Unable to continue on to third base, Sean turned back to second, only to be cut off there, forcing him toward third again. Bent dropped to the dugout floor, watching the disaster unfold from there.

Fuck.

Back and forth, the ball went between players as the opposing team squeezed Sean into an impossible box before tagging him out. Game over. Five game winning streak—over.

It wasn't the first game they'd ever lost, and it wouldn't be the last, either. The locker room was quieter than it would have been had they won, but the players were used to the you-win-some, you-lose-some nature of the game. Many found things to smile or laugh about still, including Sean Fucking Flannery.

For reasons Bent didn't want to examine, the sight of him joking around, accepting good-natured ribbing for getting caught in a rundown between bases, made his blood boil. Clenching his fists at his sides, he tried to reason with himself.

Calm down. It's not the fucking end of the world. He screwed up. It's not like you haven't done it. Shit happens. Forget it and move on.

Except, he couldn't forget it. The more Sean laughed and smiled, the more he wanted to punch his lights out.

By the time the team arrived at the restaurant where they were obliged to eat dinner as guests of one of their biggest sponsors, most of his teammates had forgotten the loss and were in good spirits. Booze flowed freely at the reception preceding dinner, from which Bent snuck away in order to call Ashley.

"Hi, Babe," he said when she answered. "It's me."

"I saw the game. I'm sorry. You were so close."

He sighed, rubbing his face. "I don't want to talk about it. I'm so pissed, I can't think straight."

"Oh, honey…don't take it so hard. Tomorrow's another day. Another game. I'm sure you'll win the next one."

The conversation wasn't helping. He didn't need or want platitudes. He wanted…to hit something. No. Not something. Someone. Sean Flannery. The fuck up.

"We won't win if people like Flannery don't get their shit together." He held the phone to his ear with one hand, clenching and unclenching the other into a fist at his side. Unable to keep still, he paced the short hallway leading to the restrooms.

"Hey, what's the matter?" Concern laced her voice. "You're upset."

"It's nothing," he lied. "I'm just tired, I guess. We've got a fucking dinner tonight, and I didn't sleep well last night. I'm sorry. I shouldn't be taking my lousy mood out on you."

"I don't mind." He could hear the smile in her soft words. "I'm glad you called me to vent. It means you trust me." She paused. "I miss you." Her voice had dropped to a low, seductive whisper guaranteed to make his cock throb.

"I miss you, too. I need you, babe. I wish you were here."

"I know. But I can't follow you around the country. However, I'm just a phone call away."

The playfulness in her tone clued him to her meaning. There was something to be said for good phone sex. "Maybe I'll call you again when I get back to the hotel. If I don't fall asleep first."

"I'd like nothing more, but please get some sleep tonight, Bent."

"I will. I promise. Talk to you tomorrow, then?"

"Tomorrow. I love you."

"I love you, too."

After a trip to the men's room, he rejoined the team. They'd already moved to the private room set up for their dinner. Stopping inside the door, he scanned the room, finding the last open seat—

directly across from Sean Flannery.
Well, shit.

CHAPTER SIX

Sean looked up from the roll he was buttering to see who'd pulled out the chair across from him and almost cut himself. Would have if the blade had been any sharper. Putting the knife down, he squashed the roll between both his hands before tossing it down on his bread plate. At least, he thought that's what they called the small dish at the top of his place setting. He wasn't much for formalities, but he'd picked up enough knowledge to keep from looking like an ass at all but the most formal of occasions. Thank God, the barbeque place they'd chosen was a paper towels-for-napkins kind of place. He felt right at home.

But at home, he chose who sat at his dinner table.

A quick glance told him the newcomer wasn't any happier about the seating arrangements than he was, but what could either of them do? Not a damned thing. He turned his attention to Tony Ramirez, seated to his right. The center fielder joined the team in the off-season, so he was still sort of a newbie himself.

"How are you liking Dallas?" he asked.

"Best move of my life." His dinner companion smiled wide. "I'm getting married during the All-Star break."

What was with the Mustangs? Two players getting married? Not that it didn't happen, but what were the odds he'd hear the same line from two players on the same team in as many days?

"No shit? Congratulations. Who's the lucky woman?"

"Clare Kincaid. She plays the organ at the stadium on game days." His smile grew wider. "I'm the lucky one. Convincing her to have me took some doing."

Sean chuckled. He couldn't help but be happy for the guy because he was so damned happy for himself. "Sounds like a smart woman," he joked. "I can't wait to meet her."

"I'll introduce you sometime. You'll love her, but hey, keep your hands to yourself. She's mine."

Holding his hands up, he replied, "No problem. Hands off the merchandise."

"Hey," Tony called across the table, "Randolph. Did I hear you're getting married, too?"

Bent looked up from the menu. His eyes went to Tony then to Sean then back to Tony. "Yeah. You've met Ashley. I finally manned up and asked her. I don't know if it was stupid or brilliant of her, but she said yes."

"Stupid." A chorus of voices sounded around them, followed by laughter interspersed with some good-natured ribbing.

Sean sat back, keeping his mouth shut. Bent went along with the teasing—his nickname seemed to have more meaning to this bunch than just a shortened version of his name.

"Yeah, yeah. I know. But I'm through playing around. I want kids, the SUV, the whole thing." He made the statement to the whole group, but his gaze locked on Sean when he got to the part about kids.

You fuckin' had to twist the knife in my gut, didn't you, asshole?

He forced a thin-lipped smile to his face.

"What do you think, Flannery? Aren't you going to congratulate me, too?"

All of a sudden, the room grew quiet. Sean sensed dozens of pairs of eyes watching him. Heat blossomed on the back of his neck, making him sweat all over. Their gazes locked across the table laden with rolls of paper towels, bottles of sauces, and galvanized buckets filled with peanuts.

In his head, he heard the words he should say, *Congratulations, Bent. I wish you all the happiness in the world.*

But, he couldn't bring himself to say it, because it wasn't true. He didn't wish him happiness—not with some woman he could never love the way she deserved to be loved. Why should the ass be happy when he was denying Sean the same opportunity? So he smiled then said what he felt, instead.

"Congratulations. I've never seen a more deserving asshole." Then he winked.

In less time than it takes a one hundred mile an hour pitch to travel from the mound to home plate, it was clear Bent comprehended his meaning. His face turned purple. A muscle twitched in his jaw.

"You fuckin' son of a bitch." The left fielder stood, placed his knuckles on the tabletop then leaned across. "You think you're hot shit, don't you, Flannery? But you're nothing but a second-rate, washed-up, wanna-be baseball player. I don't know why the Mustangs traded for you in the first place. You run like an old man. Only an idiot gets caught in a fuckin' run-down between bases."

Everyone was standing now. Those nearest to Bent had their hands on his shoulders, urging him to back away. Sean sat, unable to move as Bentley unloaded on him. The worst was, most of what he said was true. He couldn't run, not like he used to. Second rate? Yeah, it fit. Washed up? Most likely.

Clenching his hands into fists beneath the table, he absorbed the wrath coming his way.

"Why don't you get out of the game while you can still walk, huh? Because you're a coward. A fuckin' coward."

Sean blinked. Bentley Randolph was calling him a coward? No fucking way. A red haze clouded his vision. He stood. Before he could flatten his nemesis, several sets of hands were on his arms, his shoulders, yanking him back from the table. A scuffle was taking place on the other side, too.

"Enough, Randolph." Doyle Walker's voice. "Get him out of here."

He must have been talking about him, not Bent, because the hands holding him tight tugged and pushed. Chairs scraped across the painted concrete floor then he was being marched toward the door. Over his shoulder, he saw the man he both hated and loved being shoved back into his chair.

They were in the parking lot, headed toward the bus, when he dug his heels in. He shrugged them off. "Let me go."

They let him go, forming a loose but ominous circle around him. He straightened his suit coat and tie then sucked in a lungful of air.

"I'm okay. Thanks guys for getting me out of there before I broke him into little pieces." He had no doubt he would have done it, too, given the chance. He wasn't going to tell them, but the option was still on the table, he just wasn't going to do it in public.

"What gives between you two, anyway?" Todd asked.

"Nothing."

"*That* wasn't nothing," Tony said.

"Trust me, it's nothing."

"Well, whatever it is or isn't, the two of you are going to have to figure out a way to get along, at least for the remainder of the season. Last I heard, the team wasn't making any more trades, no matter what, so you're both stuck for now." Jason Holder, according to…well, everyone…had the ear of management. If anyone knew their trade plans, it was the Mustangs starting catcher.

What did it matter? He doubted he'd survive another trade, anyway. Besides, he'd have to go as a package deal with a younger player as incentive. He'd be sent down to the minors, and the kid would play. It's the way it would be for him, and they all knew it.

"I know," he said, scuffing the asphalt lot with his shoe. "I do my best to stay clear of him, but you were there. You saw what happened. He started it."

"He did," they all agreed.

"But you were about to finish it," Todd said.

"Damn right I was."

Laughter rang out around him. Startled, he glanced at his teammates. "What's so funny?"

Tony spun around, holding his ribs as he laughed. "Nothing. Tonight's the most fun I've had in ages. I thought things in Texas were going to be dull. Boy was I wrong."

"Dull?" Todd and Jason echoed each other before they too doubled over laughing.

Relieved at least these three weren't offended by his behavior, he sighed, then burst out laughing, too.

Bentley peered through the peephole then swore under his breath. *What the fuck is he doing here?*

"Open up, Randolph. I know you're in there."

"Shit." He jerked the door open. Sean stood there, still wearing the suit he'd had on at the restaurant. As it always did, the sight of the man made his mouth water and his cock twitch. Even the pissed off expression on his face looked sexy.

"What the hell do you want?"

His adversary stepped forward, forcing him back into the room. The door slid shut behind him then, all of a sudden, there was a finger poking him in the chest.

"Don't ever question my ability to play again." The guy jabbed him hard. "If you ever call me a coward again, I'll fuck you six ways to Sunday."

He locked gazes with the man who had invaded his room, his life. "Just callin' it like I see it."

Sean stopped—his finger smack in the middle of Bentley's silk tie. His eyes narrowed. He grasped the narrow fabric, wrapped it around his hand twice until his fist was at Bent's throat. One solid yank brought them nose-to-nose.

The purely masculine scent invading his nostrils made his knees weak, his dick hard. His heart slammed against his ribs. Calling the asshole's bluff had been a mistake. The man's eyes blazed, and the heat coming off his body equaled his own. He hated the way his body defied his brain.

"Who's the coward now?" Flannery taunted, his lips hovering a breath away. "Who's shivering like a fucking trapped animal?" He canted his head, moving closer. "Who's going to get fucked?"

Fear and wild desire hit him like a sucker-punch to the gut just as Sean's mouth closed over his. His lips were firebrands, taking, demanding, promising. Bent closed his eyes. Maybe if he couldn't see who was kissing him…but he didn't need his vision to know. A day's growth of beard abraded his cheeks. The hand molded to the back of his head was too large and strong to be female.

Different than anything he'd ever experienced, exciting and terrifying at the same time.

Sean shifted his weight, bringing his erection in contact with Bent's hip. Someone groaned, and he realized the sound had come from his own throat. He pressed himself closer, ground his own erection against the hipbone gouging his stomach.

Fingers fisted in his hair, yanked his head back. "Open your goddamn mouth," Sean growled.

He pressed his lips together in a tight line.

The man gave his head a hard shake. "Open it now or you're going to be on your knees sucking my cock before you know what hit you."

Panic swept through him like a wildfire. Instinct brought his clenched fist from his side to his tormenter's stomach.

The bastard grunted, caved in the center for a second. "You son of a bitch," he hissed. "You want it hard so you can say I forced you? It's what you want it, isn't it?"

Yes. No. His jaw worked but no words came out.

"Don't even try to tell me you don't want me to fuck you because we both know it would be a lie."

He drove his fist into the first baseman's stomach again, but the other man held him fast by the fist wrapped in his tie. It took the guy a moment to recover, but when he did, his eyes were aflame. The next thing he knew, Sean dragged him across the room by his neck then flung him face down on the bed.

Bent struggled to get up, but Flannery straddled him, locking him in place with his weight. His knees clenched tight around his hips, immobilizing him. He'd been here before. Paralyzed by fear of the things he wanted, needed, and he wanted to struggle as much as he needed to believe the man straddling him was forcing him. The sound of silk sliding against starched cotton rent the air. Large hands grabbed both his wrists, wrenching them to the small of his back.

Tears filled his eyes as the tie secured his hands. He made another attempt to dislodge him, but the other man wouldn't be moved.

"Fight me if you want, but I *am* going to fuck you, then you can go back to your fiancée—forget all about me. I know you think that's what's going to happen." His hands slid beneath him, working his tie free of the shirt collar then loosening the first two shirt buttons. "You want me to fuck you because you think doing it once will get the desire you feel for me out of your system. You want to believe I forced you so you won't feel guilty about wanting me every time you fuck her."

The man was reading his mind. He grabbed Bent's shirt by the collar and yanked. Buttons popped down his chest, allowing his assailant to bare him down to the waist.

"I love your back," he said. "You're strong. Have to be to make the throws you do. Christ, your shoulders are a work of art."

Bent sobbed into the coverlet as his tormentor stroked the

exposed skin. Like the time in his yard, Flannery's hands on him felt good, his praise mocked him.

Dear God, this is wrong. So fuckin' wrong.

"Shh," he soothed, sweeping broad circles across his flesh with his callused palms. "You know if you asked me to stop, I would. But you won't ask. You want it, just like I said."

Stop. Oh, please, stop. He groaned when his vocal chords refused to utter the protest.

Weight shifted from his buttocks to his thighs then hands were at his waist, unbuckling his belt and the fasteners on his slacks. He steeled himself for what was coming, but nothing could have prepared him for the rush of desire and abject terror that engulfed him when his trousers were around his thighs. His shoes hit the floor then, in a heartbeat, he was naked save for his ruined dress shirt, and the tie still looped around his neck.

Hard hands forced his ass cheeks apart.

Run. Now.

Get the hell out before…before….

His legs ignored the commands of his splintered brain. Something he didn't dare try to name held him immobile while the man, the bane of his existence, examined him in the most intimate way possible. Humiliation ate at him, but still, he allowed the probing to continue.

"I've never had virgin ass before." He kneaded the flesh with his hands. "Don't move."

Virgin ass.

For how much longer?

Not fuckin' long.

A faint hum told him the bathroom light had been turned on. If he was going to run, now was the time. His heart thudded.

Run.

Get out.

Now.

His mind sent signals to his limbs, but he didn't run. Then Sean was back, using his thighs to spread Bent's legs.

He would have caught me if I'd run.

You are such a liar.

You want him to fuck you.

"Up on your knees."

He struggled to obey, but not fast enough. Rough hands shoved him into position.

Bent closed his eyes against the shame of having his balls and hard cock exposed for another man's eyes. How could he deny he wanted to be fucked when his cock was harder than a cured-maple bat?

"Look at you." Flannery palmed his balls then grasped his erection, coating the length with cold lotion, stroking until Bent couldn't remain still. He pumped his hips, seeking an end to his torment.

"Not yet. I'll be damned if you're going to get satisfaction from the *idea* of being fucked. No, sir."

He rocked back toward the hand slathering his asshole with cold, pungent lubricant

"Hold still."

Slippery fingers reamed his asshole. There was a flash of pain that quickly gave way to a pleasant fullness. Groaning, he buried his face in the comforter, grateful he couldn't see. Feeling was bad enough.

"Fuck, you're tight." The other man worked the digits in, out, and around, forcing more moans from his lips.

He screwed his eyes shut realizing a level of mortification he'd never thought possible. His hands were tied, but he wasn't helpless. He could get away if he wanted, but…he didn't. The fingers breaching him felt too wonderful.

So fuckin' wrong.

So fuckin good.

"Don't fuckin' move."

He couldn't. Hate, fear, desire, humiliation, all held him prisoner.

Behind him, Sean cursed. A belt buckle clanked, metal against metal. The rasp of a zipper and the soft swish of fabric crumpling followed by a familiar sound of foil tearing, grounded him in reality. He lifted his head so his chin rested on the comforter. Blinking against the bright lights in the room, he knew it was now or never. His last chance. If he didn't say something, didn't escape, he was going to get fucked.

A muscle cramped in his neck. He twitched at the pain.

"I said, don't move." Long fingers gripped his hips tight then hauled his knees to the edge of the bed. "We aren't through."

All thoughts of bolting evaporated.

Switch Hitter

A stiff cock nudged at the tight ring lubricated with the hotel's hand lotion. Bent almost swallowed his tongue when the contact changed to insistent pressure. Instinctively, he clenched his ass cheeks as tight as possible.

"I'm going in, no matter what," Flannery said. "Your choice. Easy or hard."

He didn't need it spelled out for him. It was going to hurt either way, but less so if he relaxed. He sucked in a deep breath, releasing the tension in his ass on the exhale.

Sean must have taken the movement for his decision or an invitation. The pressure became unbearable for the space of a heartbeat then the massive dick he'd first seen in the shower five years ago burned its way up his ass.

He buried his face in the bedding again, taking a mouthful of fabric to muffle the scream he couldn't contain.

Shit. Shit. Shit.

The huge cock felt like a hot poker shoved up his ass.

"Goddamn, you're tight." Fingers probed the ring of fire where the two of them were connected. "You're okay, though."

Spitting the cotton out, Bent wailed, "I am not fuckin' okay! Get your goddamn horse dick out of me!" His stomach roiled with disgust.

"Not on your life. Your asshole is mine now, and I'm fucking going to enjoy it. So are you." Strong hands stroked his ass globes, massaging, soothing. "Just give it another minute."

He willed his muscles to relax.

Oh, God.

The searing pain dulled then ebbed away. The longer Sean's dick was inside him the better it felt. He *couldn't* like being fucked by a man. No way in hell was he going to enjoy being fucked.

God, no. Please. Please. Please. He had no idea what he was pleading for—mercy or the forbidden pleasure creeping into his mind and body—taking over.

The bastard was fucking right. He liked it

Feels…so fuckin' good.

"Fuck." Tears he couldn't control streamed down his face. He needed more. He wanted it all. "I can't…please…."

Sean ground his molars. His legs trembled with the effort to keep still. Everything in him called for action. After all these years, he had Bentley Randolph right where he wanted him, and he wasn't going to rush the experience for either of them.

The man needed time adjust then he would find the pleasure. He hated causing him pain, but it couldn't be helped. The first time was a bitch. Reaching around, he found his lover's bobbing appendage and wrapped his hand around it.

"Fuck." He moved his hips, bucking into Sean's fist, inadvertently sliding down the length of his cock.

"Hold still," he admonished, taking his time to drive deep, savoring the feel of the tight ass taking all of him. Heeding his own advice, he remained motionless as long as possible. Then he resumed stroking the other man's cock, waiting for a sign he was ready to continue.

He'd known plenty of guys who couldn't maintain an erection with a dick in their ass, the man beneath him wasn't one of them. His cock remained hard, throbbing as his hand slid along its length. It wasn't long before Bent began to moan. Sean realized his reluctant lover was lost in the sensations—no longer thinking about who provided them.

Flexing his hips, he pulled almost all the way out then slid back in one torturously slow inch at a time. The other man's moan assured him all was well. He did it again, increasing the speed. Again and again, he worked in and out, faster, harder with each stroke until the slap of skin on skin punctuated by male curses filled the room.

Fuck.

Bentley felt so damned good. He couldn't take his eyes off him. He was built like a god—broad shoulders, slim hips, and the most beautiful tight ass he'd ever seen. His back was smooth, rippling with powerful muscles below the surface. He couldn't resist touching him, tracing the long line of his spine down to the bunched shirt at his wrists bound with navy blue silk.

Shit. If he had it his way, he'd fuckin' tie him up every chance he got. He loved having him at his mercy, even if it was nothing more than an illusion. A lousy necktie, poorly applied was nothing against the kind of strength his lover possessed. If the man wanted to get away, he could.

But he didn't.

Sean ran his hands along toned hairy thighs then back up to smooth ass. So much power, but his to command. Using his thumbs, he held him open, watching in awe as his dick disappeared inside the tight hole. He tore his gaze away, daring to look at his lover's face.

With one cheek pressed into the mattress, his eyes closed, a watery track traversed his cheek down to his stubbled jaw. His lips parted. Incoherent, though blissful, sounds came forth. All of a sudden, it wasn't enough. He needed more. He wanted it all.

CHAPTER SEVEN

Bentley couldn't move.

Impaled on Sean's massive cock, a tangle of emotions and sensations assailed him. Unbearable pain at first had morphed into a somewhat pleasant, full feeling, followed by pleasure so intense he couldn't quantify it. Nothing in his extensive prior sexual experience equaled it. He felt small...weak...possessed. The tie binding his wrists was nothing. He sensed a few artful twists would release him, but even so, the restraint wouldn't prevent him from kicking the shit out of Sean if he wanted to.

He'd imagined sucking Sean's dick, had fantasized about fucking his ass, but he'd never considered the man might fuck him first. He'd never once considered letting any man near his ass, but he'd barely offered a protest when Flannery bound his arms and stripped him. Pressed face first into the bed, his ass reamed by the biggest cock he'd ever seen, he couldn't think of anything but how fuckin' good it felt. The pleasure scared the ever-lovin' shit out of him.

Tears stung his eyes.

Liking what they were doing was wrong on so many levels, not the least of which he was cheating on Ashley—with a man!

How could he do this to her?

How can I not?

There was no rationalization—no excuse he could utter to make his betrayal okay.

Sean's balls slapped his in a constant rhythm that sent waves of erotic pleasure coursing through his body. Every thrust made his cock throb. He ached for release.

Despite the self-loathing burning in his chest, he spoke the damning words. "Need to come…. Please."

He gasped as Sean pulled all the way out. With one hard shove to his hip, the other man rolled him to his back, pinning his hands beneath him. Bent looked up into the face of the man he hated with every fiber of his being. The first baseman's unyielding gaze swept down his body, pausing at the most visible sign of his capitulation, his turgid cock.

Long fingers closed around the aching appendage. Bent groaned, letting his head fall back while his hips rose to meet the rough strokes.

"Oh, no you don't," he said, yanking him forward by the tie still knotted around his neck. "You're going to come, all right, but when you do, you're fuckin' going to know who you're with."

In seconds, his knees were up around his ears. His tie cut into the back of his neck, causing his back to arch so his sole means of escape was to close his eyes. But he couldn't.

Sean stood between his splayed legs, still wearing his shirt, tie, and suit coat. Heat flooded Bent's face. His breath came in short pants. He'd never felt as vulnerable as he did right then.

He watched as Sean guided his cock into place. His ass was sore from the first invasion, and he wasn't sure he could stand to have it in him again so soon—especially in a position where he wouldn't be able to hide his feelings.

He was given no time to protest. Flexing his hips, the man he'd given himself to, tunneled deep.

"Fuck," Bent hissed. The pain soon gave way to the overwhelming feeling of pleasure he remembered. "Why do you have to have a goddamn battering ram for a dick?"

"Shut the fuck up." A sharp tug on the necktie wrenched a groan from his gut. "Look at me."

He stared at the man holding him a prisoner of his own desires then shifted his focus away. Another hard jerk brought his gaze up again.

"Don't fuckin' do that again." He slid almost all the way out then powered back in hard enough to send shockwaves all the way to Bent's toes. "No evasion. No denial." He repeated the same hard stroke, emphasizing his commands.

"This is you and me. This is what we've both wanted for way too long."

"Fuck you," he said, though he knew his defiance meant nothing. The man was right. He'd wanted it five years ago. He wanted it now. His shame couldn't be any greater.

Spitting into his palm, his tormentor fisted Bent's cock then began to pump. Hate for himself, for the man controlling him, rolled through him like a red tide, blurring his vision and turning his stomach.

He could make him stop. The bindings at his wrists wouldn't prevent him from rolling away, breaking the connection. But as desperate as he was to end the humiliation, he was just as enslaved to the forbidden pleasure coursing through him.

He knew the bliss of having a woman's soft hand jack him. He loved the feel of their slim fingers around his dick—loved the way they always held something back, afraid they might hurt him. But, dear God, when Sean fisted him, he'd had to clench his jaw shut or scream the rafters down.

No tentative touch. The bastard jacked as hard as he fucked. Combined, the two sensations blew his mind.

He bucked his hips, drawing a series of guttural oaths from his tormenter, and perhaps a few from himself. He couldn't be sure. All he knew was the driving urge to fuck and be fucked. He was out of his mind with the need to shove into the tight tunnel of resistance formed by Flannery's fingers.

"Ahh, Jesus…. Fuck," he ground out. He tore his gaze away from the sight of his cock's round head bursting forth from the callused hand clamped around it. The cords in his teammate's neck were tight, his jaw locked in a grimace as he rocked his hips, reaming his ass with hard, fast thrusts.

Lust flared hot and bright. He closed his eyes, conjuring the image of the first baseman's naked, hot, soapy water sluicing down his back, over his tight ass. He saw him turn. Saw the hard ridges of his chest and abdomen. Saw his cock held just as the man now held his.

Lightning struck the small of his back, sending tendrils of fire through his lower body, igniting an inferno in his balls.

Another hard jerk to his neck. "Look at me," Flannery commanded.

He locked gazes with his teammate. Bile rose in his throat. He swallowed it down, savoring the chemical burn in his esophagus as his due for what he was about to do.

His dick throbbed, and his asshole clenched. Liquid fire spattered across his bare skin. Triumph lit Sean's face. He hated the man even more for understanding what he'd done to him.

His cock softened, but his captor continued to hold it in a vise-grip. His hips had stilled, his cock buried balls deep in his ass. Released from the chokehold of his orgasm, he noticed the firm line of Sean's jaw, saw the muscles twitch there. He recognized the other man's agony. Sean needed to come as badly as he had moments ago.

"Do it," he hissed through clenched teeth. "Just fuckin' do it then get the hell out of here."

"This isn't over." He withdrew then breached him again. His face contorted in a mask of pleasure/pain Bentley couldn't mistake.

Sore as he was, he felt the pulsing contractions ripple along the cock buried up his ass. The knowledge of what was happening made the bile rise in his throat again, yet he couldn't help also feeling a wave of satisfaction at having brought such a strong man to the breaking point. He recognized the feeling as the same one he experienced when he brought Ashley to orgasm—power over another human being's body, the immense fulfillment of giving the ultimate pleasure to another.

Closing his eyes, he slumped backward. He wasn't sure if it was the weight of his shoulders that dragged the tie free, or if the other man simply let go, but the minute his shoulders touched the mattress, he wrenched his torso. Rolling to his side, he left the other man no choice but to jerk his dick free.

A twist of his wrists and he was loose. He scrambled to his feet. Globs of cooled cum slid along his chest, renewing his shame. Beside him, Flannery removed the condom, tying the open end into a simple knot before tucking his limp cock back into his pants.

The hate Bent knew so well, gripped him in its angry fist. The man looked perfect in his suit, still neat and clean while he stood naked and soiled. Scooping cum from his belly, he flung the evidence of his perverse nature at the man responsible.

"Get out." He pointed toward the door. "Get the fuck out of

my room, out of my sight."

Sean secured his zipper, looked down at his now ruined suit. His lips curved into a mocking smile. "I'm leaving," he said, "but we're far from over." He swept at a large damp spot on his lapel. He brought the finger to his mouth and licked it clean.

Mesmerized by another man tasting his cum, he was surprised when strong arms wrapped around him, hauling him up against a hard body. Lips locked his in a kiss as unbreakable as the first baseman's embrace.

He fought to get free, but one hand fisted in his hair, yanking him into submission. Mouth still gaping, he was unprepared when something cold and slimy was shoved past his lips and his jaw forced shut sealing the object inside. Surprised and sickened, his gaze met Sean's.

"Don't fuck with me, Bentley—ever again, or I'll fill every hole you've got with cum, for real. But you'd like it, wouldn't you? You'd like to feel my load filling your ass. I know you want to taste my cum, so there it is. Enjoy."

Releasing Bent's jaw from his iron grip, he stalked to the door. Stopping with his hand on the handle, he turned. "You're a fucked up asshole, in more ways than one."

Bent spit the used condom in the direction of the closing door then raced to the bathroom. Hunched over the toilet, his stomach heaved until his abdominal muscles ached. Sinking to the cool tile floor, he braced against the bathtub, letting his head fall back. His throat burned and his mouth tasted like a cesspool.

Guilt, hate, and self-loathing kept him rooted to the spot. He could no longer deny his attraction for Sean, but on the other hand, he couldn't imagine never holding Ashley again, never seeing ecstasy on her face when she came apart in his arms. He closed his eyes, recalling the same look of wonder on Sean's face. Being with him felt right, but it was so wrong.

He couldn't have both of them. Hell, he couldn't have Sean. Not now, not ever. He had to forget about what had happened tonight—let it go. It wasn't as if he was the first guy to experiment with another guy, but that's all it was or ever could be, an experiment. The results were conclusive—he could find pleasure with another man, but he didn't need the connection the way he needed a physical connection with a woman—Ashley, to be specific.

Music floated in from the other room. He groaned, recognizing the ringtone his fiancée had programmed into his phone to indicate the call was from her. For the first time since they'd become a couple he let her call go to voicemail. He couldn't talk to her at the moment, not with Sean's scent still on his body reminding him of the pleasure he'd given and received—pleasure he had no business wanting, yet he did.

Sean was right. He wanted to taste the other man's cum, wanted to take him down his throat, wanted to feel his jiz shooting up his ass. God help him, he wanted Sean to experience those things from him just as badly. Hell, his dick was getting hard again just thinking about shoving it between the man's tight butt cheeks, fucking him hard. Having a woman beneath him was one thing, but commanding a powerful athlete like Flannery, having him at his mercy would be something entirely different. Just like it had been different, but arousing for him tonight. Hard. Raw. Primal.

With Ashley he always held something back. She was too feminine, too fragile to take the kind of fucking he'd received tonight. It would break her in half. But he could bend Sean over the back of the sofa and fuck the hell out of him. Ride him without any brakes. Flannery could take it.

But it wasn't going to happen. Whatever he had with the man was over. Done. Finished.

It had to be.

He raised his knees, spread them wide then rested his forearms on top. His dick stood at attention, throbbing with need though still sore from being handled with such roughness. Eyeing the complimentary bottle of hand lotion on the counter above his head, he assessed his state of arousal. Determining nothing short of an orgasm was going to cure it, he placed his hands on the tub behind him and lifted himself to sit on the edge. The hard surface brought a tinge of discomfort, a reminder of the abuse his ass had taken, but he welcomed it.

Sighing, he reached for the lotion and filled his palm with the cool liquid. At first, he held himself with a gentle touch; much like Ashley would, pumping with slow, cautious strokes. The lotion felt nice, the smell reminiscent of the flowery oils she favored. He could see her, smiling up at him, asking with her eyes if she was doing it right. Her hand soft, her fingers barely encompassing his girth, her sweet efforts to pleasure him warmed his heart. He wouldn't trade what he had with her for a million fucks with Sean, and certainly not for one experimental evening.

Memories flooded in. He realized he'd tightened his grip and his movements were harsher, less forgiving than before. This was how Sean's hand had felt on him, his grip firm and unbreakable. He'd jacked with purpose, knowing as only another man could where the limits were to their endurance. Every guy jacked his own junk, but having someone else do it for him, someone who wasn't afraid his dick might break off, was different. Relief. No reassurances necessary. No patient coaxing or praise, just matter of fact, jack him off then let the guy breathe again. Fast. Hard. Confident.

His fingers squeezed his aching flesh. He leaned back, bracing one hand against the opposite edge of the tub in order to give himself more room to pump. Clear fluid leaked from his urethra, glistening in the harsh bathroom light. He closed his eyes, imagining his hand was Sean's ass sheathing his cock in moist heat while Bent took his pleasure in deep, forceful thrusts every man dreamed of when they were fucking a woman, but if they were any kind of gentleman wouldn't consider using.

The man could take it. Hell, he'd probably welcome it. He was that kind of an asshole.

He pictured Flannery smiling at being called an asshole. Then he envisioned those smiling lips closing around his cock, sucking hard. He came, his hot seed spilling on his flat abs once again. Curses flew—bouncing off the polished surfaces, coming back at him like the screams of sissies on a carnival ride.

Spent, his ass slid down the inside of the tub to the bottom. Scooting around, he lay prone, used his toes to turn on the faucet then lift the valve to start the shower.

Water cascaded over him, washing away the outer vestiges of his shame and humiliation, wrinkling his skin. The water rose as it overwhelmed the drain capacity. It stung the ring of muscles Sean had abused. His natural instinct was to protect the area, but he refused to move, taking the pain as punishment for his sins.

He might one day accept what he'd done with Sean, but his betrayal of Ashley would always be with him—a secret he couldn't imagine telling her. She couldn't possibly understand how he could want her, want a life with her, but still feel what he did for a man. She'd leave him in a heartbeat and never look back.

If a sore anus and bruised insides were the only price he had to pay, he'd count himself fortunate.

The hotel bar was dark, inhabited by a few people who were probably just like him. They had nowhere to go and no one to care if they did. The atmosphere was perfect for his mood. The last thing Sean needed was company.

"Scotch, neat. Three fingers."

The bartender slid the glass across the polished marble then raised an eyebrow at the hundred-dollar bill Sean plunked onto the bar.

"Keep 'em comin'." He headed to a secluded booth in the back.

The first tumbler of amber liquid loosened tight muscles and eased the physical aches from holding himself together for as long as he had. Weeks of sexual tension took a toll on a man's body, not to mention he still hadn't recovered from the locker room fight his first day with the Mustangs.

The second tumbler of liquid fire burned off the fog clouding his brain. Confronting Bentley had been stupid, not to mention, dangerous. The proof of the revelation throbbed in his lap. Hell, in his anger and frustration he'd practically raped the man then topped the assault off with a threat. Yeah, he'd handled it well. He'd be lucky if he didn't end up in jail.

The third tumbler of guilt ate at his conscience. Bentley didn't deserve the treatment he'd received. It wasn't his fault he couldn't accept who, or what, he was. Society was to blame for that. Homophobes were everywhere. Theirs was the standard for pretty much the world, and certainly for professional athletes. The guy was doing his best to fit in, even if it meant rejecting a chance at happiness.

The fourth tumbler of reality scorched truth into his heart. He had to let the man live the life he thought he wanted. He needed to forget tonight, forget the pure ecstasy on his lover's face when he came, forget the way he'd gazed at him when he'd rammed his cock up his ass, forget he knew more about the Mustangs left fielder than the man knew about himself. He was too afraid of what he would find out about himself if he looked. He'd never admit he'd enjoyed what Sean had done to him. He'd never admit his desire for another man was a natural part of him. He'd live the lie for the rest of his life rather than face up to the truth.

It *was* the truth.

Draining the last dredges from the crystal glass, Sean let his future settle on his shoulders. There wasn't anyone else—just Bentley. Out of necessity, he would find other sexual partners, he'd always managed to. But love? His was reserved for one man. If tonight proved one thing, it was the love of his life would never return the sentiment.

The fifth tumbler of forgetfulness numbed his heart and blurred the edges of his brain, so when he closed his eyes, he slept.

CHAPTER EIGHT

Sean's ass was in a sling, no two ways about it. After the bartender shook him awake, instructing him to clear out so he could close the bar, he managed to find his room all by himself. He collapsed on the bed, but not before he'd woken his roommate by knocking a half-dozen empty beer bottles onto the floor.

The bus ride to the stadium proved to be more than his stomach could handle. He'd earned the animosity of the entire team by throwing up in the bathroom at the back of the bus. Sitting on the bench, hung over and despondent, he couldn't argue with his one game time-out. He was in no shape to play baseball. Hell, he could barely see to tie his shoes, and there weren't enough painkillers in the world to ease the jackhammering going on inside his skull.

His sole consolation was, Bentley didn't look like he was doing much better. He was functioning on a normal level, but Sean could tell his nemesis was struggling to keep his head in the game. His shoulders were tight, and if he clenched his jaw any harder he was going to need dental work. It was only the fifth inning and the man in possession of his heart had struck out twice, his fielding error in the third had cost the Mustangs a run they couldn't afford to give up. But, Bentley being off his game gave Sean's mood a much needed boost.

Fucked up asshole. Deal with it, buddy.

After his third strike out in as many at bats, Randolph threw his helmet across the dugout, earning himself a reprimand from the manager and a possible fine from the organization. Sean smirked at the first thing he'd found humor in all day.

The left fielder chose then to look at Sean. A murderous look crossed his face before he turned and apologized to Doyle. He retrieved his helmet from where it had come to rest at the base of the stairs leading to the clubhouse then moved to the end of the dugout, as far away from Sean as he could get.

Fuck you, Bentley. Oh yeah, I already did, didn't I?

After his game sitting on the bench, the team traveled to Seattle for a four game series. The longest road trip of the season, from there they were headed to Minnesota for three days. Sean was back on the field playing every game. Most of his teammates had forgiven him for the incident on the bus, not because they'd forgotten, but because he'd been playing like a maniac ever since his return to the lineup.

His hip hurt like hell, but the extra hustle he exhibited on the field meant more time with the trainers and less time to think about Bentley. Which suited him just fine. Part of being a Major League player was being gracious whether you won or lost, but translating it into his personal life wasn't as easy. There was always another baseball game to win or lose, but he believed people were given just one chance at true love. In his one at bat in the game of love, he'd struck out, big time.

Being on the same team with his greatest failure, knowing he'd made his play and lost, was killing him.

Baseball was all he had left, but it, too, was in danger of telling him to shove off. If he planned to keep his position with the Mustangs, he would have to show management he was better than any of the young talent lined up to take his place.

Two days into the Seattle trip, on trainers' orders, he moved to a third floor room in the hotel—one he could climb the stairs to in order to strengthen his hip muscles. Waving goodbye to a group of his teammates heading to the elevator, he entered the stairwell off the lobby. At last, he'd gotten a private hotel room, but the price was no elevator to get to it. As he approached the second floor landing, he weighed the situation in his mind, deciding it was a fair trade. Besides, he just had to make the climb a couple of times a day, max.

Lost in his thoughts, he barely registered the door opening and closing on the floor above him. Seeing the man waiting for him on the third floor landing, he stopped short.

Bent Randolph stared down at him. His hair appeared to have been combed with a rake, and his cheeks were flushed. His hands were fisted at his sides.

Shit. Just what I need, another fight.

"Look, man, I'm beat. Whatever you have to say, can it wait?"

Bentley fidgeted, clearly undecided about what he'd come there to do. Damn, the color in his cheeks reminded Sean of the way he looked when he came. The memory pissed him off. He didn't want to be reminded of the man's passion or how much he longed to put that expression on his face every fucking day.

Sean took the last few steps to the landing. Stopping when they were on the same level, he sighed. "Spit it out, Randolph. I haven't got all day."

Before he could escape, his back hit the wall hard, forcing the air from his lungs. Gasping for breath, he hesitated. Instinct said to defend himself, but his attacker was Bentley. He didn't want to hurt the bastard, just beat the shit out of him, make him feel the same level of pain he felt every goddamn day.

"Shut the hell up, Flannery."

The man's rock-hard body pinned him to the wall from chest to hips. Through their thin dress slacks, he felt a thick cock pressing into his belly.

"Just shut the fuck up."

Large hands closed around his face. Rosy lips came closer, crushing his own, moving, demanding, taking. Hips ground hard against Sean's, startling another groan from him. Taking advantage, Bent plunged his tongue past Sean's lips.

Desire ignited like a flash-fire, searing good sense to ashes. His cock surged to attention. He held Bent's hips steady so he could do some grinding of his own.

The kiss was punishing—just what he would have expected from the man pinning him to the wall if he'd allowed himself to imagine such a thing ever occurring. His rational self had prevented any such musings, so now he had to wonder, why, as he returned the kiss with equal fervor.

Lost in the feel of the masculine mouth covering his, he froze when hands found his belt buckle, working it free.

"Not a goddamn fucking word from you," he said, his eyes blazing with intent.

Sean's heart leapt to his throat. He couldn't respond even if he'd wanted to.

Holding his lover's gaze, he let him work the fasteners loose on his trousers. When his hand closed over his erection, he groaned, arching into his touch, all the while refusing to look away from the man's gaze. *Eye jousting.* Both refusing to be the first to cave while Bent felt him up like a high school kid in the bathroom—fumbling fingers and damp palm. No hand job had ever felt as good. Sean let him know by grinding into his embrace.

"Over there." Breaking eye contact, the left fielder pointed to the metal railing where the stairs leading up a floor turned then headed down again.

Bent grabbed the lapels on Sean's suit coat. He yanked him forward, turned him, shoving his shoulder from behind. "Bend over. If you fuckin' move, I'll shove you down the stairs, so hold on tight."

The metal was cold under his hands, but he held on, sliding his left hand down the descending banister and his right up the ascending one while the horizontal bar pressed into his stomach. His belt buckle clanged like a ship's bell when it hit the two lower cross members on its way to his knees.

For a split second, he panicked over the thought of someone entering the stairwell, seeing them, then he couldn't think about anything but Bent's dick shoving dry past the tight barrier muscles of his ass. Bareback. No condom. If it had been anyone but Bentley, he would be worried, but Bent was squeaky clean. Hell, this was probably the fucker's first time without a raincoat.

His asshole burned like hellfire, but he didn't care. Bent was fucking him. Nothing else mattered. What did it mean?

"Fuck, I hate you," Bent hissed. "I. Hate. Every. Fucking. Thing. About. You." Each word was punctuated with a stinging retreat followed by a thrust hard enough to send shockwaves of pleasure all the way to Sean's toes.

"I. Can't. Get. You. Out. Of. My. Fucking. Mind."

That makes two of us.

Sean gripped the metal tighter, rocking into the thrusts. His dick slapped against the cross rail with each movement, but he welcomed the pain because Bent was fucking him—at last.

"Don't. Want. To. Want. You."

But you do. You fucking do.

"I. Hate. You."

I love you, Bentley. I love you so goddamn much.

"Feels. Fucking. Good."

Shit, yeah.

"Oh, shit!"

Sean hung his head, recognizing the signs of his lover's impending release. Clenching his jaw, he screwed his eyes shut and held still while Bentley rode out his orgasm. Hot cum flooded his ass, proof of a desire the man fucking him hated with ever fiber of his being. Sean catalogued every spurt, every spasm, committed the feeling to memory to be treasured the rest of his life.

His lover stilled, his dick buried to the hilt in Sean's ass. The cold stairwell was silent except for the wrenching sobs coming from the man whose cock was buried up his ass.

"Let me up, man. Let's talk about why you just fucked me."

They remained frozen for the space of two heartbeats then, his softened cock slipping free, the left fielder stumbled away. Sean reached for his trousers and briefs, righting his clothes before turning around.

Bentley leaned against the wall next to the door marked with a big red number three. His head was thrown back, tears forming rivers down his cheeks, the heels of his hands pressed into his eye sockets. His dick hung limp from his open zipper.

"Ahh, shit, man." Sean tucked the other man's cock back in his pants then zipped him up. "Pull yourself together, okay? My room is a couple of doors down. You want to go there so we can talk?"

He nodded, wiped at his eyes with his palms, and choked back another sob. "Yeah. We should talk, I guess."

Sean held the door for his teammate then followed him inside the room. Randolph crossed to the window, collapsing into the room's solitary chair. He turned his face to the darkened glass. Getting him to talk wasn't going to be easy. Opening the mini-bar, Sean selected two beers roughly the price of a small condominium and held out one to the man sulking in the corner.

"Beer?"

"Yeah, thanks."

He roused enough to take the cold bottle, but did so without making eye contact. Okay. At least he wasn't crying like a baby anymore, and they were in the same room without punching or fucking. It was a start.

Sean stretched out on the bed, his shoulders propped against the headboard, waiting. He'd almost finished his beer by the time his companion spoke.

"I don't want to feel this way about you."

"I know you don't, but you've tried to make it go away for over five years. How's it working out for you?"

"Not so good, obviously."

Another step in the right direction, but Sean didn't dare hope for more. He finished off his brew, placing the empty container on the nightstand, waiting.

"I love Ashley. I want to marry her. I do. I want kids with her. What I feel for her is real. This thing with you…." He shook his head.

"Is real, too, Bent. You came to me today. I didn't encourage you in any way."

"You encourage me just by being alive." The man's heartfelt confession rang with the defeated tone of a soldier surrendering the battle.

"I know the feeling," he said. "I've wanted you since the first time I saw you. You'd just come up from the Minor's, all fresh-faced and eager to make your mark on the sport. I used to fantasize about taking you in the dugout after a game—you know, when the lights are still on, but the place is empty."

Bentley nodded. "I would have killed you if you'd tried."

"I know. Why do you think I never said anything? You weren't ready. To be honest, I wasn't sure you ever would be. Then you walked into the shower, and I saw it in your eyes. You wanted me. I took a chance, stroking my dick the way I did, but I couldn't think of anything else to do. Dropping a bar of soap for you to pick up wasn't an option."

His companion's laugh was harsh, but it was another step in the right direction. "As I recall they had liquid soap dispensers."

"They did." Sean nodded, remembering. "I wanted you so damn bad. For a few minutes I knew you wanted me, too. The next thing I knew, you were on a plane to Dallas. I thought I was going to die. I missed you so damned bad, Bentley. For five years, I've wanted to strangle you for leaving."

"And I've wanted to strangle you for making me feel that way. If you'd asked me to bend over, I might have done it, but I would have killed you when it was over. I wasn't ready to handle it."

"Are you ready now?"

"No. I'm not ready, but I don't think I have any choice."

"You always have a choice, Bent."

"You think?" He shook his head. "I don't. I love Ashley. I won't leave her for you, but I can't be with you and not tell her. But if I tell her, she'll leave me."

"You aren't kidding, are you? You really love her?"

"I do, and God help me, I love fucking her."

"What about what we did?"

"I liked fucking with you, too. I'm sorry about the things I said in the restaurant the other day. I was out of line. I think I knew, deep down, if I pushed you hard enough you might do something like you did—force the issue between us. It wasn't rape or anything. I could have stopped you. We might have ended up in jail for busting up a hotel room, but I could have stopped you."

"You could have. I like to think I would have stopped, but damn it, Bent, after all these years of wanting you, I had to have you. I had to make you see."

"I saw. Too much. I saw you. I saw myself. I saw your courage and my cowardice."

"You planned tonight. You didn't just *happen* to be in the third floor stairwell at the same time I was."

"I heard the trainer tell you to take the stairs. I was the only player in my elevator, so I got off on the third floor then crossed over to the stairs. I thought once I did it, you would be out of my system and I could go back to being me."

"Did your plan work?"

"Goddamn it, Sean. You know it didn't."

Sean adjusted his legs to ease his aching package.

"You didn't come," Bent said.

"No. I couldn't."

"I can help you, if you want."

Sean had to strain to hear the softly spoken offer. "What do you have in mind?"

"Can I…you know…suck you?"

Hell, yes! "Is it something you want to do?"

"Yeah. I mean, I've wanted to ever since the shower." He closed his eyes. Sean waited for him to gather his thoughts. "I was torn between wanting to fuck you and wanting to suck you. I was so damned scared. Scared of my feelings. Scared shitless when you turned around. I saw your huge dick, and I knew you were thinking the same things I was. I was scared out of my mind someone would see us."

"What if there hadn't been any possibility of someone seeing?" Sean asked.

"I would have let you do anything you wanted to me and begged you to let me do the same."

"There's no one here now. Just us." Sean reached for his belt buckle. "Take your clothes off. All of them."

Bent stilled. Sean could almost see the wheels turning in his lover's head before he stood and removed his suit jacket.

"You, too. No clothes. If I'm going to suck your dick, I want to see all of you, just like in the shower."

Sean stood. Together they disrobed until they both stood naked, nothing but the expanse of the king-sized bed between them. Bentley Randolph, gloriously naked, willingly so, almost brought him to his knees. His fair skin was tanned except for a band of lily-white skin below his navel to the top of his thighs. Smooth-chested, his physique was one of an athlete in top physical condition. He'd trimmed his sandy pubic hair to a neat puff surrounding the base of his cock. Sean sort of remembered the manscaping from the other night. He'd been too out of his head to commit details to memory.

Bent's cock, soft when he'd first undressed, rose under Sean's gaze. Like the rest of him, it was fair, pink with a head shading more toward purple the larger it became.

"Nice grooming," he said.

"Ashley likes to do it. As long as she doesn't cut off anything important, I let her."

Bent's face flushed at the mention of the intimate details of his relationship with his fiancée. It was time to change the subject. There was room for just one other person in his bed. "Where do you want me?"

Bentley inwardly cursed. Why had he brought up Ashley at a time like this? Thankfully, Sean hadn't seemed disturbed by the slip.

But even with Sean standing naked, his enormous cock demanding attention, Bent felt as if his fiancée was there with him. She was a part of him. He couldn't just wipe her out of his mind or his heart, but if there was ever a place and time when he should, this was it. He was about to suck another man's cock.

Ashley would hate him if she knew.

"On the bed," he said, sweeping his arm to indicate the giant piece of furniture in the center of the room.

Don't hate me, Ashley. Please don't hate me. I hate myself enough for what I'm going to do, but I want to suck his cock so damn bad. I have to do it.

Sean's body was the epitome of strength and good health. Tight, bronzed skin defined every muscle in his torso. Even the skin below his belt was dusky, indicating it was his natural coloring. His dark cock bobbed as he bent to turn the covers back then adjusted the pillows. Bent caught a glimpse of his firm ass before he lay down on the white sheets.

His feet seemed glued to the floor. Blood rushed past his ears to pool in his groin. Licking his dry lips, he stared at Sean's hand shifting his balls to rest on top of his thighs.

"Just lay with me a while." Sean patted the expanse of white cotton beside him.

"I…I can do that." He forced one foot off the floor, placing his knee on the edge of the mattress. He moved like molasses to lie stiff as a board on his back beside Sean. They weren't even touching, but he could feel the heat radiating off Sean's body, could smell him. He hadn't been this nervous when he'd gone down on his first girlfriend in the back seat of his car following Junior Prom.

"I can't believe I'm doing this," he said.

"You've been around naked men almost every day of your Major League career," Sean reasoned.

"This is different. I've never been in bed with any of them."

"I know. Why don't you start by touching me? Anywhere. We've sort of skipped the getting to know each other phase."

Closing his eyes, Bent blew out a breath, willing himself to relax. "I guess we have." He rolled to his side, propping up on one elbow. His free hand hovered over Sean's chest.

"I won't break, Bent. Touch me."

He lowered his palm to the center of the other man's chest as if expecting a bomb to detonate on contact. Sean hissed in a sharp breath, but otherwise remained still.

"You take good care of yourself," he said, admiring the firm skin and muscle beneath his hand.

"For an old guy?" Sean teased.

"You're just a couple of years older than me."

"In years, yeah, but I'm not the man I used to be."

He trailed his hand lower to Sean's left hip, his arm hovering above his engorged cock. "The hip injury?"

"Yeah. It's better. I can play on most days."

"I'm sorry." He traced the scar that hadn't been there five years ago. "I heard about it when it happened. You're lucky you came back from it at all."

"You're killing me, Bentley. I said I wouldn't push, but if you're going to help me, could you get on with it? I promise to let you touch all you want…after."

He stared at the massive appendage twitching with need, inches from his face. He'd never been close to a cock before. The reality of what he was going to do hit him square in the gut.

"Okay," he breathed. "Cut me some slack, will you? I've never done this before."

"Just open your goddamn mouth and put it in, for Christ sakes."

Bent smiled at the tension in Sean's voice, so different from the kitten pleas Ashley made when she needed to come. Knowing Sean's powerful body was enslaved to him for even the next few minutes filled him with masculine satisfaction and pride. He closed his hand around the base then raised the head to his lips.

How does Ashley do it?

He flicked his tongue over the head. Sean bucked his hips.

"Fuckin' asshole. Suck it. Now!"

Bent opened wide, taking in as much as he could.

Sean arched his back, forcing his cock farther toward the back of his throat. "Ahh, Christ almighty that feels so fuckin' good."

God, he tasted good, salty and like nothing he'd ever tasted before. Forced to breathe through his nose, he reveled in Sean's clean scent, enhanced by the heat emanating off his body. It didn't take long to figure out how to drive Sean crazy, he just remembered the things Ashley did to him that sucked his brains out through his dick then tried them himself.

With his fiancée, he was careful not to move too much, afraid being so much stronger than she was he might hurt her, but Sean had no such sensibilities. He bucked, arched, and gyrated to an almost non-stop litany of curses. At some point, he placed a hand on the back of Bent's head and it remained there holding him in place, as if he had any intention of stopping now. No, controlling Sean by his dick was too much fun.

Bent shifted in order to use both hands. Sean raised his left knee allowing him better access to the goodies. Taking advantage of the new position, he cupped Sean's balls in the palm of his hand then tugged hard.

"Shit!" Sean's hips came off the bed.

Bent tugged his scrotum again, adding a not too gentle twist. He smiled inside as Sean tried to rip a chunk of his hair out. Sucking dick was more fun than he could have imagined. Like sex with Sean, it was rough, almost primal, yet there was an element of sweetness about the act that warmed him to the core. He knew how much trust it took to let a woman suck his dick, but to let another man? Yeah, that took some big balls.

Remembering another move Ashley was especially fond of, he dipped his middle finger lower to stroke the soft skin between Sean's scrotum and his anus. A hissed insult to his parentage told him he'd found the right spot. He pressed hard.

Sean jerked Bent's mouth free then rolled to a kneeling position.

"Fuck that, asshole," Sean said. "On your knees."

Power drained from his body, replaced by the surprising contentment of submission as he positioned himself in front of Sean, his shoulders to the mattress, his ass in the air.

"Show me your ass," Sean commanded.

Bent spread his cheeks, exposing himself literally and figuratively to his lover. This was what he craved with Sean. No flowery words, just raw, elemental fucking.

Sean drove deep in one powerful thrust, then wrapping his arms around Bent's waist, he lifted him so he sat on his thighs, his back to Sean's chest.

"Jack yourself," Sean said. "I want to see you come." He pried Bent's right hand from between them, bringing it to his mouth. Sean's tongue swiped over Bent's palm in a gesture so tender it made his heart ache. After moistening Bent's palm, Sean placed a kiss in the center then guided it to his cock.

"I won't last long, so you better work fast."

Ashley never demanded. She was never crude. He loved her lady-like ways, but he loved Sean's no bullshit language, too. He loved the way Sean ordered him around, the way he took charge, the way he didn't hold anything back.

"It won't break off," he said when Bent slowed his pace. "Harder. Faster."

Bent jacked himself, his hand sliding along his length while the other held his ass open for Sean. He was still a little sore from the last time, but after the pain of the initial penetration, he was able to enjoy the fullness, the push and pull of the cock reaming him.

"Harder," he pleaded. "Fuck me harder."

"Ah, shit, Bent."

Sean tightened his arms around Bent's waist, half lifted him. Bent let go of his ass cheek and thrust his hand forward to brace himself off the mattress. Sean rocked him to the core, his balls slapping Bent's with each savage thrust. His own cock swelled in his grasp. It was a matter of minutes before he came with a gut-wrenching orgasm that weakened him, leaving him completely at the mercy of the man at his back.

"Fuck, you're killing me," Sean said. With one more powerful thrust, he filled Bent's ass with hot cum.

CHAPTER NINE

They lay side by side, their arms making contact from shoulder to wrist. Bent hadn't made any effort to leave, yet. He would have to. No way could he be seen leaving Sean's room in the morning.

Watching the play of city lights from the street and adjacent buildings cross the ceiling, Sean hated to bring the subject up. But someone needed to.

"Where do we go from here?" he asked.

"I don't have a fuckin' clue."

"Are we going to do this again?"

Bent was silent for so long he began to think the worst.

"Yeah."

Sean breathed a sigh of relief.

"You were right, you know. I'm messed up. I can't stop thinking of ways to fuck you, but at the same time, I want to tell Ashley all about it. How's this for fucked up? I want you to watch me fuck her. Maybe play with my ass while I do her."

"That's fucked up all right." Sean mulled the possible scene over in his mind. "Do you think she'd do it?"

"No."

"Then you're screwed."

"Yeah, I figured that out on my own."

"I think I'd like to watch you fuck her. You ride her while I ride you. It could be fun."

"She'd never go for it."

"How do you know?"

Silence stretched while he supposed Bent contemplated asking his fiancée to do a threesome with his male lover.

"If she won't, and I keep you, I'm going to lose her. If I keep her, am I going to lose you?"

"You mean if you don't tell her?"

"Yeah. If I don't tell her about us. Would you walk?"

Sean took his time answering. One thing he was sure of, Bentley was in love with his fiancée. He wasn't going to let her go if he had any choice in the matter.

"I guess it depends on how you feel about me. I love you, Bentley. I always have, and I always will. I believe you when you say you love Ashley, so the question is, do you love me, too? Or am I just a novelty you'll tire of one day?"

"I don't think I'm going to get tired of you. Maybe we could just let things play out for a while, see where it goes between us?"

"You aren't going to tell Ashley about us?"

"No. Not right away. I feel like I'm cheating on her, but I need some time to figure this out before I tell her."

Sean remained silent letting him collect his thoughts. Whatever Bent decided, he had no choice but to go along, no matter how much it hurt. Bent was the one with everything to lose, a successful career, a fiancée, as well as a family in the future. He, on the other hand, had nothing but Bent.

"I'll tell her, Sean. I promise. Give me some time, okay?"

"So, while you're figuring out what to tell your fiancée and when, how does our relationship work? I get you on road trips, she gets you during home stands?"

Bentley groaned. "I'm doing the best I can here, asshole. I don't hear any constructive ideas coming from you, so just shut the fuck up."

"Point taken." Sighing, Sean rolled to his side so he could see his lover's face. "I don't know what to tell you to do. All I know is I've waited a long time to be with you, and I don't want to lose you. I don't think I could share you with another man, but I might be able to come to terms with you and Ashley being together."

"That's all I'm asking, a little patience and understanding. I had no intention of cheating on Ashley. I never would have if you hadn't showed up. When you were thousands of miles away, it was easy to forget you. But having you here…I tried to fight my feelings for you. I gave it everything I had. But seeing you every fucking day drove me out of my mind."

"I know the feeling. I'm sorry, Bentley. I didn't want to be traded to the Mustangs. I did everything I could to keep the trade from happening. You can't imagine how much I hated you for leaving the Pioneers."

"I left because—"

"Because of me. I know. Hating you was easier than loving you."

"I hate you, too." Bent smiled.

Sean kissed him, putting five years of longing and a lifetime of hope into it.

CHAPTER TEN

Guilt ate at Bentley, but every time he thought he'd found the words to tell Ashley, they dried in his throat, almost choking him. Fear could be a great motivator, but in his case, it held him captive, robbing him of the ability to speak.

The team returned to town for a ten game home stand. Thanks to their crazy schedules, he managed to avoid Ashley for three days.

"I've been busy," was his answer to her tearful questioning of his absence. She had every right to be upset. What kind of man didn't put his fiancée first when he'd been out of town?

"You could have answered your phone," she argued. "I've been busy, too, but I found time to leave you messages."

Excuses died on his lips. "I'm sorry, babe. I'm an ass." *Truer words were never spoken.* "But I'm here now."

She melted into his embrace. When she turned her tear-streaked face up to him, all he wanted to do was make the hurt go away—for both of them.

He kissed her, angling his mouth across hers in a flash of heat guaranteed to fan the flames of desire. God, he wanted her, couldn't imagine not being with her. He moved his hands over her back, to her ass, hauling her up against his hardening cock. Tearing one hand away from her firm backside, he palmed her breast. Moaning, she squirmed against him. In his lust-fueled mind, he took her actions to mean she wanted more. He closed his fingers over her and squeezed.

"Ouch!" Ashley broke the kiss, pushing away from him.

Stunned by the pain on her face and the way she'd brought her arms up to cover herself, he reached for her. "What? Did I hurt you? Oh, God. Please tell me I didn't hurt you."

She shook her head. "No, I'm fine."

Holy shit. Had his being with Sean caused him to forget what it was like to hold a woman? He mentally kicked himself for not tempering his strength. "I'm sorry." He held his hand out in supplication. "I didn't mean to hurt you."

She looked at him with clear eyes. He breathed a sigh of relief, seeing the pain had eased.

"I know, Bentley." She took a deep breath then let it out, straightening her shoulders as she did so. "I'm glad I caught up to you today."

She reached out to him. He grasped her fingers, relieved to see she still trusted him—though God knew he hadn't earned it. Guilt over his betrayal loosened his tongue.

"Ashley—"

"No talking." She tugged him forward. "I've missed you. Make love to me, please?"

Like the low-down, lying, cheating ass he was, he followed her up the stairs to the bedroom.

Bentley needed to get his head in the game.

You are such a fucked up coward. You don't deserve her. God knows she doesn't deserve a fucked up mess like you, but she's stuck with you now.

Jogging out to left field, he pulled his sunglasses off the bill of his cap, settling them into place where they belonged. His focus was shit today.

He'd taken the coward's way out last night, making love to Ashley instead of telling her about Sean, and now he was glad he hadn't said anything. Their conversation this morning made it clear he'd waited too long.

She'd looked so damn sweet, standing there in the kitchen wearing nothing but the rumpled T-shirt with his number on it she liked to sleep in and a bad case of bed head. He'd been tempted to scoop her up to the counter then fuck her senseless. It still amazed him how much he wanted her, considering. "Good morning," he'd said from his perch at the bar. The Mustangs were playing the Marauders at one o'clock, which meant he needed to be at the stadium in a few hours. He was capable of making his own breakfast, so he'd let her sleep. She'd seemed particularly tired last night after their lovemaking. Coward that he was, he'd been damn grateful for the reprieve when she'd curled up beside him and gone to sleep.

"Morning." She shuffled around, getting a glass from the cabinet then pouring herself orange juice from the jar in the refrigerator before sitting on the stool next to him.

"You okay? You conked out early last night. Are you coming down with something?"

He picked up the slice of toast he'd been eating while checking the news on his iPad then slid the plate containing the extra slice toward her. She helped herself.

"I'm fine. Just tired. We've been working on some new programming ideas. The whole process is making me crazy. I've been at the office late every night you've been gone."

"You should take a day off, get some rest."

"I can't. At least not right now." She bit into the slice of toast, chewed and swallowed. "On top of everything going on at work, my mother is bugging me about setting a date for the wedding. She's thinking about fall or winter—in the off-season. I think a winter wedding sounds fun. We'd have to hustle to get it all done, but the right planner could make it happen. What do you think?"

I think I'm screwed. He smiled. "Whatever you want, babe."

You are a lying, sniveling coward, Bentley Randolph.

The crack of the bat hitting the ball jerked his attention back to the game. Instinct took over. He tracked the ball, a grounder to the right side of the field. No play for him, but he moved toward third base anyway, just in case he'd be needed for backup. The lead runner held at second, and Sean took the easy throw from right field for the out at first. Forcing his gaze off the first baseman's fluid motions, he returned to his position.

Stay calm. No need to panic.

The idea of telling Sean they'd set a date for the wedding made him sick to his stomach. For the last month, they'd had nothing but stolen moments on the road. Thanks to his hip injury, Sean continued to get a single room on a lower floor. Surprisingly, the stair climbing seemed to do some good. Or maybe it was all the sex. Sean was moving easier on the field, favoring his left leg less than when he'd first joined the team. He only complained about it when they were in bed together, and then because he knew Bent wouldn't say anything to anyone on the Mustangs.

Always careful not to be seen together, they'd worked out a system to avoid detection, but the few hours they managed to be alone never seemed to be enough.

Now this. He had a wedding date.

He had no idea what Sean would think when he told him.

Hell, yes you know what he would think. He's going to think you're a coward.

He's always known you weren't going to leave her.

Stretching to loosen his tight shoulders, he blindly scanned the crowd.

A Christmas wedding. Jesus, what a mess.

I have to tell her about Sean.

She'll leave you.

He couldn't take his eyes off the man in question. He was poetry in motion. Every play he made, Bent imagined the muscles he'd come to know so well, bunching and stretching beneath bronze skin. If there was some way he could have them both…but he couldn't. He knew that now.

The knowledge almost crushed him.

Sean knew something was wrong. Bentley played the final games of their home stand like a zombie. He went through the motions, but the enthusiasm the Mustangs left fielder usually exhibited for the game wasn't there. He didn't think many people noticed—that's how good Bentley Randolph was at the game. He played better than most, even when he wasn't trying.

But Sean knew. And he had a sinking feeling in his stomach he knew what was coming.

They were always careful around each other, keeping a distance explained by the earlier violent encounters in front of their teammates. Officially, they hated each other. For the sake of the team, they'd called a truce of sorts, but off the record, they kept their distance for a whole different reason. When they were within reach, they couldn't keep their hands off each other—but the world they lived in wasn't ready for their kind of relationship.

Watching Bent step into the hotel elevator at the far end of the alcove, he cursed under his breath. By the time he reached the fourth floor where his room was, it would be a matter of minutes before Bent came to him.

Taking the stairs two at a time, he tried to focus on planting his feet just right so as not to tweak the very muscles the exercise was supposed to strengthen. Because, if his gut was telling him the truth, his shaky career was all he would have left in a few minutes.

He sprang to answer the knock on his door—a full hour later than he'd expected it. One look at his lover's face confirmed his fears.

Closing the door behind him, Sean resisted the urge to put his fist through a wall. *Maybe I'm wrong. Please, God, let me be wrong.*

"What took you so long?" he asked in what he hoped was a normal tone.

Bentley stood facing the window, his hands fisted on his hips, his head dipped low. It was tempting to go to him, to offer comfort, but he sensed it wouldn't be welcome. Whatever put his friend in his current mood was something he couldn't fix. He was sure of it.

He raised his head without turning around. "I almost didn't come at all."

Sean helped himself to a beer from the mini-bar then, after twisting the lid off, sank to the edge of the bed facing away from the window. Whatever Bent had to say, he didn't want to look at him when he said it. "Why?"

The room's AC came on, went off again. Sean waited. The hell if he was going to drag it out of the man.

"I don't know any other way to say this, Sean, but to just say it. We're done. We can't see each other again."

A chill not attributable to the room's temperature raced along his spine. He'd expected Bent to end their relationship, but the reality of it hit him harder than a fastball to the head. Tears blurred his vision. He blinked, trying to keep them from falling.

"Why?" He cringed at the pathetic whimper of the word.

"Ashley and I have set a date for the wedding. Christmas."

"What the fuck?" He was off the bed, rage burning hot enough to melt the ice around his heart spurred him into action. "Why haven't you told her about me? About us?"

Rounding the bed, he took a few steps but stopped before he got close enough to do something he would regret, like throwing Bentley through the window. "You're seriously going to marry her. I don't fucking believe this." *Un-fucking-believable.*

Bent turned to him. The anguish on his handsome face almost brought Sean to his knees. But anger won over hurt. "So, what? You're feeling like a man now? You're going to throw away what we have together because you're too much of a coward to tell her the truth?"

Bent raised his gaze to Sean's. "I've never lied to you about my relationship with Ashley. I'm a fucked up son of a bitch, but I'm not going to let the perverted side of me ruin the rest of my life."

"*Perverted?* You think what we have together is perverted?" That one word was all he'd heard, and it felt like a knife to the gut. "God, you're an ass, Bentley. You deserve to be miserable for the rest of your life if that's what you believe."

"I'm sorry. I don't know what else to say. I just want to be like everyone else, Sean. Can't you see? I want a wife and kids. I want to be *normal.* Ashley is my chance at the kind of life I want. I have no intention of sneaking around for the rest of my years seeing my gay lover on the side, worrying every second about someone finding out and telling the world."

Tears streamed down Bent's cheeks, his shoulders shaking. "I love you, Sean, but I can't keep going back and forth between the two of you. I hate myself for what I'm doing to Ashley. Face it—there's no future for us. There never was."

The weight of reality all but crushed him. *Bentley is right.* He'd let himself imagine a future with this man when there wasn't one. At least not one they could show in public, and sneaking around was for teenagers, not grown men.

Ah hell.

"Come here," he said, forcing his feet to move.

Bent leaned into Sean's embrace. It felt good to be held, comforted, even though the last person who should be showing him compassion was Sean Flannery. But for the first time since he'd committed to the wedding date, he began to believe he might survive.

"You don't hate me?" he sniffed against one strong shoulder.

"No. I don't hate you. I love you. I'll always love you, Bent. No matter what." Sean's big hands stroking his back were as reassuring as his words. "I understand why you're walking. I was stupid to think we could make a relationship work."

"I hate doing this to you."

Sean pushed him away enough so he could look him in the eye. "I'm sorry, Bent. I dragged you into a relationship that was doomed from the start. I knew better, but I couldn't help myself. I've wanted you for so long."

Bent sniffed back tears. "I could have said no, but I didn't. If we lived in a perfect world, I wouldn't have to choose, but we don't. If we continue like we are, I'm going to lose you, *and* Ashley."

"You're right. We can't continue seeing each other this way. I want you to be happy. That's all I want."

His heart swelled with love for Sean. He hadn't expected him to understand any more than he expected Ashley to if he'd ever found the courage to tell her.

"I have no right to ask…but can I stay…for a little while?" He let every bit of desire he felt for him show in his eyes, praying it was enough.

"You know what's going to happen if you do."

The gravel in his voice encouraged him. He leaned in, placed his lips on Sean's jaw, and murmured, "I know. I need you, one last time." His fingers went to work on Sean's belt buckle.

"Goddamn it." He pressed down on his lover's shoulders, forcing him to his knees.

Letting Bent stay was so not a good idea, but he couldn't bring himself to say no. Just a few weeks ago, he would have given anything to hear this man say those words. They'd come a long way in a short period of time, but it was over. Fuck if he was going to pass on one final night with the man he loved. He might be an idiot, but he wasn't stupid.

Shifting his feet to keep from toppling over, he let his head fall back. He stared sightless at the ceiling while the man worked to free his cock. His trousers pooled around his ankles. His skin tingled, and his cock strained against his tight briefs.

Bentley cupped him through the fabric, teasing the beast within.

"Goddamn it," he hissed. "Don't fuck with me, asshole, or you'll regret asking to stay. I swear to God, you will."

"Don't fucking move," he warned, continuing his exploration, "unless I tell you to."

The command in his lover's voice, tinged with a hint of sadness was like a stab to the heart. He glanced down. His eyes were closed, his hand hidden by Sean's shirttails.

"What the fuck are you doing?" he demanded. Did he not have any idea what he was doing to him?

Bent looked up at him. "Memorizing, asshole. Unbutton your shirt. Leave it and your coat on—just keep them out of my way."

Memorizing. Oh, fuck.

Sean clenched his jaw tight, loosened his tie then he unbuttoned his shirt. When he worked the last button free, anchoring the sides open with his fists on his hips, Bent dragged his briefs down to his knees. His cock sprang out like a rookie player taking the field for his first Major League game—proud and eager to please.

"You're fucking huge."

He flexed his hips, stabbing his appendage toward the place it wanted to be. Bent slapped it away, and Sean saw stars.

"Shit."

"I told you not to move." Bent gripped his thighs. Wrapping his fingers around to the back, he slid his hands up to grope Sean's ass cheeks. "I want to take my time. I want to memorize everything about you then I'm going to drive you out of your mind, so you won't forget me."

"Jesus, Bent. I won't forget you."

"What do you want? Tell me what you want." His mouth was so close to his cock his hot breath washed over it.

"I want you to shut the fuck up and suck my dick."

Without another word, Bent gave him what he wanted.

"Ah, fuck, that feels good," he hissed, fighting the urge to shove his cock down his lover's throat. In the few months they'd been together, Bent had learned exactly what he liked. Alternating between taking him deep then sucking just the head while he swirled his tongue over him, he brought Sean to the brink.

"Jesus," he said through gritted teeth. Unable to remain still, he wrapped his hands around the back of Bent's head to hold him steady. The man grunted once, but then he wrapped his arms around Sean's thighs and relaxed his facial muscles.

He fucked his mouth hard, pumping with short, jerky thrusts that pounded his stomach against his lover's face. He didn't care. Like a freight train out of control, he barreled toward the inevitable crash. When it came, it buckled his knees. If not for the strong arms supporting him, he would have fallen as wave after wave of ecstasy rolled through him.

When he had spent himself completely, Bent eased away from him. With a not too gentle shove, he pushed him back on the bed. Weak, Sean made no protest when his lover rolled him to his stomach, parted him, then with no ceremony, drove his cock home.

"Christ!" He shifted, easing his entry, allowing him to go deeper. God, it felt good. Like always, the man fucked hard. Never cautious, he was always physical—demanding complete surrender, and surrender was something Sean was always willing to give.

Lying beneath him today, he opened his heart and his body in an effort to absorb his lover's pain. He'd do anything to prevent his suffering, but in the end, this was all he could do—be there for him now then let him go later.

The fucking was raw, brutal, and unforgiving—intentionally so. They'd both be sore tomorrow, a reminder of tonight. As if he would ever forget.

The rod shoved up his ass grew harder, and Sean braced for the violent finish he sensed coming. The thrusts grew shorter, faster. With an oath, Bent erupted. Sean savored each throbbing spurt, savored the flush of liquid heat signaling his lover's satisfaction.

Long moments passed while the only sound in the room was the soft swoosh of the air conditioner and their ragged breathing. Sean fisted his hands in the bedspread, waiting. Softening, Bent slipped from him. The sound of him adjusting his clothing tore at Sean's heart. Christ. They hadn't even bothered to undress. They were right back where they'd started—fucking like strangers meeting in cheap hotel rooms.

It hurt more than he wanted to admit that all the man had wanted from him was a quick, hard fuck, but damned if he would say anything. His ass stung from the brutal assault. His dick, half-aroused despite its recent satisfaction, ached for something it could never have again.

It was over. He'd been well and truly fucked, in more ways than one.

A gentle but firm hand touched his ass a moment before sliding beneath his shirt and suit coat to the small of his back. It rested there for the span of a heartbeat. A benediction. A thank you. An acknowledgement. A declaration.

Then it was gone, leaving behind an invisible brand he would carry with him the rest of his days.

Sean lay silent, eyes shut, listening to Bent's footsteps cross the carpet—the door opening then closing as his heart walked out of his life.

Bentley made it to the stairwell, climbed up two flights before he collapsed in the corner of a landing. His chest felt like someone had used a rusty can opener to pry open his ribcage and remove his heart.

Fuck. Fuck. Fuck. Fuck.

Wrapping his arms tight around himself, he tried to breathe through the pain, but each breath was another one he took without Sean in his life, and there was no comfort in it.

You did what you had to do.

He sat there until the cold from the concrete surrounding him numbed the pain.

CHAPTER ELEVEN

Shit.

Everything on him hurt, including his dick, which hadn't seen anything but hand action since Bentley sucked him off almost two months ago. It was nothing short of torture to be around him almost every day while acting as if nothing was wrong. At least they had eased into a tentative friendship the other players seemed to accept without question.

A small part of him hated Bentley for the way their relationship ended, but deep down he understood there was no other choice. Even though it killed him to pretend in front of the world, he wouldn't trade a single minute of time spent with him.

The day after their breakup, he'd made a decision. He couldn't risk another trade that would take him away from Bentley, which meant he had to get his shit together. He had to play harder than he'd ever played in his life. First base was his, and he was going to keep it. The team had recently brought up a kid from the Minor's who had his eye on Sean's position.

Not going to happen.

The way he figured it, he had two options. He could hustle to keep his job, or he could die trying. Either way, he'd stay in Dallas. He didn't dare hope anything would change in regard to Bentley, but he was going to stick around, just in case—he'd never thought Bent would admit his feelings for him, but he had. There was always hope.

Bent swore under his breath.

What the fuck is he trying to do? Kill himself?

It wasn't the first time since he'd walked out of Sean's hotel room he'd questioned the workings of his former lover's mind. He'd become a loose cannon on the field. He slid into impossible situations and went after foul balls no one had any prayer of catching. His stats were better than they'd ever been.

Watching him slide into second base, Bent cringed. Every time, he worried if their first baseman would get up, and if he did, would he still be able to walk. Holding his breath, he glared across the field. Sean rolled to his good hip, came up on one knee, and rising, brushed red dirt from his uniform. The crowd cheered along with everyone in the dugout except him. He wanted to throttle him, not cheer for him.

Yeah, having a runner in scoring position was huge. Tied at three runs each in the eighth inning, if the Mustangs were going to win, they needed to score now, not later. A go-ahead run would bring Jeff Holder to the mound in the bottom of the inning. With the best record in the League, Jeff was the closer no one wanted to face. He could pitch two shutout innings, easy, but the offense had to put a run on the board, or they'd be wasting his talents.

Bent was surprised to realize none of it mattered to him if Sean's career was the price paid for it. There were other games, other ways to win this one.

"He's going to do that one too many times," he muttered, "then where will we be?"

"Accepting our World Series rings?" Chip Matthews, a bench sitting, second-rate, green behind the ears infielder clapped him on the back. "At least the old man is showing some hustle."

"You think all it takes to win is hustle?" He was in the kid's face. "Let me tell you, asshole, all the hustle in the world won't make up for a lack of common sense. Another injury could end his career, not to mention put a serious hole in our lineup. So why don't you—"

"Stand down, Randolph." Doyle Walker's firm hand on his

shoulder urged him to back away. "Flannery is fine. Leave the kid alone, all right? Don't you remember your first week up from the Minor's?"

Bent shrugged, stepping back. "I was never as stupid as he is."

"Yes, you were. You just don't remember." He advised the rookie to watch and learn before sending him to join the rest of the team at the railing.

"I don't know what's got into you, Bentley, but whatever burr you have up your ass, you better pull it out—fast. You haven't had your head in the game for a couple of weeks. If we're going to make the playoffs, we need you to give one hundred percent." His tone brooked no argument. He wiped a hand over his face then sighed. "Look, if you need someone to listen, I'm here for you. Anytime."

"Thanks. Maybe I'll take you up on the offer sometime," he lied. No way in hell was he telling the team manager he was fucked up because he'd broken up with his gay lover who just happened to be the Mustangs first baseman, or he was afraid his fiancée would leave him if she found out. That conversation had career killer written all over it.

"You good?" Walker asked.

"I'm good. Sorry. The kid got under my skin. I won't let it happen again."

Thwack!

The sound had them both jockeying to see what was happening on the field. Having hit a grounder past the second baseman, Ramirez sped toward first trying to beat the throw from right field. With two outs, Sean had been running almost before the ball left the bat. He rounded third base then headed home.

A seasoned player, Flannery didn't look up to see what was happening on the field. The play was at home plate, and his only chance was to slide in under the throw.

Bent held his breath. Sean folded in two then launched himself, head first at the plate. The hometown crowd roared their approval. Hands extended, Sean belly slid the last six feet. Dust flew. His hand brushed the white rubber pentagon a fraction of a second before the catcher's glove brushed his arm.

The dugout emptied. Bent didn't move, didn't breathe, until Sean popped to his feet, a big smile lighting his face, then he joined the throng celebrating the go-ahead run. When it was his turn to congratulate the man of the hour, he grabbed him in a man hug, clapping him on the back.

"You're a crazy son of a bitch. You know that, don't you?"

"I know."

They broke apart then walked back to the dugout with their arms slung over each other's shoulders.

Bentley dropped his duffle bag in the laundry room off the kitchen and, after grabbing a beer from the refrigerator, trudged into the den. He wasn't surprised to see Ashley curled up on the man cave-sized sofa. Glancing at the television screen, he stifled a groan.

"Why are you watching the press conference?" Coming around to sit next to her, he slung his arm over her shoulders, pulling her in close.

"Sorry I missed your game," she said, turning into him for a quick kiss. "I had another late night." She pointed to the screen where a repeat of the night's post-game press conference ran. "Can you introduce me to him?"

"Sean Flannery?" His heart almost leapt from his chest. "Why on earth would you want to meet him?"

"Are you blind? Look at him. I was so pissed at you the day he came to the house I hardly noticed, but I'm noticing now. He's gorgeous. Listen to his voice. See the way he handles himself? He's a natural on-screen personality."

"You do know he has a job," he warned.

"I know, but Ray Walters is going to retire at the end of the year, and we're looking for someone to replace him."

"I repeat, Sean has a job—one he loves, I might add, so what makes you think he would even listen to your offer."

"I didn't say I was going to make an offer. I just want to talk to him. You know, get a feel for the guy, maybe ask a few questions."

"I don't think that's a good idea. He's having what could be his best season ever. A guy doesn't just walk away from that."

Sean's segment ended. Ashley reached for the remote, rewinding the taped interview back to the beginning. Bent tried to remain calm. Damn, she was right. Sean had an easy, relaxed way about him on camera. He was quick on his feet, answering the reporter's questions then transitioning from one subject to the next without hesitation. He could see him taking over the anchor seat on the weekly sports-talk show.

Ashley's attention was on the screen for the better part of Sean's interview, then she hit the pause button and turned to him. Her eyes sparkled with excitement as she crawled into his lap. She wrapped one hand around his nape, toying with the hair above his collar while the other stroked his tie in a suggestive manner. His dick twitched, anticipating the same sort of treatment.

"Please, Bent? The team has a day off next week, right? Invite him over for lunch."

"He won't come." *Please, God.*

"Why ever not? He's your friend, isn't he? Ask him, for me? Please? I could call him myself, but I don't want him to know what I'm thinking yet. I just want to spend some time with him in a casual atmosphere, see what he's like. See if he's all show for the cameras but a jackass the rest of the time."

"You think he'd be my friend if he was a jackass?"

"No, I don't, but how well do you know him?"

Well enough. "He's a great guy, you can take my word for it. But he isn't interested in leaving baseball."

"Then we'll have a nice lunch together, and that will be that."

"No." The last thing he wanted was to bring the two of them together.

"Then I guess I'll have to make the call myself." She sighed, and he recognized he was fighting a losing battle. She hadn't gotten where she was in her profession by taking no for an answer.

"Okay, I'll ask, but don't be surprised when he turns me down. We haven't always been on the best of terms."

She stilled in his lap, and he knew he'd said too much.

"He's the one you fought with, isn't he?"

"Yeah. Like I said, he's a nice guy, but we've had our differences."

"I saw you walking off the field with him earlier. It looked like you were getting along okay."

"We have our moments."

"Then you need to spend some time together off the field. This lunch will kill two birds with one stone, as they say."

More likely kill two relationships. For a split second, he considered telling her the truth, but then he remembered why he couldn't. *Time to change the subject.* He asked, "How's work? Any light at the end of the tunnel?"

"Work is fine. Crazy. Exciting. I love what I do."

"Don't let them take advantage of you."

"I won't. I promise." She kissed him, slow and sensuous. "Make love to me, Bent. I need you."

He reached for the remote, clicking the button to remove Sean's face from the screen. He was his past. Ashley was his future. He laid her back on the sofa then covered her with his body.

She was soft beneath him, and he wanted her with every fiber of his being. But even as he took her breast in his mouth, another image flashed through his mind, an image of a hard-muscled chest with flat nipples he'd learned could be sensitive, too. As he worked his way down his fiancée's body, he tried to banish the memories of being with Sean, but they'd become a part of him, and he hated himself for it.

Ashley deserved all of him, not the half-man he'd become. But every time he thought about telling her, he remembered what he had to lose if she didn't understand, and he chickened out.

Half a man in his heart, his body responded wholly to hers. Another sin heaped on the pyre of guilt building inside him, ready to spark into flame and consume him, body and soul.

You're a sick bastard.

Sick or not, he *needed* her, needed to be inside her, needed to feel her heart below his palm when he closed his hand over her breast. He *wanted* her.

She opened for him, offered her essence to him. He took it greedily, lapping at her folds, burying his face in her wet pussy, biting and sucking until he was drunk on her scent and her juices. She clawed at his scalp, begging him for more. Out of his mind with lust, need, and crazy-assed guilt, he drove into her hard. She cried out, her head thrown back. The pain of her fingernails digging into his ass was fuel to the raging fire burning inside him.

He couldn't stop, couldn't temper his thrusts, even though a tiny rational voice in his head screamed for him to ease up on her.

She's not Sean. She's not Sean. She's not Sean.

"Bent!" Her body convulsed, quivered with the powerful spasms gripping his cock. Garbled sounds came from her throat, but he still couldn't stop. He pounded into her tight sheath, hard, punishing thrusts that rocked her body in increments toward the arm of the sofa. His ass burned where she clung to him, dragging him along with her until pleasure blinded him. He erupted inside her, shaking and shuddering his release, pouring his heart, his anguish, into her, one scalding spurt at a time.

Gulping air into raw lungs, he held himself above her, his one concession to her femininity. His shoulders screamed with the effort imposed upon them, but he absorbed the pain as penance for what he'd done. Still hard, he rocked his hips, reveling in the feel of their mingled fluids bathing his cock.

"I'm so sorry, babe. So fucking sorry."

"What is it?" Concern laced her voice as she framed his face with her hands. Her thumbs brushed his cheeks. He thought he might die when he realized she was brushing tears from his cheeks.

"Bentley." Her voice had hardened, and he realized he'd fucked up royally. "Tell me. What's going on? What do you mean, you're sorry?"

She wiggled out from under him, reaching for any scrap of clothing she could reach from the pile on the floor. She found his suit coat, pulling it over her like a shield. My God, she looked so vulnerable it broke his heart to look at her. He scooted away, grabbed his pants. Not trusting his legs to hold him, he pulled his pants on without trying to stand.

"Bentley. Tell me what's going on in your head. Is it what we just did? You didn't hurt me. I swear."

God, how could she still be thinking of ways to excuse his behavior? *Because she doesn't know the half of it, that's how.*

"I fucked up, Ashley." He sucked in a deep breath, held it then used it to push the next words out. "I cheated on you."

She sat like a statue, curled up under his coat, staring at him as if he'd grown two heads. Her post-coital glow faded to a deathly pallor. Her mouth opened and closed then she uttered the one word he dreaded most.

"Who. Who, Bentley? Who is she?"

"Not she. He. Sean Flannery."

"Sean Flannery," she repeated without emotion. "You slept with Sean Flannery?"

Nodding he looked away, unable to watch as she processed the information. "I'm sorry. It…it just happened."

Silence rang in his ears. He barely dared breathe, waiting for the inevitable.

"Are you telling me you're gay? Don't bother trying to convince me, because I'll never believe it."

"I'm not gay." He jerked his gaze to her. "Not gay. I swear it."

"Then why, Bent? Why did you do it?"

"I don't know." He shrugged. "I had to. I don't understand it any more than you do. All I know is, I had to. And God help me, I liked it."

He hated the confused look on Ashley's face, but it felt good to tell her, even if doing so meant he would lose her. Keeping it from her was killing him.

"Make me understand. Tell me everything, Bentley."

He nodded. "Let's get cleaned up, put some clothes on then I'll tell you." Her pink-tipped toes peeked out from the hem of his coat. Reaching out, he touched her big toe, marveling at how feminine it was with the daisy/star thing painted on it. "I'm so sorry. I never wanted to hurt you."

Famous last words.

"Wait here." She stood, slipped her arms through the sleeves of his coat. Her arms crossed tight over her middle, acting as a belt. "I'll be right back."

When she was out of sight, he pulled on his shirt. Gathering the rest of their scattered clothes, he took them to the laundry room. He paused, listening to the hum of the shower running in the bathroom above him.

Fuck.

He scrubbed his face with his hands, freezing when he caught the scent of her on his fingers. Her sweet surrender a few minutes ago washed over him in a hot wave, followed by a red tide of shame and humiliation for the way he'd repaid her trust. He'd taken her with the same physical abandon he would have taken Sean, and then she'd crushed him by saying he hadn't hurt her.

Like hell.

On his way back to the den, he started to grab another beer but opted for a soda instead. Selecting a bottled water for Ashley, he went back to wait for her.

A few minutes later, she returned, wearing a pair of cut-offs, and a T-shirt. Over the last few months, more and more of her clothes had ended up at his house, something he once thought intrusive now added a level of security to their relationship he had played false. She took the cold bottle he offered her. After settling in the far corner of the sofa, she screwed the top off and took a long drink.

"I don't know what to think, Bentley. Explain it to me."

Unable to look at her, he sat on the edge of the sofa, his elbows braced on his knees, staring at the soda can clutched in his hands. "I don't think I can explain because I don't understand how it happened myself. It goes back over five years, but nothing happened between us until a couple of months ago."

"Before or after you asked me to marry you?"

"After."

She tensed as if he'd struck her.

Yeah, I waited until we were engaged to fuck someone else.

You deserve to lose her, asshole.

"How many times?"

Does it matter? Once was too many.

"I don't know. More than once. Less than a dozen. Once I started, I couldn't stop. I tried to stay away from him, Ashley. I honestly did. I hate myself for wanting him, but it's like…."

"Like what?"

Like he's part of me.

"I feel the same things for him I feel for you." He sat up, placed the soda can on the coffee table then faced her. "I love you. I know you probably don't believe me right now, but it's true. I love you more than I love my own life. I can't imagine living my life without you."

"But," she prompted.

"But I love Sean, too. I can't imagine living my life without him, either, though I know I'm going to have to."

"He doesn't feel the same way?"

"We agreed to break it off."

An awkward silence filled the room. Ashley's gaze bored a hole straight through him. He refused to look away, letting her see what she would on his face, in his posture.

"God damn you, Bentley." Her quiet curse sounded as if he'd reached in and yanked her guts out with his bare hand. The hell of it was, he knew he had.

"I'm sorry. That's all I know to say. Now you see why I can't ask him to come over for lunch. He'd never come anyway."

Another heated silence hung between them, only this time he prayed for her to do something—yell at him or throw something. Anything but look at him with pain in her eyes.

"Were you ever going to tell me?"

He nodded. "I wanted to from the beginning, but I never found the balls to do it. I was going to, the day we set the wedding date. Then…I couldn't. I know it was cowardly. I broke it off with Sean a few days later—on the road trip."

Closing her eyes, she let her head fall back. "I don't want to imagine you…with him, but it's all I can see." She looked at him again. "I don't know what to think, what to do. Part of me wants to hate you, but another part of me says I never can."

"Sean said the same thing. Don't worry. I hate myself enough for both of you."

"Why do you hate yourself?"

"Because I've hurt the two people I love most in the world, and there's nothing I can do to change it. I can't change the way I feel. Believe me—I've tried. I've put you both in the middle of something neither of you deserve. I'm fucked up, Ashley. No one knows that better than I do."

"What do you want to happen? If you had exactly what you wanted, what would it be?"

"Does it matter? We live in the real world. What I *want* doesn't matter as much as what I *can have* does."

"Did you tell *him* what you want?"

He nodded. "Yeah."

"You told *him*, but you can't tell me."

Her words sliced him to the core. "I told him I wanted it all. Both of you."

"What did he say?"

"Goodbye."

"He let you go? Just like that?"

"It wasn't easy for him, but he knows how much you mean to me."

"He wants you to be happy."

"So he says."

"But you aren't happy."

"No. Half my heart died when…when we said goodbye. The other half will die when you leave me."

"Who said I was going to leave you?"

"Do you have a choice? I'm in love with two people, and one of them is a man. What kind of woman wants to stick around for that?"

"The kind who loves you and wants you to be happy."

Hope surged through him like lightening. He lifted his gaze to hers, searching for anything to indicate he hadn't imagined her intent.

She shook her head, a wry smile lifting one side of her mouth. "I must be insane, but I think I want to meet Sean Flannery. Convince him to come to the lunch we discussed. You can tell him I'm thinking about offering him a broadcasting job. Tell him anything, except don't tell him I know about the two of you. I want to see what you're talking about with my own eyes. Maybe then I'll know what to do."

Oh, Bentley. Her heart ached for him, but a little part of her couldn't help wondering why she wasn't enough for him. But then again, she'd always felt as if he was holding back some portion of himself. It hadn't been enough to keep her from falling hopelessly in love with him, but it had always been there, a small invisible gulf between them.

Now you know. He loves someone else—not in place of you, but beside you. She didn't know where her need to meet the man who held part of her fiancé's heart had come from, but everything in her told her it was imperative—for Bentley's sake and her own. If they were ever going to have any kind of real marriage, she had to know who stood between them.

He tore himself in half for you.

All the more reason you have to meet Sean, see for yourself if what Bentley says is true.

And if it is?

You have to find a way to fix the problem.

One thing was for certain. She wasn't going to give up her half without a fight.

CHAPTER TWELVE

Sean sat in the shade of the cabana, watching Bent at the grill. The day was hot, and his former lover wore nothing but loose swim trunks hanging low on his trim hips along with a pair of flip-flop sandals to protect his feet from the stone patio.

They hadn't touched in months, and they never would again. Seeing the play of sunlight on his lover's broad shoulders made him ache with need. Every movement reminded him of the man's strength, the way it felt to give himself to him, and the heady sense of power that coursed through him when Bent submitted to him.

His teammate reached for his beer on the granite counter next to the built-in grill and lifted it to his lips. It was all Sean could do to remain in his seat when what he wanted to do was press himself against that wall of heated male flesh. He'd kiss those shoulders, wrap his arms around his slim waist then trace every line of his six-pack abs before slipping his fingers past the elastic waistband on his trunks. But he couldn't do any of the things he wanted to do with the man's fiancée sitting across the table from him. Not to mention, he still didn't have a clue why he was here.

All he knew was Randolph had mumbled something about a possible job offer. What the fuck? He didn't need a job. He had one. But after days of asking, he outright begged, and Sean had acquiesced. Though God only knew why. Playing nice with the affianced couple was pure torture for him. The groom-to-be looked like he had a live wire stuck up his ass—a prospect Sean was beginning to think held merit. The man deserved to be put through an equal amount of anguish.

"Thanks for coming today."

The soft, feminine voice startled him back to reality. Tearing his gaze away from the man at the grill, he prayed Ashley hadn't noticed the way he'd been ogling her fiancé.

"Thanks for having me. Bent's the only person I know in Dallas." He could afford a little bit of kindness until he knew why he was here. Besides, there was no indication she knew anything about his relationship with her fiancé. She was more of a pawn than he was. At least he knew his lover was fucking her.

"You're welcome anytime. With his schedule, he doesn't have much time to make friends outside of his teammates, so we don't socialize much." Her gaze wandered to their grill master. "He's happier than I've seen him in a long time. It can't be because of the way he's been playing the last few weeks, so it must be because you're here."

"He looks a little tense to me, but as you say, he hasn't been playing well. He needs to relax." He lifted his own beer, pointing the neck toward the man at the grill. "I know he's glad to be home for a few days. He misses you when he's on the road."

"That's good to hear, I guess. I mean, I don't want him to be miserable, but it's nice to know he thinks about me. I miss him, too, but my job keeps me busy. It helps."

"He said you're some kind of hot-shot media executive."

Ashley laughed, her smile lighting up her face. It was easy to see what he saw in her. She was beautiful, even he could see that, and intelligent.

"He exaggerates, but I won't hold it against him. I'm the News Director in charge of programming for one of the major sports networks. We met when I called to ask if he would be on one of our shows—a casual interview kind of thing. He asked me out over the phone. We've been together ever since."

"The man has good taste." A wave of uncertainty washed over him. When it was just Bent and him alone in a hotel room, it was easy to forget about Ashley. Hell, he'd even fantasized about his lover leaving her to be with him, but since he'd met her...he half wanted her himself.

"Steaks are done." Bentley approached the table, a platter heaped with grilled meat and veggies in his hand. He placed the feast in the center of the table then leaned down to place a lingering kiss on Ashley's lips. She seemed to stiffen at first, but maybe he was seeing what he wanted to see. There was something going on here. He just wished to hell they would clue him in, sooner rather than later.

He watched the display of affection for a split second then turned his gaze to the pool sparkling in the sunlight a few feet away. He was drowning in a chaotic mix of jealousy, desire, guilt, and dread. It wouldn't do to let it show on his face, so he did his best to put on a mask of polite friendship. Anything else would be hurtful to Bentley, and he loved him too much to cause him any discord.

When he turned back, the couple had broken apart, but an unmistakable air of intimacy tinged with what?…secret knowledge, surrounded them. He'd known the man was in love with Ashley, but seeing the physical manifestation of their love made it real in a way his lover's declarations never could.

This is what he was trying to tell you. You can't compete with what they have.

She passed him a filled plate while their host placed fresh beer bottles on the table for the men along with a cold water bottle for his fiancée. They worked together like an old married couple, easy with each other, anticipating each other's moves.

They're a team.

There's no room for you on their team, so get used to it, buddy.

Conversation flowed throughout the meal, primarily because Ashley asked lots of questions. *Probably why she holds such a prestigious job at her age.* She knew how to draw people out, as a result, he told her more about himself than he wanted to.

"Have you found a place to live?" She passed the bowl of fresh fruit to him.

"Thanks." He spooned out a good-sized serving. "No. Haven't even looked. The Mustangs relocation service called. They have a few places they want me to see, but I don't know when I'm going to find time."

"I have a crazy idea." She glanced at her fiancé as if apologizing in advance then turned back to Sean. "I think Bentley would be okay with it. I'm surprised he hasn't thought of it himself."

She hesitated, played with the cubes of melon on her plate. She glanced at the man seated next to her.

"What? Did I miss something?" he asked.

"The pool house," she said. "Sean could move into the pool house. It's more than big enough for a single person, and no one ever uses it." Throughout her little speech, her eyes shifted between the two men. There was a hint of nervousness in her voice as if she wasn't sure if she was overstepping. From the stricken look on the man's face, she was. Big time. Sean schooled his own features. Lord, she couldn't know what she was doing. Could she?

"What do you think, honey? Ya'll have the same schedule, and he can't live in a hotel until the season is over when he'll have time to look for the right place."

He leaned back in his chair, a beer in his hand. Tension radiated off him like heat waves off blacktop in the middle of a Texas summer. His gaze traveled over the landscaped backyard to the pool house at the back—a mini-McMansion to go with the full-sized one facing the street. Sean didn't dare breathe. Did Bent want him so close? If he said yes, should he accept the offer? Could he live there knowing the two of them shared a bed in the main house? Hell no. He'd have to be insane to accept.

The insane bastard smiled, wrapped one hand around Ashley's nape, and pulled her in for a kiss. "Brilliant idea, babe." He turned a smiling face to Sean. "What do you say?"

Are you out of your fucking mind? It was all he could do not to yank the man out of his chair and drag him off somewhere for what Texans called a Come to Jesus talk. Plastering what he hoped was a smile on his face, he held his hand up in protest. "Really, guys, thanks, but…I shouldn't."

He couldn't be that close to the man he loved…every fucking night. Keeping his hands off him would be impossible. *Not happening.*

"I don't see why not," Ashley said.

Let me tell you, honey.

"I think it's perfect. I know Bentley will love having you around. Honestly, Sean, if it was anyone else, I wouldn't offer, but ya'll seem to get along so well. It won't be forever, just a few months. When the season is over, you'll have plenty of time to find the right place."

"She's right, Sean. You know she is." His smile wasn't quite genuine, but his eyes blazed with banked desire and something else it took him a second to decipher.

He wants me to say yes. Mother fuckin' son of a bitch! You are out of your fuckin' mind, asshole, if you think you can keep our relationship from her with me living here. But, have it your way. Was this why he'd been summoned today? Just what the fuck is going on here?

"Bent, why don't you show Sean the pool house while I clean up out here? Maybe seeing it will convince him."

Sean looked at the home's owner, dared him to end the insanity swirling around them. A small aircraft droned overhead. *Probably writing DISASTER in puffs of white smoke.*

"Sure, babe." His chair scraped across the paving stones as he stood. "You don't get to play domestic goddess often, so who am I to cheat you out of the opportunity." He smiled at his fiancée, flicked her ponytail before placing his hand on her shoulder bared by her strapless sundress.

Are you trying to piss me off? Fucking bastard, flaunting his relationship in front of him. *'Cause if you are, you're doing a damned fine job.*

"Come on, Sean. Let me show you your new digs."

"I haven't said yes, yet," he said, standing. He thanked Ashley for lunch then followed Bentley's perfect, soon to be kicked to Kingdom Come, ass around the pool.

Well, that was that.

Ashley watched the two men walk away. It had taken all of five seconds to see everything her fiancé had told her was true. Hell, a blind man could see the sparks flying between those two. She could see how they'd turned to public animosity to throw people off—but anyone with half a brain could tell there were deep feelings between them. Whether the person saw love or hate depended on their perspective.

Love it was. The physical attraction between them did things to her she never expected. Once she'd seen them together, the vague images she'd conjured when he'd first told her came back, magnified and enhanced by real knowledge of the man her fiancé desired.

She cleared the table, grateful for the activity to direct her thoughts in a less disturbing and inappropriate direction. Though, as time passed and the men hadn't returned, she couldn't help but wonder what was going on between them, and how, exactly it would affect her. She began to regret offering Sean the pool house, but what else could she have done? Keeping Sean Flannery close was the only way she would figure out what to about their situation.

As soon as the door to the pool house closed behind him, Sean railed on his host. "Are you fucking insane? You want to keep your gay lover on the same property with your straight fiancée? Do you have any idea how crazy that is?"

"Hold on." Bent's hand was a stop sign between them. "Number one, Ashley doesn't live here, though she's here more than she's not. And, two…she knows."

She knows? She knows. "She fuckin' knows?"

He found the closest chair. Dropping into it, he scrubbed his hands over his face. "You told her?"

Bentley sat on the sofa facing him. "Last week. I know I said I wasn't going to, but I…well, I snapped. She said she wanted to meet you, size you up for a broadcasting job opening up soon. She wasn't going to take no for answer, so I told her why I couldn't ask you to lunch."

"The job thing. That was real?"

"Yeah. I wasn't lying to you about the job. I don't know much about it, but I told her you wouldn't be interested. After I told her about us, she came up with the idea of using the job as an excuse to get to know you. What could I say, Sean? All I could think was she wasn't leaving me, at least not right away. I had to take a chance."

Sean held his face in his hands, his elbows braced on his knees. He peered up at his lunatic lover. He still wanted to beat the shit out of him—for general purposes. But the pain etched on his face reminded him how much the man had to lose.

"Why didn't you tell me before I came over here?"

"I didn't think you'd come. But honest to God, I never expected her to ask you to move in. Her offer was as much a surprise to me as it was to you."

"*Surprise* doesn't begin to cover it." He sat back, determined to hear it all. "What did she do when you told her?" He held up a staying hand. "Wait. Wait. What, exactly did you tell her?"

"I told her I'd been unfaithful to her. She was pissed, wanted to know who the woman was. She was hurt. I won't lie to you, I considered making up some random woman then swearing I wouldn't ever do it again, but then I thought about you." He shook his head. "I couldn't do it. I couldn't lie to her again. I told her the truth."

"What is the truth?"

"I've been half in love with you for years." Their gazes met. "I finally got up the courage to do something about it."

A curl of warmth unfurled to wrap around his heart. At last, the man was being honest with himself. Maybe there was hope for them yet. "You risked losing her, over me?"

He nodded. "I did. I had to after…."

"After what?"

Closing his eyes, he sighed. "I fucked her that night. Hard. Harder than I should have."

"Jesus, Bent!"

"She said I didn't hurt her, but I went at her like she was you, like she was strong enough to take it, and all the time it was you I was fucking in my head. I felt like an ass. It was time to come clean, tell her everything. I knew I had to let her decide for herself if she could live with me, could accept that I loved you, needed what you could give me."

"She wanted to see for herself?"

"Yeah, she did. She said she knew something had gone down between us the day you came to the house. I proposed to her right after you left. She's smart, Sean. She questioned me then, said my proposal was too abrupt, but she wasn't going to turn it down. She loves me."

"So what's this about?" He swung his arm to indicate the small house they occupied. "Why invite me to live on the premises?"

"She saw what she needed to see, I guess. She said she knew I loved her, but she needed to see what kind of man I could have the same kind of feelings for."

"Sweet Jesus, Bent!" Sean stood, paced to a window overlooking the pool. He couldn't see the cabana where they'd had lunch from there. He turned to face his lover. "So, what? Are we going to trade? She gets you on even numbered days, I get you on odd numbered ones? Or does she just want me close, so she can keep an eye on me? What the fuck is going on here?"

"I don't know. I didn't know she was going to invite you to

move in. I had no idea, Sean. I swear. She said she'd make up her mind once she got to know you."

"Make up her mind about what?"

"If she was going to stay with me or not."

"Inviting me to move in means she's going to stay?"

A knock sounded on the door. Sean jumped, turning toward the sound.

Ashley stepped inside. "Mind if I come in?"

Bentley stood. "No. We were just talking." He shoved his hands in his pockets.

Sean took a step back. It was one thing to talk to her when she didn't know, but now…he was scared spitless. If she had a mind to, she could destroy both their careers with one well-placed comment—not to mention the power she held over their relationship. Maybe that was what this was all about.

She shut the door behind her. Holding onto the knob, she leaned her shoulders against the dark wood. "I think we all need to talk." Her gaze shifted between them, landed on Sean. "I saw the way you looked at Bentley today when you thought I wasn't looking. He told me how he feels about you. Maybe it wasn't fair, the way I went about getting to know you, but I had to see with my own eyes if what he said was true." She looked at her fiancé. "I believe it is. You've made love with this man—"

"It was sex—"

She shook her head. "Let's call it what it is, okay? I should be shocked, outraged, but I'm not. I know you love me." She fisted one hand over her heart. "I know it. In here." She looked at Sean. "He loves me."

"I know." His voice sounded like it had been dragged over gravel.

"We both love him," she stated.

Sean nodded.

She looked back at her fiancé who stood statue still in the center of the room. "Do you still want to marry me?"

"Yes, I do," he stated without hesitation.

"What about him?" She waved her hand in Sean's direction. "You can't marry us both."

"I know. It's fucked up. Like I told you last night, I'm fucked up. I need you both. I need you by my side, in my bed. I told you I want kids with you. That's the God's honest truth. But I need Sean, too. It's different with him, but I want…need him, too."

The room was quiet for a long time while she leaned against the door, studying them both. Sean was afraid to breathe, afraid any movement on his part would break the fragile air surrounding them.

Bent moved, and Sean emptied his lungs. Then he realized he was reaching for his hand. By rote, he let his fingers twine with his lover's. Mesmerized by the sight of their joined hands, he stumbled when the other man tugged him forward.

Bent offered his other hand to Ashley. She hesitated then she took it, threading her fingers with his.

"Let me show you, Ashley," he said. "Come to the bedroom with us. Let me show you how it is between us. Let me make love to both of you."

"Please?" Bent's knees felt like jelly as he waited for her response. He silently prayed for her to give him a chance to convince her what they shared was real. Since Sean moving into the pool house had been her idea, he held out hope she was coming to terms with what he'd said.

He saw withdrawal in her eyes before he felt her hand slipping from his. She shook her head, and his heart sank.

"No. Not yet. Maybe not ever. I'm sorry. It's too soon." She looked at Sean. "I still think you should move in here. Maybe with time…."

Her gaze fell away then she looked at him again. "Give me some time…to get to know Sean…to think about what this all means. If we're all here together, it will be easier…to…um…to…if we decide to." She dropped her chin to her chest. "I've never done anything like…what you're asking."

He reached for her, folded her into his arms, tucking her head under his chin. "Take all the time you need. I just thought…if you saw…. But I understand." She shivered, so he held her tighter. He hated what his confession was doing to her. She was always so decisive, so strong. To see her uncertain and quivering in his arms confirmed what he all ready knew—he was an ass. "Thank you for having an open mind. I don't deserve you, but I'm damn glad I have you."

"Maybe I should go." Sean took a step toward the door.

"No." She raised her head. "Please, Sean. Stay. I want you to move in here. It would be safer for both of you, anyway. If ya'll are going to be seeing each other, being on the same property will make it easier."

"She's right," Bent said. "As much as I'd like to tell the world to go fuck themselves, we can't, not if we want to keep our jobs. I'm tired of sneaking around. If you move in here, at least we'll be together when the team is in Dallas."

"Am I the only one who thinks this is fucked up?" Sean asked.

"No," the other man said. "I think we can all agree on that." He looked at Ashley for confirmation.

"Yeah. I think fucked up pretty much covers it," she said.

"Another thing we can all agree on is you're an amazing woman. I'm so sorry. I was so afraid you would leave me. I should have told you from the start."

"I might have run screaming." She eased out of his arms. "I'm still not sure I won't. I wasn't thinking about a threesome when I suggested Sean move in. I was thinking about protecting your secret. Ya'll know as well as I do you can't go public with your relationship. If we…if I decide to stay—"

"If anyone is going, it's me," Sean said. "I won't come between the two of you. If we can't figure out a way to have what he wants— the three of us together—then I'm the one who will leave."

"Let's give it some time, okay?" she said.

"We'll find a way," Bent said. *We have to.*

"Then let Sean go get his things. The only way we're going to figure out if we can make this work is for us all to be together—for as long as it takes."

CHAPTER THIRTEEN

"So. What does this mean?" Sean dropped a stack of folded T-shirts into a drawer in the bedroom of Bentley's pool house. He closed the drawer, leaned his hips against the dresser then crossed his arms over his chest. It was taking a Herculean effort to keep his hands off the man. It was a toss-up whether he would strangle him or kiss him when he lost the battle. "I understand why I'm here, but what, are we doing?"

"Fuck if I know," His lover said from his perch on the end of the king-sized bed. "Ashley wants to get to know you. That's all I know."

"Smooth move, asshole, inviting her for a threesome without any warning you were thinking along those lines."

"Not one of my finer moments, but it would have solved a lot of problems if she had agreed. I know her. After a she got over the shock, she would have loved it."

"Love it or not, showing her what the rest of her life would be like might have scared her off for good."

The other man nodded. "Yeah. It could have gone that way, too."

"Which brings me back to my original question. What are we doing? Are you a fucking ping-pong ball, bouncing from one bed to the other?"

"My answer is the same. Fuck if I know."

"Then you better go talk to her, find out what the ground rules are before we start playing the game for real."

"I'm going. Promise me you won't change your mind. Right now, convincing Ashley to stick it out is my priority. I don't need to be worrying about you, too."

"I'm not going anywhere. I like her, man. She's everything you said she was. Her actions today proved she has more going for her than just good looks and brains. She has guts. She might be a little kinky, too." He smiled, wiggling his eyebrows.

Laughter eased the worry lines on his friend's face, making Sean's heart lighter. The drama was taking its toll on all of them. But he'd survive. He had to.

Bent slid into the bed beside Ashley. He had no idea what to expect. The three of them had ordered pizza then sat around the table in the kitchen, trying to act as if they were normal. There was nothing normal about his fiancée and his male lover sitting at the same table. At least when Sean had been across town, the issue of whom he would sleep with had been clear. With him ensconced in the pool house, the lines were blurred.

The most awkward moment came when they were through eating and the conversation had dwindled out. Sean stood first, making his polite excuses. Following him to the back door, he asked, "You got everything you need?"

Sean smirked, casting a glance back at the table where Ashley sat watching them. "Everything, except you."

Before he knew what was happening, Sean cupped his face between his big palms and covered his mouth with his. Startled, he tried to protest, but only managed to provide opportunity. Sean's tongue swept inside. Bent melted against him. It had been so long since they'd had any real physical contact, he lost himself in the kiss. Sean's lips were hungry, devouring, and demanding. It felt so fucking good to touch him again. He kissed him back, pressing his body close so the hard ridges of their arousal brushed. His lover groaned, moving his hips to let him know how much he wanted him, too. He forgot they had an audience, forgot why kissing Sean was a bad idea all around and just went with it.

When Sean broke the kiss, they were both breathing heavily.

He held Bent's face in the cradle of his roughened hands a moment longer. His eyes were dark with meaning and unfulfilled lust. He took a step back, nodded to Ashley then he left. Dazed, he stared at the man's retreating back, desperate to go after him so they could finish what they'd started. He wasn't through tasting him, loving him. Another minute and he would have had a cock in his mouth.

A movement in his peripheral drew his attention to the table. The expression on his fiancée's face snapped him back to reality.

He couldn't abandon her tonight. Not after everything he'd put her through the last few days. The Mustangs would be on the road again at the end of the week. He'd have time with Sean then. He could wait.

She appeared shell-shocked. Her eyes were wide, her mouth open in mute disbelief.

Fuck. Sean had kissed him on purpose—to see her reaction. *Look what you did, asshole.*

"Babe…."

"That was…." She shook her head. "I don't know what to say."

"He shouldn't have done it. I shouldn't have…."

"No." Her voice was brittle. "He has every right. You have every right…I guess. I don't know…I hadn't expected the two of you to…while he's…I mean, in front of me. But of course you will. It's only natural."

"I didn't know he was going to kiss me," he said. "If it bothers you so much, I'll tell him not to…we won't…. Ah, hell. I'm sorry." *Goddamn, Sean!* But he was as much to blame—he'd returned the kiss, turned it into a make-out session by grinding against him. *You're a class A ass, Bentley Randolph. A real fuck-up.*

She looked down at her lap where her fingers were busy shredding a paper napkin. "No. Don't do…not on my account. It just took me by surprise. It won't be as much of a shock next time."

He approached the table—she stood, gathering the dirty plates.

"Let me help you."

They worked together in silence. When everything was clean, he took her in his arms. She was as forgiving as a stone column, but he was determined to get past the barriers she'd put between them. He needed to show her how much he still loved her. He'd apologized in every way he knew how. Now it was up to his actions to speak for him.

He started with her lips, tracing them with the tip of his finger until they softened and parted for him—the first glimmer of hope sparked in his chest. She was scared, uncertain of him, of their relationship. He needed to show her the physical connection they shared was still there, solid and unchanged.

Leaning in, he covered her mouth with his while he cradled her cheek in his palm. Her initial reticence made his heart ache, but he refused to give up on his mission.

"I love you," he murmured against her lips before he let her see just how hungry she made him. Backing her up until she was pressed against the counter, he divested her of her tank top, sucking in a harsh breath when he found her braless. He took a moment to enjoy the perfection of her then his hands went to work dismantling the invisible wall she'd built between them, one ice-cold brick at a time.

He took his time, not pushing, but not allowing her time to think either. He told her he loved her, breathing the words against the most sensitive parts of her body, punctuating each verbal reminder with a physical one. Words and actions. If one didn't get through to her, perhaps the other would.

"I love you," he whispered against her breast, his breath causing her nipple to bead. Sucking the tight bud into his mouth, he laved it with his tongue, nipped at it with his teeth. She arched beneath him, her body responding though he suspected her mind had yet to get with the program. He moved to the other breast, giving it the same attention. He wanted her mindless, unable to think. If he could get past her brain, her heart would be defenseless.

Back and forth he went, from one breast to the other, while she cradled his head in her hands. The smell of her arousal sent a primitive surge of power through him. Dipping one hand between her legs, he coated his fingers with her juices then brought them up to spread the elixir over her nipple. Groaning, she offered the candy-coated crest to him.

God, he loved the way she tasted—like the rarest honey known to man. The sample wasn't enough.

"More." She shifted from foot to foot as he divested her of her clothes. Her hands slipped from his head as he descended to the open juncture of her thighs. On his knees, he buried his face in her mound. "God, you're beautiful. Got to have you." He grabbed her around the waist, lifting her to sit on the edge of the counter.

"Bent," she moaned as he guided her feet over his shoulders, anchoring them there by wrapping his arms around her thighs.

"So damned perfect." He parted her with his thumbs, her hips rose in silent invitation. He made love to her pussy. Lips to lips, he teased, tasted, and aroused until she uttered the word he had prayed to hear.

"Please. Please, Bent."

With one last flick of his tongue over her clit, he looked up at her. "Please, what?"

"Please, Bent. I need you. Inside me. Now."

"I love it when you beg," he said. In a heartbeat, his jeans were around his knees, his cock pressed against her vagina. "Tell me again. Tell me what you want."

"You." She dug her fingernails into his ass. "I want you."

Searching her eyes, he found the same love and desire he'd seen so many times before. "I love you," he said, nudging his erection forward so her heat warmed the head. "Do you love me, Ashley?"

"I hate you," she said, though her eyes made her declaration a lie.

He filled her with one hard stroke, burrowed deep inside her. He stilled. "Do you love me?" he asked again.

"I hate you," she moaned.

Withdrawing, he tunneled deep again, filling her one slow inch at a time. When she'd taken all of him, he rocked against her. "Do you love me?"

Closing her eyes, she sighed. When she opened them again, she met his gaze. "Goddamn it, I love you, Bentley. I hate it, but I love you."

"Then we'll work it out, babe. We'll work this out."

I hope so. Oh, God, I hope you're right.

When Bentley made love to her, she forgot everything except how perfect he felt inside her. Tonight was no different. She'd tried so hard to resist him, had insisted for days he keep his hands to himself. He'd honored her wishes until this evening, then with a few whispered words and magic hands, he'd found his way past her barriers, all the way to her core.

I love him. No matter what he's done, I love him.

He continued his sensual assault on her body, stroking inside her, touching, kissing, savoring every inch of skin he could reach until she was mindless, lost in the maelstrom of feelings swirling around in her heart.

Love for him, hate for what he'd done, shattering disappointment knowing he loved another when he was everything to her—the crushing feeling she'd lost something precious and nothing they did or said in the future would fix it.

Yet she loved him. Couldn't bring herself to let him go. A war waged between her heart and her head, but for this blessed amount of time when Bentley commanded her body, she was free of the turmoil, free of the doubts and indecision. Free of the hurt. There was nothing but their love for each other. Her body recognized it, craved it. Though her heart was raw from days of crippling pain, it opened tonight, accepting his love like it was an enchanted potion capable of fixing everything.

"Mine," he growled in her ear, his breath hot and fast as he drove into her.

Her arms closed around him, reveled in the power evident in his hard muscles. The way he tempered his strength for her made her feel cherished. Bentley was the man she loved. He was physically capable of hurting her, but always gentle, careful. Except for one time when he'd shown her another side of himself.

A side she had liked.

Flashes of that night came back to her. He'd taken her hard, so much harder than ever before, more like he had the afternoon in the grass, but harder. Always so in control, it was as if he'd been caged for years, then suddenly, the door had sprung open. He'd been wild and free. God, she'd loved it.

He'd apologized before she'd had a chance to tell him how much she had liked the new side of him. The pleasurable memories were buried beneath the crushing weight of his confession and the shock she'd had to absorb. She was still trying to process it.

I liked it.

She stilled, willing the memory to come back. "Bent. Stop."

Freezing in mid-stroke, he gazed at her with such tender concern she wanted to cry. "Did I hurt you? What is it?"

"No." She shook her head. "You didn't hurt me." She took a deep breath and let it out. "You know the night you told me? Do you remember how you made love to me?"

He closed his eyes. A muscle ticked along his jaw line then he opened his eyes again. "I remember. God, I'm sorry, babe. I shouldn't have. I—"

"Stop. No more apologies—at least not for the things you did."

She met his gaze, held it. "I liked it, Bent. I *really* liked it. I never got a chance to tell you because you were apologizing. Then…well, I forgot. I forgot to tell you no apology was needed. I *liked* it."

"You liked it." His concerned expression gave way to confused desire. He didn't move, didn't say a thing for so long she began to think she should have waited to tell him. "What are you saying?" he asked.

"I don't know what I'm saying," she answered. Was she asking for him to make love to her that way again? "I just wanted you to know you didn't hurt me. It felt good. You were so…strong…decisive…assertive. I won't break."

"God, babe." His eyes gleamed then a wicked smile broke across his face. He pulled out of her. "I hope you know I'm going to fuck you six ways to Sunday now."

"I know. I want you, too."

"Bedroom." He yanked his jeans up. Lifting her into his arms, he carried her up the stairs as if she weighed nothing.

She liked this side of him—masterful, determined. He deposited her on the bed, undressed then joined her. She opened her legs, inviting him to take her any way he wanted.

His first hard thrust scooted her up the mattress then he rose to his knees. Sitting back on his heels, he lifted her ass in the air. "Spread your legs. Knees up. Hold them there."

She did as he asked. He took her hard, one powerful thrust after another. She tried to move with him, but what the position lacked in freedom of movement, it made up for with visibility. It enabled her to see his thick cock impaling her. Watching the joining of their bodies was the most erotic thing she'd ever seen in her life.

Sweat glistened on his toned body, but he never let up or looked away from her face.

"Fuck, you feel good." He found her clit and rubbed. He applied just the right amount of pressure, circling. "Come for me, babe. Milk my dick."

His words were crude, demanding. He took what he wanted from her but gave so much back. She loved watching the play of muscles in his magnificent body—reminders of who he was, what he was—an athlete in his prime. Like before, the sensations were different but not unpleasant. The same things she'd felt before came back in a rush. Her body tingled and sparked with each powerful thrust. Her head swam, overwhelmed with the raw, primitive nature of their coupling.

Clenching the bedcovers in her fists, she held on. A familiar tension began to build in her stomach, but this time there was something wild about it. She felt like she was on a runaway roller coaster—exhilarating in the headlong rush of dips and curves, climbing fast toward the moment when the world would fall away and for a moment, she would fly.

He reached out, squeezed her breast then pinched her nipple. She came off the rails. Arching her neck, she flew. The tightly wound tension inside her uncoiled, catapulted her faster and faster. Out of control—her body bucked. She writhed in his hold, grasping for every bit of pleasure until the crazed ride slowed. She braced for the crash, but his hands, cradled her, brought her safely back to earth.

"Hold on, babe. We aren't done yet."

Boneless, she thought she couldn't possible experience anything more. Her hands slipped from her thighs. Her feet fell to the mattress. Rough hands replaced hers, held her wide. Bentley rode her, slamming into her with short, almost brutal thrusts. Tension built. The roller coaster launched, and once again, she rode the waves of ecstasy.

His cock throbbed inside her. The rhythm of his thrusts became erratic right before he came with a muffled curse. Hot cum bathed her inner walls. Grasping for sanity, she followed him down the big hill, screaming her pleasure all the way.

The writing was on the wall. Their arrangement would never work. One glimpse of Ashley's face after he'd kissed her fiancé was all the confirmation Sean needed. The idea of him and Bent together confused her, possibly disgusted her.

She's always going to be between us.

The mantra repeated in his head as he returned the few items he'd unpacked to his suitcase. Bent was going to be pissed tomorrow when he discovered Sean had left.

Better now than later.

Hanging around was just going to make the complete dissolution of their affair more painful.

She's always going to be between us.

He loves her too much to let her go. She's never going to accept him being in love with a man, too.

Yeah, moving in had been her idea, but he saw it in her eyes—shock. Hearing your fiancé say he was in a sexual relationship with a man was one thing, seeing it was something altogether different. But he'd be damned if he was going to live on the same property with the man he loved and not have him any goddamn time he wanted him. That was shit.

They'd been right to call it off when they did. Dredging it up today had been a huge mistake—one he was going to correct right this minute. Hauling his suitcase to his car, he glanced up at the main house. One light was on, a dim one, perhaps a hallway light, illuminating one of the upstairs windows.

Were they up there right now having sex? She'd call it *making love*. She thought she was in love with the man, but she wasn't. Not deep down, I'd-sell-my-soul-for-him, in love. If she was, she wouldn't have looked horrified when he kissed him. Hell, she'd looked as if he'd violated *her. Her!*

"Shit."

Driving away, he focused on the road ahead and nothing else. No looking back. No regrets. If only one of them could be happy, he wanted it to be Bentley.

She doesn't love you the way I do, Bent. I'd sell my soul for you.
Hell, I already have.

CHAPTER FOURTEEN

It was possible to avoid someone for weeks. It took determination and focus, but it could be done. Checking into a cheap, by-the-month, chain motel after leaving Bentley's pool house had been a stroke of genius. He'd told no one where he was living these days. No one on the team would suspect he would choose such a place given the Mustangs were giving him a stipend to cover living expenses until he found a place to buy or rent. Why choose austere when you could have luxury?

Because it suits me.

Paring down his life to the bare essentials so he could concentrate on his future was the only way he could survive. No reminders of the past. No looking back. Just looking forward from now on. He'd start from the bottom again, work his way up—with his personal life and the team.

Avoiding Bentley at the stadium and on road trips took more planning, but he'd managed thus far to insure they were never alone anywhere, putting as much distance between them as possible at every function. He tried not to look at the left fielder, but every once and a while, he couldn't help it. He needed to see his face, if even for a brief second. Mostly, he managed to glimpse him when the man wouldn't know he was looking, but a few times their gazes had locked across a crowded room. The pain in his former lover's eyes would almost convince him to change his mind, to try to make it work, one more time. But then he'd remember Ashley. He couldn't forget the look on her face the night she'd seem them kiss. That alone was enough to shake loose any lingering hope he had for his relationship with Bentley. Nothing good could come of reopening that particular wound.

Refocusing his energy on his career was paying off in small increments. His averages were improving all around, and he'd moved up in the batting order. Thanks to extra training sessions as well as religious adherence to his PT schedule, his hip felt better than it had in years. The season was shaping up to be one of his best ever, if not *the* best. Management was talking contract renewal, which was nothing short of a miracle given the way he'd begun with the Mustangs—brawling on the locker room floor with one of their star players.

Professionally, he'd come a long way in the last few weeks. Personally, he was a wreck. Not a minute went by he didn't think about the man he loved and want him. A few times he'd considered going to a bar searching for a casual hookup—anything to relieve the pressure—but when it got right down to it, he couldn't bring himself to follow through. If he couldn't have Bentley Randolph, he didn't want anyone.

He'd become so adept at avoiding the one person he most wanted to be with, his techniques had become second nature to him. He no longer gave conscious thought to taking the longer way around, or waiting until everyone else had chosen their seat on the plane before choosing his. The other man's lack of interest in figuring out his methods in order to thwart them was proof he'd done the right thing by sneaking out of the pool house. If the man wanted to talk to him, he could find a way.

"Hello, Sean."

A familiar figure blocking the hallway stopped him in his tracks. *Well, hell.*

"What are you doing here?" Few people other than delivery people and maintenance personnel used the narrow passageway connecting the back exits of the various rooms in the Clubhouse. It had become Sean's primary means of traversing the underground warren over the last few weeks.

"Looking for you. You've been avoiding me."

"I've been avoiding everybody, in case you haven't noticed. Don't think you're special." He took a step, intending to go around, but the man put his arm out to block the hall.

"Move out of my way, Randolph. We don't have time for your bullshit. The game starts in ten minutes."

"Fuck the game. Why did you leave?"

Scraps of memory flashed through his brain. All those years ago—the paralyzing pain when he realized the man had fled to the Mustangs to avoid him. The loneliness. The gut-wrenching despair.

"You have the nerve to ask me why I left? After what you did to me in St. Louis?" He sneered. "Don't fuck with me."

"I'm *not* fucking with you. Isn't that the problem? I've already apologized for asking to be traded, and you said you understood why I did it. But the situation is different now. We found a way to be together then you left without a word. After you…after we…in the kitchen. I thought we were going to make it work."

"What planet are you living on? Did you see the look on your fiancée's face? She might have been saying the words, but that's all they were, words. She fuckin' hated what she saw. It scared the shit out of her."

"She was okay with it."

Sean noted the uncertainty in the man's voice. "No she wasn't. Don't fool yourself into believing otherwise. She has no intention of sharing you with anyone, especially not me. I did what I had to do. I left. So, go back to the little woman, Bentley. Marry her. Have enough kids to have your own baseball team. Be happy. Whatever you do, just stay the fuck out of my life."

Saying those words turned his stomach, but he needed to say them. In his own way Bent had chosen this road for both of them by choosing to ignore the signals Ashley was giving off.

"You don't mean that," he said, his voice low and laced with pain. "She'll come around. I know she will. We just have to give her time to get used to the idea."

"She isn't going to come around no matter how much time we give her. She loves you, but not enough to give you what you want."

"What about you?"

"I'm not part of the equation." He took a deep, cleansing breath then let it out. "Tell me something. You took her to bed after I left, didn't you?"

Bentley nodded.

"Did you think about me when you were fucking her?"

Silence.

"I thought so. You're good at compartmentalizing. There's just one thing wrong with your neat little compartments. You can't keep them separate forever. Once the contents start mixing together, they're going to destroy each other." He pushed Bent's arm out of the way. "You made the choice to keep the compartments separate when you let me walk out of your kitchen the other night. Go home to your woman, and forget about me."

He took a few steps along the hallway then turned. "Have a nice life. Name a kid after me."

Bentley leaned his shoulders against the wall, listening to the sound of Sean's metal-spiked cleats grinding against the concrete floor, growing fainter with each step. Was he right? Had he subconsciously chosen Ashley? Had he made a choice when he didn't insist on his lover staying?

Would things have blown up if he had stayed?

Stunned to find every trace of Sean gone from the property the following morning, he tried calling him but got a disconnect message for his cell phone. He'd gone back to the house to tell Ashley. What had she said? Something like, "I guess he decided he didn't want to share, after all."

Was that it? He couldn't remember. He'd been too lost in his own thoughts, wondering what the hell happened, and where the man he loved had disappeared to.

Since then, Ashley had thrown herself headfirst into planning their wedding. He nodded his agreement on every decision from the color of the bridesmaid's dresses to the color of ribbon on her bouquet. He couldn't have cared less about any of it. None of it mattered. Once he'd seen the first baseman was alive, he'd focused on one thing, finding a way to talk to the man alone.

Easier said than done. He'd become a ghost, flitting in and out of the shadows, gone before you were sure you'd seen him at all. When he did see him, he was surrounded by a crowd—inaccessible. He'd known the evasion was deliberate from the beginning but figured it would run its course. His irate lover would get over it, whatever *it* was then they'd talk. Except that never happened. After almost three weeks, feeling as though he might crawl out of his skin with need, he decided he had to find a way to talk to him.

A door opened somewhere around the corner followed by the Batboy's voice.

"There you are. They're looking for you. The game is about to start. Have you seen Mr. Randolph?"

"Yeah. He's down the hall."

The door shut, followed by the echo of quick footsteps growing closer.

Time to go. He shoved away from the wall.

The other man's accusations followed him all the way to left field. How could he think his leaving now had anything to do with what happened back in St. Louis? It wasn't the same. He'd run in order to put distance between himself and a temptation that scared the life out of him. Sean had left because he couldn't have everything he wanted.

Fuck you, Flannery. We could have made it work. You were just too chicken to try. Your fault, not mine.

Distracted was the nice word for his condition on the field. Fucked up was the accurate word. His fielding error in the first inning almost cost them a run, and his appearances at home plate were dismal, at best. He was zero for three—all strikeouts. Big, ugly, whiff at dead air, strikeouts.

The Claim Jumpers were on their third relief pitcher, down by just one run. Stepping into the batter's box once more, with a runner on base and one out in the inning, Bentley had a chance to put the game almost out of reach. If he could hit the damn ball.

Focus, asshole.

He stepped out of the box.

"Time," the umpire called.

He needed to do something to get back into the game. Naturally right-handed, he most often batted right, but he could hit from either side of the plate. Switching sides was sometimes a matter of strategy—where to place the ball or to disconcert the pitcher, but batting left-handed required his complete concentration on his body mechanics as well as on the pitch. God knew, he needed to concentrate.

Decision made, he stepped to the other side of the plate. He scanned the field, noted the runner on first base, the shortstop shifting toward second, the outfield adjusting to the new dynamics. They were well aware of the percentages. Chances were, if he hit it, the ball would go to the right side of the field.

Switch Hitter

The umpire waved him to the plate. Time to play fuckin' ball.

He dug his left foot into the dirt until the grip felt good then planted his right foot. Gaze locked on the pitcher, he brought the bat to his shoulder.

He opened his mind to the subtle strain on seldom-used muscles—used it to distill his focus. Everything dropped away except the weight of the bat in his hand and the pitcher on the mound.

The first pitch went wide. Ball one.

On the next one, the pitcher over-compensated, and Bent had to jump backward or take a hit on the kneecap. Ball two.

The third pitch was inside, but good enough he swung, cringing at the sound of leather smacking against leather. Strike one.

Another pitch went high out of the strike zone for ball three.

Fuck. He's throwing everything but the kitchen sink. Bent stepped out of the box to adjust his batting gloves—giving himself a moment to contemplate where the pitcher would go with the next one. He needed to even the count so it would be a strike. He'd most likely paint the outside edge of home plate, hoping to get a foul ball strike. Speed? Fast. He'd be crazy to shave velocity off a pitch at this point.

Muscles tensed, he stepped back into the box, shrugged to loosen up.

You and me, buddy. No one else.

The instant the ball left the pitcher's hand, Bent knew it was his. Instinct? A lifetime of watching pitches, looking for the perfect one? It didn't matter. His brain made the almost instantaneous calculations, calling on muscle memory trained into his body to do the rest.

He swung.

His eyes never left the ball, using the sensory information to guide his hands, position his arms, his shoulders, his hips and legs. Everything in perfect alignment to hit the ball—crush it.

Thwack!

The smooth vibration traveling from his hands, along his arms to the rest of his body confirmed what he already knew. That ball was going.

He tracked it until it bounced off an empty seat in the right field bleachers.

A fuckin' homerun!

Crossing home plate seconds behind Jason Holder, who'd been

the runner on first base, he joined in the jubilant celebration taking place. He couldn't help scanning the group, looking for one teammate in particular. Sean stood at the dugout railing, watching. Their gazes met, holding for the span of a heartbeat, then Sean shook his head and ducked inside.

He felt like a starving puppy turned away from the back door of the butcher shop. "No scraps for you today."

Fuck off, Sean. I don't need you. Never did. Ashley loves me. I'd name a kid after you, but asshole wouldn't look good on a birth certificate.

Sean locked gazes with Bentley. For a heartbeat or two, blinding heat sizzled between them. He looked away, dropping down from the raised fence to the dugout floor. Just because he'd said the words to sever their relationship didn't mean his feelings for the left fielder had died. He'd long since realized they never would.

He'd wished for many things in his life, and rarely gotten any of them, so why was this any different? As long as the asshole insisted on walking through life with blinders on, he'd see what he wanted to see. Bentley didn't want to see anything outside the path he thought he should walk.

Face it, Ashley is smack in the middle of his path, and you *are not.*

Ashley is safe. She'll never challenge him to be more than an adequate husband or an attentive father.

You challenge everything he believes.

Not a thing had changed since St. Louis. He might have admitted to himself he had desires beyond the social norm, but he sure as hell wasn't going to let the world know. When push came to shove, he retreated back into the small closet society said was appropriate and pulled the door shut.

He wasn't much better. He loved playing baseball, but telling the world he was gay would pretty much end his career. At the very least, he'd always be known as the gay player. Everything he did, any record he might achieve would be prefaced by the words "openly gay player, Sean Flannery." He did not want that to be his identity or his legacy.

He'd much rather be known as "two time All-Star player, Sean Flannery" or even "Major League veteran, Sean Flannery." Why his sexual preferences had anything to do with his ability to play baseball was beyond his understanding. But he wasn't stupid enough to believe the press wouldn't have a field day with the information if they got their hands on it.

Fuck you, Randolph.

He grabbed his glove from the bench. Following the third out, he took his place on the field. Just three outs away from a win, he cleared his mind except for the game and his part in it. Jeff Holder, the Mustangs' ace closer, came in from the bullpen, shutting down the first two batters with ease.

One more out, then we're done. I can get the hell away from here.

His mouth watered, imagining the first taste of the cold beer he intended to down as soon as he could find a bar. Getting rip-roaring drunk sounded like a plan. The team had tomorrow off, perfect timing in his opinion.

The next batter swung at and missed the first two pitches. Sean relaxed as Jeff consulted with the catcher, his brother, Jason, on what pitch to throw next. The umpire broke up the discussion, and the players resumed their positions. Sean settled in, focused on the batter.

Make it quick, Jeff. I want to get the hell out of here.

As soon as the bat connected, Sean's feet were moving, tracking the popped up ball with his eyes. He lifted his gloved hand high to block the glare from the stadium lights that had come on midway through the game to chase away the early evening shadows.

I've got it. I've got it.

He shuffled to the left another foot then suddenly the ball was gone. Lost in the lights. His heart jumped into overdrive.

Fuck. Where is it?

He wavered, spotted the spinning orb again. Realizing it had traveled farther foul, he stretched his arm out, glove up. His feet left the ground as he launched himself toward the spot where his glove might, with a dose of diamond dust luck, intercept the ball for the final out.

He felt the impact of the ball against his palm at the exact same time someone slammed a sledgehammer into his left hip. Stars blinded him. He reached out with his free hand for anything solid to stop his momentum but came up empty handed.

Time slowed as he tumbled over the railing like a rag doll. Life flashed across his retinas like a Picasso painting—jumbled fragments came together to create a surreal tableau he had no control over. Railings. Concrete. Faces. The lineup card on the dugout wall. A television camera.

Pain clouded his brain. His hip. His ribs. His knee. They all hurt. He was flying. Then he wasn't.

He landed face-up on the dugout floor. For a heartbeat, he saw nothing but white pain. Someone called his name. He opened his eyes, saw open sky above him, then everything went black.

CHAPTER FIFTEEN

Holy shit!

Bentley froze. He watched from his position in left field as Sean disappeared head, then feet-first over the dugout rail.

Blood roared past his ears as he waited, breathless for him to pop up, laughing and smiling triumphantly at having caught the final out of the game. Except he didn't pop up. Not the first heartbeat, the second, or the third. A sick feeling took hold in his stomach.

He'd never seen an uglier fall in all his years playing baseball.

No.

No.

No.

He forced his feet to move, the mantra playing through his mind with each running step.

Please, God. Let him be okay.

He pushed his way through the crowd blocking the steps.

"Move. Goddamn it. Out of my way!"

Doyle Walker stopped him with a hand on his chest. "Hold on. Let the medical personnel do what they do."

Bent looked over the older man's shoulder at his lover's crumpled body. Tears blurred his vision, clogging his throat.

"Is he…?"

"He's alive."

Closing his eyes, he silently thanked God for the miracle.

"Clear out folks." Doyle's voice was calm as he urged the players to make room. "Go on to the clubhouse. I'll update you as soon as we know something."

Bentley wasn't going anywhere. When the Mustangs' manager pushed against his chest, he balked. "I'm staying."

"Nothing you can do here," he said.

"I'm staying," he repeated, his gaze locked on Sean's pale face. The Mustangs' trainers and team physician knelt over him, their faces screwed up with concern.

"The EMT's are here, Randolph. We have to make room for them," Doyle reasoned.

Bent glanced up, saw the uniformed crew spilling out of the ambulance parked on the field. His gut twisted. They never called the emergency people unless the injury was life threatening. He took a step back then another as they piled into the dugout with their cases of equipment.

"Bring a backboard," one of them called to the last guy out of the truck.

He was going to be sick. He swallowed back the bile rising in his throat, clenching his fists at his side to steady himself. Going to pieces now wouldn't help Sean. He had to be there for him.

Bits of their last conversation flashed through his brain, and he fought the urge to wail. He'd been so stupid. So fucking stupid. He'd let the man down by not fighting for their love. He wasn't going to let him down now.

I'm here for you. I love you.

He'd never felt so helpless in his life. The EMTs worked like a well-oiled team. In minutes, they pronounced the injured man stable, strapped him to the bright orange backboard, and carried him up the stairs to the field level where a stretcher waited at the open ambulance door.

No one stopped him as he followed them up the steps. After they secured their patient to the gurney, he stepped forward.

"I'm going with him."

"We've got it," one guy said after a silent consultation with his co-workers.

"I don't give a shit if you've got it or not. I'm going with him."

"Bentley." Doyle Walker's voice. "Let them do their job. I'm going to the hospital as soon as I change clothes. You can ride with me."

He shook his head. "No." He toed off his cleats then kicked them toward the dugout. "I'm going with him. Bring me some shoes when you come."

Doyle regarded him with questioning eyes, then nodded to the emergency crew. "Let him go along."

Nothing more was said as they loaded Sean into the ambulance, and Bentley climbed in. He'd never been in an ambulance. The ride was harrowing, but he held on, his focus trained on the man on the stretcher.

"Is he going to be all right?" he asked.

"He's unconscious," the guy who'd ordered the backboard said. "Probable concussion. Possible broken bones. He could have a spinal cord injury, but there's no way we can tell for sure without tests."

Spinal cord injury.

The words sent a chill through his body. Baseball players didn't come back from that kind of injury.

"They'll do all kinds of tests at the hospital. You should know more in a few hours."

Panic screamed louder than the sirens clearing their way through the Dallas traffic.

I'm here. No matter what happens, I'm here. I'm so damned sorry. We're going to get you through this. I won't leave you.

In sock-clad feet, he paced the emergency waiting room for what seemed like an eternity. Belatedly, he understood why Doyle had taken the time to change out of his uniform. Everyone recognized him. Some knew why he was there, had seen him on TV getting in the ambulance with his teammate. All wanted his autograph. Some wanted news about the condition of the player he'd accompanied.

He'd never been so glad to see his team manager as he was when he arrived carrying a familiar duffle. Doyle brought his civilian clothes from his locker. Such a little thing, but once he was dressed, he felt more in control. Miserable, but more in control.

Team management threw their weight around, getting them moved to a private waiting room. They all looked at him with questions in their eyes. Why was he here? Didn't he hate Flannery? Of all the players on the team, why was he the one who refused to leave?

There was an answer to all their unspoken questions. He wanted to tell them, but he had to talk to Sean first. He had to make it right with him before he told these people what they wanted to know. Until then, he kept his own council, quietly praying for the man to recover soon.

"Why don't you go home," Doyle asked late in the night when they still had no answers. "There's nothing you can do here."

"Maybe not, but I'm not leaving."

"Don't you have a fiancée to go home to?"

For the first time since he'd seen his lover tumble into the dugout, he thought about Ashley. He searched his pockets for his cell phone. "I'll call her. She'll understand."

"Just so you know, you don't have to stay. We aren't going to leave him alone."

"I know. He doesn't have much family." One of the many nights, exhausted from a game then sex in his hotel room, they'd lain in bed talking about their families.

"We called his sister. She'll be here in a few hours."

Bent nodded. "That's good. He likes her."

"She saw it on TV. Said she was halfway out the door when we called."

"He'll be glad to see her. Siobhan, right? Lives in D.C.?"

Doyle nodded. "I didn't know you two were close. After the brawl in the clubhouse…."

"Yeah, well, that was old business." Business he didn't want to discuss. "I'll call Ashley." He held up his phone. "Let her know where I am." With the help of a friendly nurse, he found the nearest exit not swarmed by the media and powered up his phone. He had half a dozen missed calls—all from his fiancée. He hit redial on the latest one then pressed the phone to his ear.

"Bentley!" she screamed in his ear. "Where are you?"

"At the hospital. Sean…." His throat closed up, and he couldn't continue. Damn. He needed to get a grip.

"I saw it on TV. Is he all right? The news people are saying how awful it could be."

"I don't know anything yet. They're still doing tests. He was still unconscious when we got to the hospital."

"I'm sorry. I really am." She paused, and he couldn't think of a single thing to fill the silence. "When are you coming home?"

"Not until I see him. We had another fight, a verbal one this time, right before the game. I can't leave him…not until we talk."

"I understand." Her voice was softer, almost sad. But what the hell did she have to be sad about? "Look. I've been getting calls from the network. They know we're engaged. They want information. I promise, I won't tell them anything you tell me. If you need to talk, I'm here."

"Thanks." He scrubbed a hand over his face. "I appreciate it. I'm sure he will, too, when he comes to."

"Bentley…I'm sorry. Tell Sean, I'm sorry." She disconnected before he could ask her what she meant. *Sorry? For what?* As long as she didn't feed private information to the press vultures, she had nothing to be sorry for.

If only you could say the same for yourself. You're a grade A asshole, Bentley Randolph.

He was unraveling, one silent minute at a time. When the team of physicians treating the first baseman stepped into the waiting room, he was one taut rubber band away from snapping.

"Gentlemen."

Bentley recognized Phillip Sanderson, the Mustangs doctor. Of course, he would be at the hospital—it was his job to keep the players healthy. He introduced the others—an orthopedic surgeon, a trauma specialist, and a neurologist. From the introductions, it sounded as if they'd called in the best, but impatience ate at him. He didn't want to hear how many Board certifications they had.

"How is he?" he interrupted.

Dr. Sanderson glanced at him, blinked as if he was seeing things then stammered. "Uh. He's…well…there's a lot to discuss." His gaze traveled over the group. "Does he have family here?"

"His sister is on the way," Doyle said.

"Okay, then. I can tell you he's awake. He knows what happened to him. He's in a lot of pain from a variety of injuries. I'll let the others here tell you, as they're treating him within their own specialties." He looked at the orthopedist. "Dr. Williams, why don't you go first?"

Dr. Williams didn't look more than thirty years old. Bent wanted to ask if they had anyone with more experience but held his tongue. There'd be time for that later, if need be. He'd move whatever mountains stood in the way to see Sean had the best care possible.

"Mr. Flannery has two cracked ribs he sustained in the fall, as well as a broken hip. The break is severe and will require surgery, but we've elected to postpone it for a few days so other issues can be addressed first."

"What other issues," Bent asked.

The shorter doctor stepped forward, clearing his throat. "I'm Dr. Schmidt," he said. "Mr. Flannery has some bruising along his spinal cord, and a CT scan revealed a minor concussion. Because of the concussion, I've advised against surgery until we know more. There doesn't appear to be any permanent spinal injury. He has use of all his limbs, and he responded appropriately to stimuli. For the time being, he's on mild pain killers to be increased as needed once we're sure he's out of danger from the concussion."

Dr. Schmidt stepped back to allow the last of the team to come forward. "I'm Dr. Hollowell," he said. "I get to deliver the best news. Mr. Flannery doesn't appear to have any damage to internal organs, but we're going to keep a close watch on him over the next few days. It appears he landed hard, and there could be internal bleeding we can't detect right away. But, all things considered, his injuries appear to be more skeletal than anything else, and bones heal."

"When can I see him?" Bent asked.

Dr. Sanderson stepped up, taking charge once more. "His family is on the way?" he asked the general gathering.

"It's going to be a few hours, at least," Doyle said. "Bentley knows Sean as well as anyone on the team. I don't see why he can't go in."

The doctor nodded. "Okay." He turned to Bentley. "Let him sleep as much as possible. Try to keep the jokes to a minimum. It's going to be a while before he feels like laughing."

The medical team left with promises to keep Mustangs management informed of Sean's progress. Bent was aware of the curious glances as he left the waiting room with Dr. Sanderson, but none of it mattered to him any longer. All that mattered was seeing the man he loved.

He was asleep when they entered his private room. The doctor checked the monitors hooked up to his patient then with a whispered reminder to let the man sleep, he departed.

Bent stood for a few minutes, watching his chest rise and fall, reassured by the steady rhythm. Every once in a while a grimace would pull at Sean's face, and he'd moan a little. His color was better than it had been when he was lying on the dugout floor, but he was far from having a healthy glow. There was a scrape on his left cheekbone, and bruises were rising to the surface along both arms. *Christ! He must have bounced around like a pinball before he hit the ground.*

Satisfied he was sleeping as comfortable as possible given his injuries, Bent pulled a chair up close to the bed and sat. Sean's hand was outside the covers, a clothespin style heart monitor clamped to one finger. He placed his palm over the back of his hand then closing his eyes, dropped his forehead to the edge of the mattress.

I'm so fucking sorry. Everything you said before the game was true.

His back ached like he'd slept in the back seat of a Volkswagen Beetle. Strange sounds stirred his consciousness. He opened his eyes. His eyeballs stung, and he had to blink twice to make sense of his surroundings. A nurse in flower print scrubs stood on the opposite side of the bed, writing something on a clipboard.

Bent sat up, rubbing both palms over his face. Damn, he needed a shave.

"Good morning," nurse flowers said.

"Mornin'." He glanced at the man in the bed. He appeared to be sleeping, which was a good thing. Every couple of hours through the night someone had come in, woken him, asked stupid questions, looked at his pupils then told him to go back to sleep. At least he knew Bent was there. They hadn't exchanged more than a few words all night long. They would talk later.

"Mr. Flannery's sister is here. She's in the waiting room talking with Dr. Sanderson."

He took the hint. "I guess I should go talk to her, too."

"I'll look out for him while you're gone. He's doing well. No signs of complications from the concussion. We should be able to give him something a little stronger for the pain in a few hours."

"I'm glad." He covered Sean's hand with his, reassuring himself the man he loved was alive. "If he wakes up, tell him I'll be right back?"

"I will. There's coffee at the nurses station. Grab a cup if you want. It's better than the stuff in the waiting room."

"Thanks." He smiled at her kindness. "I appreciate it."

Coffee in hand, he stepped into the waiting room. Dr. Sanderson, freshly shaved and wearing a lab coat over crisp chinos with a blue shirt, was talking to a dark haired woman Bent assumed was Sean's younger sister, Siobhan.

"Good Morning," he said, approaching. The woman turned. He knew he'd been correct. She was a full head shorter, but the sibling resemblance was striking. She was a female version of her brother, which meant she was beautiful. "I'm Bentley Randolph."

She shook the hand he offered. "Siobhan Flannery. Dr. Sanderson said you haven't left my brother's side. I appreciate you sticking by him." Her gaze seemed too astute then he remembered she knew about Sean's sexual orientation.

"I couldn't leave him alone, but since you're here...."

"Dr. Sanderson assures me my brother is going to be fine, eventually, but it's going to be a long road for him, especially with the hip injury." She didn't correct Bent's assumption she would want him to leave, nor did she acknowledge it. He took it as a good sign.

"I figured as much." He turned to the doctor. "This will end his career, won't it?"

"It could. It's a bad break—worse than the one he suffered a few years ago. As I was telling Ms. Flannery, the hip socket and pelvic bones are shattered. He could come back, but it's going to take time."

He wondered if they'd told Sean or if he remained unaware his life had irrevocably changed when he caught that pop up.

"At least he caught the ball," he said.

Siobhan smiled. "He did. He'll be glad to hear, if he doesn't remember."

"He isn't going to want to hear the rest," Bentley said.

"No, he's not. He loves baseball. Not playing is going to take some adjusting if it comes to that."

"Let's just focus on getting him through the surgery for now," Dr. Sanderson interjected. "We can deal with his post-baseball life once he's back on his feet. He may play again. It's possible, if he wants it bad enough."

"Good to know," Bentley said. "I won't mention it then, unless he brings it up."

"Sounds like a plan," Siobhan said, "but he's going to bring it up."

"We'll deal with it when we have to. From the way it sounds, he doesn't have much choice but to have the surgery, right?" He turned to Dr. Sanderson for his answer.

"No. Not if he wants to walk."

A chill ran down Bent's spine at the realization of how serious the man's injuries were. "Then that's our primary goal."

Having done all he could for the time being, Dr. Sanderson excused himself to see to his patients from his private practice.

"You should go home, get some rest," Siobhan said.

"I don't want to leave him."

"I'll be here. If he wonders where you are, I'll tell him I sent you home but you'll be back. You will be back, won't you?"

"I will." He shifted his feet, looking around the empty waiting room. "Look, you should know...."

"No need to explain. I can tell. He means a great deal to you, doesn't he?"

"I love him." He was surprised at how easily he spoke the truth to a complete stranger, even more surprised she didn't appear in the least taken aback by his declaration.

"Then go home, get some rest. He'll still be here when you get back." She smiled at her joke. Bent couldn't help it, he smiled back.

"It's not like he's going to walk out of here, is it?"

"No. He may try to wheel himself out, but I'll stop him before he gets far."

"Come on," he said, leading the way. "I'll show you where his room is, then I'll go get cleaned up. I need to make some arrangements with the team, then I'll be back."

CHAPTER SIXTEEN

Things hurt he didn't even know he had. How was that possible? Even the slightest movement brought on more pain, enough sometimes he thought he might pass out. But nothing hurt worse than seeing Bentley hovering over him, suffering right along with him.

Damn him.

The man had been there every time he opened his eyes—except the last time. Siobhan had sent him away. Thank God. He could always count on his sister to have his back. Not so for the rest of his family, but Siobhan loved him the way family should—unconditionally.

They'd given him some better pain meds, allowing him to sleep for longer stretches of time. Though he was getting more rest, waking up took more effort.

Lying still, he listened. A game show, it sounded like, was on the television, the volume down low. Off to his left, the steady clicking of computer keys. *Siobhan.* Always working, though she swore the romance books she wrote weren't work at all. It sure as hell looked like work to him, but then again, he did good to compose an email.

He risked turning his head, found the neck pain to be bearable, and watched her type. She looked so serious, her brows knit, her lips drawn into a tight line. "What kind of scene are you writing?"

She jumped at the sound of his voice. He smiled as she caught her laptop before it slid to the floor. "Don't do that!" she scolded, setting the computer aside then coming to stand over him. "You almost gave me heart failure." Her words chastised, but her smile said she wasn't going to hold a grudge. She never did where he was concerned.

"Hey, sis. What are you writing?"

"Oh. Nothing much. My hero is being an ass to my heroine. I don't like him very much right now."

"I could tell. You were scowling at the screen."

"Maybe I was. I get carried away sometimes."

He chuckled. The small action rocked his injured ribs, making his entire torso ache. "Ow," he groaned.

"Are you okay? Do you need the nurse?"

"Hell, no! I just have to remember nothing is funny, and I'll be fine. No laughing."

"No laughing," she agreed. "Seriously, can I get you anything?"

"No. Just talk to me. Tell me what's going on. I feel like I've been run over by a truck, and about half of what's been said to me since I got here, I haven't heard."

She told him as much as she knew about his injuries, which amounted to what Dr. Sanderson had told her when she arrived. Everything she said confirmed what he thought he knew.

"I was hoping I was having nightmares, but I wasn't. My career is over. I won't be coming back from this."

"You don't know that, Sean. It's too soon to tell. Bentley said you would be out for a while, maybe most of next season, but he thinks you'll be back."

He closed his eyes against a different kind of pain. There weren't enough drugs in the world to ease his heartache where Bent was concerned. While they had him on the operating table, perhaps they could sew up the rip in his heart, too. He opened his eyes and looked at his sister, wanting her to hear him. She had to understand. "Don't listen to him. As a matter of fact, don't let him back in my room. I don't want him here."

He'd stunned her. Clearly, Bentley led her to believe they were close. He hated to burst her happily ever after bubble, but there was no other way.

"But…he loves you."

"He thinks he loves me. Did he tell you he has a fiancée? A female fiancée?"

"No. No, he didn't." She contemplated the news for a second. "But…why?"

"I know all the questions you want to ask, but I don't have any of the answers. Look, we had a thing…for a while. He had a chance to man up, to choose me, but he didn't. I told him we were through…what day is it?"

"Tuesday."

God, he'd lost an entire day somewhere. "I told him on Sunday, before the game. He's feeling guilty or something. I don't know. I don't care. I just don't want him around. If he comes back, send him away, okay?"

He could tell she wasn't convinced he was telling the truth, but she nodded. "Okay. I'll do my best, but I got the impression he planned to be with you through everything."

"Don't go getting all sappy on me. You don't know the half of it, and I'm not going to tell you. Just trust me, he might come back, but then again, he might not. He's scared to death of his feelings. Once he gets home and his fiancée coaxes him back into bed, he might stay there."

"But…he told me he loves you."

"I'm sure he meant it, but he has another life, Siobhan—a safe one. One that doesn't require him to risk anything. I've been on an emotional roller coaster with him for years. I gave up. This—" He waved his hand to indicate his injured state. "—doesn't change anything, except maybe to make me more certain breaking it off was the right thing to do. It's going to take every ounce of strength I can muster to get back on my feet. I can't waste any of it on a man who can't make up his mind what he wants."

"You're sure."

"I am. So, please. If he comes back, send him away." The physical pain combined with the strain of telling his sister about his sorry love life took its toll. Closing his eyes, he tried to relax, but the pain was taking hold again, smothering him. "The surgery is tomorrow?"

"Bright and early."

"You'll be here?"

"I'll be here as long as you need me. My work is portable.

Where are you staying? Did you rent a house?"

"Not yet." He named the motel he'd moved into then told her where to find the key to his room. "Doesn't look like I'll be going back there anytime soon. Can you get my stuff for me?"

"I'll take care of it," she promised.

He was drifting off to sleep again. At least he didn't hurt when he was sleeping.

Bentley dropped his keys on the kitchen island then headed straight for the fridge. Who the fuck cared if it wasn't yet noon? He needed a beer in the worst way. His body ached from sleeping in a chair all night, and the antiseptic hospital smell had given him a bitch of a sinus headache. But he was going back—just as soon as he showered.

He pulled a bottle from the refrigerator then pressed it to his forehead for a few seconds before removing the cap and taking a long swig.

"Good morning."

He almost choked on the beer. "Christ, Ashley! You scared me."

"I didn't mean to. I heard you come in." She wrapped her arms around him from behind, resting her head between his shoulder blades. It felt good to be held. "How's Sean?"

"Hurting. It's bad, Ashley, really bad. There's a strong likelihood he won't ever play again."

She tightened her arms around him for a moment. "I'm sorry. Does he know?"

"I think so. I don't know. Maybe." Had anyone told Sean? "I think the orthopedic surgeon told him, but he's been in a lot of pain. They didn't want to give him the good meds because of his concussion, but this morning they did another CT scan. The doctor said it was looking much better, so they gave him something stronger. He was asleep when I left."

Turning, he took her in his arms and held her, resting his chin on the top of her head. "I've got to go back."

She nodded. "I understand. He needs you."

"No. I'm sure he doesn't, but I want to be there for him. I owe him as much."

"Why would you think you owe him anything?"

The scene in the bowels of the stadium right before the game came back to him. Maybe if he had left Sean alone—hadn't cornered him. Maybe. "We had an argument before the game. He was pissed. Hurt. I feel like I pushed him over the railing, in a way."

"You didn't, and you know it. It was an accident. He's not the first player to fall into the dugout."

"I know, but I couldn't concentrate on the game, so I'd bet he was distracted, too. If I'd waited until after the game…."

Straightening, she looked up at him. "What happened? I thought it was over between ya'll."

He hated the worry in her eyes. Seems he was doomed to hurt those he loved. "It was over. But I couldn't stop thinking about him. I wanted to find out why he left without a word. Why he wasn't answering my calls. Why he was avoiding me."

"Did he tell you?"

He looked away. "Yeah, he did." Everything appeared so peaceful in the backyard. The grass sparkled with water droplets not yet evaporated following the morning's automatic watering. Beyond the yard, the pool shimmered as tiny waves spanned out from the circulating pump. Nothing out of the ordinary.

Why the fuck can't you be ordinary?

He'd given up searching for the answer to that particular question. There wasn't one.

She slipped her hand in his, tugging him toward the door. "Come on. Let's go in the den." When they were settled side-by-side on the sofa, her fingers were still entwined with his. "Okay. Tell me what he said. Why did he leave here?"

He shook his head. "You don't really want to hear this."

"Yes, I do. You've been miserable since he left. I want to know why he hurt you the way he did."

Her hand felt good in his, soft yet strong. He didn't want to hurt her, but she deserved the truth. "He said I didn't stand up for us—him and me. He said he saw the look of disgust on your face when he kissed me. He said I'd made my choice when I didn't invite him to stay—to be with us—you and me. He knew I made love to you afterward, then he asked me if…."

"If what?"

"If I thought of him while I was with you."

She was still for a long time. "Did you think about Sean when you were with me?"

"I let him think I didn't."

"You lied to him."

"Yeah. I'm sorry, Ashley. When I'm with you I think about being with Sean, then when I'm with him I think about being with you."

"Did you want to ask him to stay? Did you want to make love to both of us?"

"Yeah, I did. But I saw the look on your face, too. You weren't ready for it. Maybe Sean was right. Maybe you won't ever be ready for it. He was right to leave."

"What happened afterward? Did he say anything else?"

"No. He said we were through. I'd made my choice, and he'd made his. His meaning was clear. He doesn't want to see me again."

"But you rode in the ambulance with him."

"He didn't have much choice in the decision. He was unconscious." He paused, seeing a replay of the accident in his mind. "I never want to feel that helpless again. I was scared out of my mind. I thought he was dead when I saw him lying there. All I could think was, he thought I didn't love him enough to fight for him.

"Everything he said to me before the game was true, and I hated myself for it. I didn't give the three of us a chance. I didn't give you a chance to get to know him. I know you talked a couple of times, but you don't really know him. I guess the kiss was a test—for us. We both flunked.

"You know, if he'd sat up in the dugout, I would have been so relieved, I would have kissed him in front of everybody. I don't care who was watching. I swear I would have done it."

"I'm sorry. I admit I was shocked. I suppose it showed on my face, but shock wasn't all I felt. It took me a few minutes to get past seeing you kiss a man, but once the initial shock wore off, other feelings began to surface. I didn't tell you what I was thinking. Maybe if I had, you could have stopped him from leaving."

"What are you talking about?"

"That kiss was hot, Bentley. Seriously hot. It's all I could think about when we were in bed together. You know how you tried to explain to me about it being different between two guys? I couldn't imagine it, couldn't fathom what you were talking about, but then ya'll were kissing, and I saw it. I *saw* it. It scared the shit out of me, but yeah, I saw what you meant. There's some serious chemistry between the two of you."

"It didn't turn you off?"

"Oh, hell no! I'm sorry. If I'd said something…."

He shook his head. "No. You weren't ready. Sean was right about everything. Neither one of us was ready—except him. I hurt him, made him feel like he was on the outside looking in."

"The kid looking in the candy store window with no money in his pockets."

"Yeah."

"Have you talked to him?"

"No. They kept waking him up all through the night—making sure he was okay—the concussion…he knows I was there."

"You need to talk to him. Tell him the things you've told me."

"I will. He needs to get past the surgery first, though. For now, I just want him to know I'm there for him."

"When he gets better…I think I'm ready, Bentley. I've been thinking about it, the three of us together. I want to do it. Maybe if you tell him that first…."

"Thanks." Their hands were still clasped, resting on his thigh. He brought his free hand up to cup her cheek. "I love you. I always knew you were an incredible woman." He brushed his lips across hers. "I don't deserve you."

She smiled, stroking his jaw. "You look tired."

"I'm not too tired for *that.*"

Her lips were soft and warm against his. "Will you talk dirty to me? Tell me what if feels like to be with him?"

"Anything you want, babe. Anything you want."

"I want you."

Instantly aroused, he pinned her to the sofa cushions in the blink of an eye. "I want to fuck you so bad, you can't even imagine."

She moaned, arching up to fuse her mouth to his. Her tongue flicked against his lips, and he opened for her. She'd never been the aggressive one in bed, but he liked this new side of her. It reminded him of Sean, except he didn't yield when Bentley tried to take the lead.

They dueled for supremacy until he was crazy with need. He broke the kiss then making quick work of removing her clothes, he made his way down her body, tasting, taking, and taunting. She wanted dirty, he'd give her dirty.

"I fuckin' love your tits," he said, handling them roughly. She moaned and writhed when he squeezed them hard then bit down on one distended nipple. "Beautiful goddamn tits." He turned his attention to the neglected one, sucking and biting until the scent of her arousal drew his attention lower.

"Spread 'em," he growled, clasping his hand around one thigh, showing her exactly how he wanted her. "Yeah, just like that."

Kneeling between her splayed legs, he covered her heated sex with his hand, applying pressure to the most sensitive area. "I love wet pussy, don't think I don't."

He speared her with two fingers, fast and hard. Her hips rose off the sofa cushion as her cry rose to the vaulted ceiling. "Your pussy is wet and hot. So fuckin' tight. I want it. Now."

"Bent," she moaned, arching her neck, thrusting against his fingers.

One handed, he freed his cock. He withdrew his fingers, replacing them with his dick. "Yessss," he hissed, rocking into her with almost savage thrusts. "My fuckin' pussy. All mine. Say it's mine, babe. Say it's mine."

"Oh, God, Bent. It's yours. I'm yours."

"I want all of you, babe. You want to know what it's like fucking Sean? I'm going to show you."

She protested when he pulled out of her. He shushed her. "Turn over. Give me your ass, babe. Just like Sean does."

He expected her to balk. He'd never asked her before, but she surprised him by flipping to her stomach and spreading her legs.

His heart almost hammered right out of his chest. "What the fuck are you doing?" his conscience asked as he knelt there, staring at her perfect round ass. So damned sweet. So damned innocent.

"Bent?"

Her voice snapped him out of his coma. "Babe."

"Do I need to do something? Is this the way you want me?"

Oh, God. I'm really going to do fuck her in the ass. "No, babe. I'll do all the work."

She wiggled her butt, and it was all he could do to hold onto the seams of his control. "Please, Bentley. Hurry."

Jesus, he was fucked. He swiped three fingers through her wet slit, gathering her slick juices. With one hand, he spread her while he slathered her tight, pink rosebud with her honey. Going back for more, he considered warning her, but she wanted to know what it was like, he was going to show her.

He coated his dick with her sweet juices then gritting his teeth against the exquisite pleasure awaiting him, he positioned the head of his cock and pushed into her.

"Fucking, Christ," he said through his clenched jaw. He froze.

She was utterly still. He counted to ten, watching, waiting until her back rose and fell when she sucked in a breath. Her muscles rippled along her spine. He knew everything she was feeling—the absolute wonder of being possessed—the peace that comes with surrendering everything to the person you love—knowing without a doubt they cherish your surrender.

"Babe. My God, babe."

"Bentley."

He heard the tears in her voice, knew he needed to be skin to skin with her. Careful not to disengage from her, he removed his shirt, tossing it to the floor atop her clothes. Deciding he couldn't do anything about his pants that were down to his knees, he lay atop her, giving her his heat and his heart.

"I've got you, babe. I treasure what you've given me." He flexed his hips, taking her deeper. "Talk to me. Tell me what you feel. Am I hurting you?"

"Bent. No. Not hurting me. Oh, God. I…I feel…."

"Loved? Possessed? Cherished?"

"Yes," she whispered.

He kissed the temple, her cheek, the corner of her mouth. "You are all those things, babe. I love you."

He continued to kiss her, showing her how precious her gift was to him. He stroked his hands down her sides until he gripped her hips. Holding her steady, he inched inside her until she'd taken all of him.

"Babe. You make me feel like a king. You've given me a gift beyond measure."

She moaned his name.

"Let me show you how much it means to me."

Pushing to his hands, he braced above her, slowly retreating then pushing back in. God, she was perfect. He couldn't wait for Sean to see how perfect she was.

"Sean is going to love you. He's going to love watching me fuck your pussy and your sweet ass."

Her hands were tiny fists, her eyelashes a dark fan across her cheekbone. Her lips were parted, her mouth working to take in air then expel soft moans of encouragement. He increased the tempo, doing all he could to prolong her pleasure while delaying his own. With each retreat and thrust, it became more difficult.

Dropping to one elbow, he reached beneath her and found her clit. She made an unintelligible sound, bucked her hips like a mare in heat, then she imploded.

"Ah, Jeeezusss," he cried as her ass tightened around his cock in erratic waves. It was all he could do to remain still, to let her experience every bit of pleasure.

When she lay beneath him, panting but relaxed, he pushed back up so his hands were braced on either side of her then with a few quick, forceful thrusts, he found his own release.

CHAPTER SEVENTEEN

"That's what you feel when…with Sean?" Still inside her, he'd rolled so his back was to the sofa, pulling her back tight against his front. Staring sightless at the empty fireplace across the room, she pressed her hand over his where it rested against her stomach, stroking lazy circles. Still intimately connected, she felt at peace in his arms.

"I suppose. I love being with you. I always feel like a conquering hero when I make you come. God knows you steal my sanity when I come, but being with Sean…. It's different. He's my equal, physically, so fucking him, having him submit to me—me submitting to him…it's different, but the same, I guess."

"I think I understand. I've never felt closer to you than I did, than I do now."

"I know. There's so much trust involved in giving someone that kind of power over your body."

His cock softened. He slipped out of her. She wiggled her ass closer to his groin, reluctant to give up the connection.

"I can't do it again for a while, babe," he said, nibbling on her ear lobe.

"It's like I can't get close enough to you. I'm not horny, just…needy, I guess."

"Mmm. I know the feeling."

"You do?"

"Sure. I've felt it with you before, and with Sean, especially after a particularly satisfying orgasm. It's like you've given the other person a part of yourself you can't get back, but if you can get close enough, you'll feel whole again."

"That's it. That's how I feel." Who knew her baseball player was a poet? "You should write that down."

"I don't think so. I already have a gay lover and a straight fiancée. The last thing I need is for someone to run across my sappy writings when I'm gone and start calling me a romantic or something."

"You are a romantic."

"No. Just a stupid fuck who's in love with two people."

"What are we going to do, Bent?"

"About Sean? I don't know. Putting pressure on him right now about our relationship won't do."

"You need to get back to the hospital."

"I do." He pushed up so he was sitting on one hip behind her. "You okay with that?"

"I am. Sean needs you."

"What do you mean, he doesn't want me here?"

Siobhan Flannery had his arm in a chokehold, dragging him toward the elevator. He had no choice but to go along or cause a scene in the middle of the busy hospital corridor.

"I'm just doing what my brother asked me to do. He said to tell you to leave if you came back."

Bentley dug his heels in, tugging his arm loose. This was unbelievable. "Why?"

"I don't know, but he said to tell you the things he said before the game…he meant them. Nothing has changed for him."

"Fuck." Setting his hands on his hips, Bent stared at the floor.

"I'm sorry. If it's any consolation, I think he loves you, but it sounds like your relationship has been a roller coaster. He doesn't need the turmoil right now. Getting back on his feet is all he can handle for the time being."

He looked at her again. Her eyes, so much like Sean's, gazed at him with pity. "The roller coaster has come to a stop," he said, his voice laced with steel. "I know he needs to concentrate on his recovery, and I have no intention of rocking the boat. I want...I need to be there for him."

She shook her head. "He doesn't want you there. I know he's being stubborn, but he's hurting—not just physically. He's facing the real possibility he's never going to be able to play baseball again, Bent. I can't imagine what that's like for him. It's been his life since he was a kid. I don't think he even wants me around, but he has little choice in the matter. He knows he can't manage the physical therapy by himself, at least not for a long time, so he's willing to let me stay."

"He's being stubborn."

Siobhan smiled. "He excels at stubborn." Her smile faded. "Give him some time. I'll talk to him after the surgery. When he has a better idea of what his limitations are going to be I'll try to convince him to see you."

He hated her logic, but she was right. Her brother had made up his mind, and there wasn't going to be any changing it. "When's the surgery?"

"Tomorrow morning. Six a.m."

"I'll be here." He'd already told the Mustangs he wasn't traveling with them to Los Angeles. They hadn't liked it, but had agreed to take him out of the lineup for one day. "No need to tell him. Besides, someone needs to hold your hand through it. And what Sean doesn't know, won't hurt him."

"I appreciate it, Bentley. I'll be grateful for the company." She cocked her head to one side then smiled at him. "Besides, technically you won't be here for him—you'll be here for *me*. Right?"

"Right." He smiled back.

Bentley was at the hospital early. Siobhan met him in the waiting room after they'd wheeled her brother off to the operating room.

"Thanks for coming," she said, walking into his outstretched arms.

"No need for you to suffer just because Sean is being an ass."

She broke away from him, swiping her fingertips over her cheek to capture a rogue tear. "I know he's going to be all right. His surgeon is the best, but still...."

"It's nerve-wracking," he finished for her. "It's going to be hours. There's nothing we can do here, so why don't we go find some breakfast and coffee that isn't made with ground up asphalt? There's a place on the next block I know."

She looked around at the dingy waiting room and the smattering of others somberly awaiting news. If there was a more depressing place on earth, he had no idea where it was. "Okay," she said. "Anything is better than here."

"How was he this morning?" he asked once they were seated at a booth along the back wall of a popular breakfast place.

"Better, I think. He had a good night, thanks to the heavier meds they gave him."

"I understand if you don't want to answer, but I was wondering if the doctors have said anything more about his chances of playing again."

She opened her mouth to speak, but their waitress chose then to appear with coffee and menus. They took a few minutes to savor the hot liquid while they made their selections.

"To answer your question, no. They haven't said any more, to me or to Sean. The consensus is, he could make it back if the surgery goes well, and if he plays nice with the physical therapist they've assigned to him."

"The standard bullshit," he said. "How did he do with the PT the last time he injured his hip? Did he cooperate then?"

"For the most part. I stayed with him a few months then, too. He wasn't what I would call a model patient, but he was motivated. He wanted to get back into playing condition."

There was something in her voice that put him on alert, but their waitress was back, and he was forced to hold his question until she'd taken their order.

"Is he motivated now?" he asked as soon as they were alone again.

"I don't know, Bentley, I really don't. Last time, all he could talk about, even before the surgery, was when and how he was going to get back in the game. This time…he hasn't said a word. I have no idea what he's thinking."

He took a sip of his coffee then rested his forearms on the table, cradling the warm mug in his hands. "Do you think he might have given up?"

"On playing? I honestly don't know." She straightened her

silverware. "I don't know what he would do if he didn't play. It's all he's ever wanted to do."

"I know the feeling. The idea of retiring scares me to death. I don't know what I'll do with myself when the time comes."

"I'm sure you'll find something. I suspect money won't be an issue for you, so you can do anything you want, or nothing at all."

He'd been fortunate, and he knew it. His contracts had gotten bigger with each renewal, and he'd made some good investments. "I won't starve in my later years," he said. "Sean hasn't done as well, has he?"

"He isn't in the poor house, but I suspect he isn't in your league either. If he doesn't play again, he'll need some kind of income to supplement the investments he's made over the years."

"I want to see him play again. He was having one of his best seasons ever—if not *the* best—this year."

"I know. He was proud of himself. He said he was doing pretty good for a washed up cripple." She smiled. "I tried to tell him he wasn't either, but I'm afraid it's the way he's seen himself for the last few years."

Guilt dropped like a ball of lead into his stomach. "I should have been there for him," he said, keeping his gaze focused on his cooling coffee. "But I wasn't. I don't know if he told you, but I hurt him when I asked to be traded from the Pioneers. If I'd stayed…confronted my feelings for him then…. Maybe things would have been different for him."

"Bentley, you aren't responsible for anything that's happened to Sean. He's had some bad breaks, pardon the pun, but they come with the game. How he deals with them is all on him."

"This is killing me. I finally found my balls—" He glanced up apologetically. "—and he won't let me help him."

Their food arrived, and they ate in silence. Bentley paid the check then ushered Siobhan out to the sidewalk.

"I've got to go to L.A. tomorrow. I pulled some strings and bought myself a twenty-four hour reprieve, but if I'm not on the field tomorrow I could be in serious trouble."

"I'm glad you're here today. I'll be sure to tell the Mustangs how much it meant to me the first chance I get. Even if Sean did say he didn't want you here, I know he would be grateful for your support."

They walked the block back to the hospital where a quick check at the desk confirmed there was still no news on their patient.

"Do you have a place to stay while you're here?" he asked.

"I was going to stay with Sean, but he doesn't have any place to go when he gets out of here." She shook her head. "He's been living in a monthly hotel. I got his things for him yesterday, but I don't know what I'm going to do when he gets out of the hospital. I guess I'll have to find a place to rent."

"You can both stay at my place. I offered my pool house to Sean a few weeks ago, but he wouldn't take it. I doubt he'll change his mind, but it's perfect for him. One story, easy access for someone on crutches. I've got more bedrooms in the main house than I know what to do with. You're welcome to stay there."

"That's very generous of you."

"Like I said, he probably won't hear of it, but if he doesn't want it, it's there for you. You can tell him I won't bother him. He won't even see me. Hell, I'm never home anyway."

"Thanks," she said. "It sounds like a perfect solution to the problem. Can I let you know?"

"Sure." He made sure she had his phone number. "Write these down, too," he said, rattling off Ashley's cell and work numbers. "Ashley is my fiancée. She isn't at the house much either, but feel free to call her anytime. She'll be happy to help with anything you need."

"You really do have a fiancée." The surprise in her voice took him back a notch.

"Sean didn't tell you?"

"Yes. He mentioned it, but I didn't think he was serious."

"Yeah, well…he was serious. It's one of the things complicating our situation."

"I bet it is," she said.

"Anyway, you'll love her, she's fabulous." He couldn't help remembering how she'd encouraged him to do what he could for Sean. The three of them were going to be happy together—eventually. He couldn't imagine it any other way. "Whatever you or Sean need while I'm out of town, just ask. She'll be there for you."

"She knows?"

"About me and Sean? Yeah. I've managed to screw up quite a few lives, but I'm going to fix every last one of them or die trying."

"This is beginning to sound like a very bad romance novel," she said, staring at the phone numbers she'd written down.

"Romance novels all have happy endings, don't they?"

"Yes, they do."

"Then I'm okay with bad. I can live with it as long as it doesn't turn into a tragedy instead." *And if Sean doesn't get his head out of his ass, that's exactly what it's going to be.*

Sean stared out the windshield at the familiar and unwelcome sight of Bentley Randolph's pool house. He'd argued his way out of a twenty-four/seven stay in a rehab facility partly because his sister had sworn he would have the best of everything in the house she'd rented for him. He'd been so damned grateful for her support he hadn't thought to question where their new digs were.

"You've lost your mind if you think I'm going in there."

Siobhan turned the key, and the air conditioner died along with the engine. "Suit yourself, big brother." She opened the door then reached behind his seat for her purse. "I'm going in where it's cool. If you change your mind, honk the horn. "

"Siobhan! Get your ass back here!" Damn her hide. She didn't even look back. He watched her disappear around the winding walk leading to the side-facing front door.

"Siobhan!" He jerked his door open, leaning out to yell at her again. A wall of heat slapped him in the face, and he cursed under his breath.

What the hell am I going to do now? Damn her meddling hide.

He sat, a helpless captive, trying to come up with a solution. If he'd taken the initiative and found a place to rent when he first arrived in Dallas, he wouldn't be in his present situation. Hell, he'd had multiple opportunities to get a place but had passed on every one because he knew deep down he couldn't live in the same city with Bentley for long. Dallas was a temporary stop or his last stop.

He'd never known which until he'd woken up in the hospital.

Last stop, Flannery. Toot! Toot! Everybody off! End of the line!

End of the line.

He scrubbed a palm over his face, looked at the red brick structure before him, and mentally catalogued his piss-poor options.

He could sit there until he died of heat stroke or he could honk the horn to get his sister back out there. Maybe once she was out of the house, he could convince her to take him somewhere else. Hell, even the rehab facility was an option now. Anything was better than Bentley's pool house.

The horn grated on his ears, but he kept honking until Siobhan appeared. She looked like a pissed off teenager in her jeans and pink T-shirt with her long main of dark hair pulled into a high ponytail.

"Enough! I heard you," she said, jerking his door open. With one hand on the top of the door, she leaned down to glare at him. "Have you come to your senses?"

"Take me to the rehab hellhole."

"No." She started to leave.

He grabbed her wrist to stop her. "Sis, please."

"No." Her tone was softer, but the single syllable held all the conciliation of a mules' bray. She wasn't going to back down.

"I hate you."

"No you don't," she said. "I tried to find another place, Sean. You have some special needs right now, and I didn't want to sign a long-term lease on anything. I didn't have many choices. When it got right down to it, the pool house was the best thing I could find. Bentley swore to me he wouldn't bother you."

He stared through the windshield, unwelcome memories flooding back. "I don't want to be here," he said though his gut told him he didn't have a choice.

"I know. I promise it's just until you get on your feet. We'll make other arrangements as soon as possible, but for now, this will have to do."

"Fuck."

"I'll take your eloquent utterance as agreement. Hang on," she said. "I'll get the walker out of the trunk."

She trailed along behind him, one excruciatingly slow step at a time until he crossed the pool house's low threshold. It took a second to figure out what was different, but then the change registered. Someone had removed a few of the larger chairs in the living area and rearranged the furniture, to make it easier for him to get around.

"Where to?" his sister asked. "Here or the bedroom?"

"Here's fine." He propelled himself to the sofa. It took some doing, but he managed to sit without ending up on the floor.

"Can I get you anything?"

"No," he grumbled, reaching for the television remote control.

"At least let me get you an ice pack. The doctor said—"

"I know what he said. I was there, remember?"

"Don't yell at me!" She stalked to the kitchen. For the next few minutes, the rattle of ice cubes almost covered her pissed off mutterings.

He knew he shouldn't take his frustrations out on his sister, but she was the only human around, so she had taken the brunt of it since his surgery.

"I'm sorry," he said when she came back in the room, ice pack and a cold soda in hand.

"Here." She handed him the pack wrapped in a dishtowel then set the soda on the end table where he could reach it. Without ceremony, she hauled an ottoman around the coffee table, placed it in front of him, and helped him raise his injured leg. He positioned the ice pack against his hip.

"Do you need anything else?"

She wasn't ready to forgive him for being an ungrateful ass, but she would. Siobhan had never been able to hold a grudge where he was concerned.

"I'm fine. Thanks, sis." He hoped she heard the apology in his tone.

"Okay." She ignored his polite overture. He guessed he deserved her cold shoulder. "In that case," she continued, "I'm going to leave you alone for a while. I'm behind on my manuscript. I could use a few hours of uninterrupted writing time."

She slung her purse over her shoulder then grabbed a key ring off the table by the door.

"Where are you going?"

"Over to the main house. I'm staying there. Oh!" She dug around in her purse, coming up with his cell phone. "Here. If you need anything, call me. I'll be here in a matter of minutes."

He stared at the phone in his hand for a few seconds. "You aren't staying here, with me?"

"No. There's just one bedroom, and this way you'll have some privacy. I'll be back in a couple of hours to fix us some dinner, but in the meantime, call me if you need anything. Don't be stupid, big brother. If you need help, ask for it. I don't want to come back to find you in a heap on the floor and have to call 9-1-1 to get you back up."

He didn't know what to say.

"Promise me, Sean. Promise you won't do anything stupid."

"I promise," he said, wondering what qualified as stupid and what didn't. He wasn't a stranger to hobbling around with a walker. He'd done it before and managed well enough. He didn't care what his doctors said—give him a few days of PT then he'd be up on crutches, and walking with nothing more than a cane in a week—two at the most.

"Get some rest. You're going to need it 'cause the hard stuff begins tomorrow."

He waved as she walked out the door. *So…she's staying in Bentley's house.* He wasn't sure how he felt about her living there for the time being. He was grateful she had a nice place to stay, but shit, she didn't need to be mixed up in his fucked up personal life, but what choice did he have?

The sad truth was, he had no choices. He'd screwed around, ignored the help offered from the relocation service, and now he had nowhere to go but Bentley's pool house—the last place on earth he wanted to be.

Well, maybe not the last place. He was certain the accommodations beat the hell out of the rehab facility. Whoever had chosen the sofa knew what furniture was supposed to be.

It felt like heaven after almost two weeks lying on a hard hospital bed. Closing his eyes, he willed his muscles to relax. As the tension left his body, he realized how wonderful it was to have peace and quiet. No beeping monitors. No shoes squeaking on tile floors. No people shuffling past his door or worse, coming in to poke or prod him.

The remote slipped from his fingers as sleep claimed him.

CHAPTER EIGHTEEN

"He's getting better every day," Siobhan said. "He still refuses to talk about his goals. I have no idea if he's going to try to play again or not."

"Bentley was afraid of that." Ashley took a bite of her sandwich, chewed, and swallowed.

"What?"

"That he would shut everyone out. He says your brother can be an ass sometimes. I think he was referring to the four-legged kind."

"He can be stubborn. It's a Flannery family trait, but I think there's something else going on." She took a long sip of her soda then set it back down. In the two weeks since she'd brought her brother to live in the pool house, she and Ashley had become friends. It was also nice to have someone to visit with while Sean was at his PT sessions. The sandwich shop they met at was next door to where Ashley worked, which happened to be a few blocks from Sean's physical therapist. As long as she didn't think too hard about her new friend's relationship with her brother and his lover, she was all right. She'd found even romance novelists had their limits.

"The doctors must have talked to him," Ashley coaxed.

"I know they have, but he wouldn't let me sit in on their

meetings, and he isn't talking."

"You think they told him he wouldn't play again?"

She shrugged. "I don't know. If they did, he's keeping the information to himself."

"But he's doing the PT."

"Yep. As I said, it seems to be going well."

"Maybe Bentley should talk to him."

"No!" She shook her head. "No, don't ask him to. The only way Sean is still living in the pool house is because your fiancé has kept his word and left him alone. He doesn't have the time or the energy to be moving to another place yet."

"I won't say anything to him then, if you're sure. I know it gives him a little peace knowing Sean is close by, even if he's hardly ever home."

"The season is going to be over soon, and he'll be home all the time. Is that going to be a problem?"

"I hope not. I'll do my best to keep him busy. We're getting married right after Christmas. He's going to hate it, but I've got a million details for him to deal with, once he has the time."

Siobhan laughed. "He doesn't strike me as the type to be picking out flowers."

"He's not." Ashley smiled. "But he'll have more time than I will, so I'm not giving him any choice. Besides, I've already made most of the *girly* decisions. He's getting the easy stuff like putting invitations into envelopes and making sure they get to the post office on time."

"If he has trouble with it, let me know. I'm not much good at organizing, but I can stuff envelopes."

"How long do you plan to be here? Can you stay for the wedding?"

"Oh, please…no. You don't have to invite me!"

"We'd love to have you there. Please? Can you stay?"

"Truthfully? I have no idea how long I'm going to be here. As long as it takes Sean to get back on his feet, I guess. I don't want to leave him until I know he can make it the rest of the way on his own."

"Well, if you're here through the end of the year, then you will come, won't you?"

There was so much sincerity in her voice and in her eyes Siobhan couldn't say no. "I'd love to."

Fuck!

Sean clenched his jaw against the stabbing pain radiating out from his hip in all directions. Hell and damnation. Even his balls and dick shriveled away from the pain.

He forced his spine to straighten then tightened his hold on the handgrips. Two more reps on this machine would end today's torture session.

"You can do it, Mr. Flannery."

God, he hated her voice. Why couldn't he have a physical therapist who wasn't fresh out of the cradle? Someone who wasn't so goddamn perky?

Closing his eyes, he forced the weighted machinery to move again. And again.

"Excellent! You're all done, Mr. Flannery." Perky came around to stand in front of him. The nametag on her baby pink polo shirt said, "Tiffany." Why couldn't he remember that? Probably because the name conjured up images of sweet young things without malice in their bones. Pixy or not, perky Tiffany was a sadist at heart. She loved pushing him to the breaking point, sometimes beyond, but he wouldn't trade her for anyone else.

"Thank God." He collapsed against the back support. "I hate you."

Smiling, Tiffany handed him a towel. "No you don't. You love me. Why else would you come to see me every day for the last two months?"

He wiped the sweat from his face and hands before easing to his feet. "Maybe I like to be punished," he said with a wink.

"I don't think so. If you did, you'd beg for more. I hear a lot of words come out of your mouth during our sessions, but *please* has never been one of them."

"You have a point."

"Never fear. Despite your lack of requests for longer sessions, you've come a long way."

"I guess I have, but it doesn't seem like it sometimes."

"What did the Mustangs' trainers say?"

They'd come to watch his workout the day before and talked to him afterward. He hadn't told anyone what they'd discussed. "The same as before. Keep working." The lie tripped off his tongue.

"Well, I've got good news for you," his sadistic pixy said. "I met with your doctors yesterday. We agreed you're ready for the pool. As of tomorrow, we're adding swimming to your daily workout. Start with one lap tomorrow, then add a lap each day until you get to ten a day."

He glanced in the direction of their pool. The idea of sharing the facilities with a bunch of people he didn't know bothered him. "I have access to a pool where I'm…at home…. Would that be okay?"

They discussed dimensions, agreeing on one and a half laps in the smaller pool to one in the facilities larger one.

"Don't push it, Sean," she said, using his given name for the first time. "I know therapy is difficult, but you have to give the bones time to heal. You didn't just crack your hip like before, you shattered it. The doctors put you back together like a jigsaw puzzle. It's going to take time."

He left with a promise to swim no more than the prescribed distance before coming in for his torture session. He didn't care what the Mustangs' trainers said, he was going to be on the field next season. If necessary, he'd bow to his Pixy of Pain every day until he made it happen.

Bentley stood at the kitchen window, sipping his coffee while he watched Sean's sleek body slice through his pool. He was up to ten and a half laps. It seemed he was going to stay at that level for a while. Yesterday had been the third day in a row he stopped when he reached that number.

"He's dedicated," Siobhan said, joining him at the window.

"Seems so," he offered, not taking his gaze off the man in the pool. "The question is—dedicated to what? He isn't going to make it back. Not with the Mustangs, at least."

"You're certain?"

"Yeah." He'd had to do some pretty underhanded things to get the information as it wasn't the official stance of the team, but he'd long suspected it to be the case. The optimistic press releases had dwindled to nothing in the last few weeks, a sure sign Sean's future with the Mustangs didn't look bright. "He hasn't said anything to you?"

"Not a thing," his sister confirmed.

"How's he doing?" Ashley asked as she entered the kitchen, dressed for work. She wrapped her arm around his waist then placed a kiss on his jaw. He turned his head, capturing her mouth for a more satisfying kiss. She tasted like mint toothpaste and smelled like an entire rose garden in bloom.

"Same as yesterday," he said. "I don't know what's keeping him going. He has to know he isn't going to play again."

Ashley moved in front of him. "What? Are you positive? How do you know?" Her eyes mirrored the concern in her voice. They'd had plenty of time to discuss what they referred to as The Sean Situation over the previous weeks and come to the conclusion neither one of them wanted him to leave. They'd also agreed to give him all the time he needed to deal with his injury, observing him through shaded windows as he traversed the backyard walkways, first using a walker, then canes, and now one careful, independent step at a time.

Watching him climb from the pool, his body looking fit and sexy as hell had become one of their favorite morning pastimes over the last week. After seeing him the first day, she'd dragged Bentley back to their bedroom, confessing if the other man wasn't gay, she'd want to jump his bones herself. She was as anxious as he was to invite him to join them as a sexual partner as soon as he was ready.

"I'm sure, and I'm sure he knows it, too," he said in answer to her questions.

"What's he going to do?" She turned to Siobhan for an answer when her fiancé shrugged.

"I have no idea." Sean's sister shook her head. "He hasn't mentioned a thing to me about not playing again. Up until Bentley confirmed he wasn't, I assumed he was planning to return next season."

They all watched him swim the tenth lap then the eleventh.

"He added half a lap today," Bent noted.

"I'm going to go talk to him." Siobhan snapped.

"No," Ashley said.

The younger woman stopped, turning to face them.

"Let me," Ashley added.

"Why?"

"Well…he hasn't talked to you, you said so yourself. He doesn't want to talk to Bentley. Maybe he'll talk to me."

He watched the two women. Siobhan had looked ready to murder her brother before his fiancée stopped her. Now the women faced off across the kitchen, one not ready to relinquish her fratricidal rights, the other with a gleam of mischief in her eyes. The woman was up to something. His cock stirred as he imagined the things they'd talked about doing with Sean. Surely she had better sense than to approach the man about being their sex partner when he was trying to save a career he'd already lost.

"Ashley," he warned.

She glanced at him. "I promise I won't upset him. I have something he needs to hear." The look in her eyes begged him to believe in her.

"Oh, go ahead," Siobhan said. "I can kill him another time." She refilled her coffee mug then left them alone in the kitchen.

"You think talking to him is wise?" he asked.

Ashley nodded. "I do. I think it might make all the difference for him personally and professionally. I promise I'll tell you how it goes."

"Okay then. You better catch him before he leaves for his PT session."

He was going to have to find another place to live. There was no reason for him to stay in Bentley's pool house any longer. He was ambulatory, and he was down to taking over-the-counter meds to control the lingering pain, which meant he was cleared to drive himself around. Siobhan could go home. If he rented a place with a pool, there would be the added bonus of not having an audience every morning while he swam.

He made the turn in the deep end, pushing off the wall with his good leg then headed in the other direction, adding another lap to the running total in his head. Halfway done.

They thought he didn't know. It almost made him laugh, an activity he'd given up until his ribs healed. He felt like a lab rat, always being watched, his behavior catalogued then discussed. It would feel good to laugh again, but there wasn't a goddamn thing in his life he found humorous.

He was a washed up ball player with enough savings and investments to provide him some security in his old age, but if he was fortunate, there were several decades in between in which he'd need to find a way to support himself. Unfortunately, the one thing he was good at was out of the question. His hip was mending, but not fast enough. The doctors couldn't guarantee the bones would ever be strong enough to take the normal abuse of a game again. He had enough metal screws, plates, and rods in his left hip to make an airport metal detector light up like a Christmas tree.

He was better. Much better. He was certain his audience could see the improvement. He was beginning to feel normal in other ways, too. So knowing Bentley was watching him added another level of torture to his recovery. Yet another reason he needed to find another place to live. He might spend the rest of his life jacking himself off because he couldn't have the man he loved, but he be damned if he'd do it on that man's property while the bastard in question shared his bed with a woman.

Oh, hell no.

After his PT session today, he would ditch his sister then go look at some of the places the relocation team had sent over. The sooner he was out of there, the better.

He made the last turn, and feeling as if he was, if not taking his dick in hand, at least he was taking his life in hand, he swam to the end of the pool then added another lap. It felt good to make decisions again for himself—even if they were small ones.

Climbing the stairs in the shallow end, he held the handrail, placing his feet with caution on each step. He might have pushed things a bit with the extra lap, but he'd heard his doctors' warnings loud and clear. Another break and all the king's men wouldn't be able to put him back together again.

He picked up the towel he'd left on the nearest table, drying his face first then dragging it over his head to scrub his hair. When he dropped the towel and opened his eyes, he was no longer alone. His heart knocked so hard he thought it might have cracked another rib.

"Shit." *What the hell is she doing here?* He felt the ridiculous urge to cover himself, though his board short style swim trunks were more than respectable.

"Sean," she said. Her smile was disarming. "Do you have a minute?"

He had a lifetime, but he wasn't going to tell her. "Did Bentley send you?" He rubbed the towel over his torso.

"No." She fell in behind him as he headed toward his temporary home.

"Must have been my sister, then. Knew I should have killed her in her crib."

"Wasn't her, either."

He stopped before stepping inside, pushing his wet swim trunks to his ankles. Tossing them over the manicured shrub next to the door to dry, he walked bare-assed naked into the house.

"Nice ass." She shut the door behind her.

Ignoring her, he continued on to the bedroom. He was stepping into a pair of boxers when she caught up to him.

"If you're trying to shock me so I'll go away, it isn't working."

He pulled a pair of workout shorts over his boxers then rummaged in a drawer for a T-shirt. "What *will* make you go away?"

She leaned against the doorframe, one perfect red fingernail tapping against her chin, her eyes turned up to the ceiling as if she was giving his question serious thought. "Hmm…I don't think there is anything you could do or say to would make me leave right this minute." She turned her gaze on him. "Are you through being an ass? No pun intended."

"Depends on why you're here." He pushed past her, heading straight to the refrigerator. After selecting a protein drink, he crossed to the sofa and sat.

She followed him, taking a seat across from him. "Rumor has it you aren't going to play again."

Direct hit. How the hell did she know? He took a swig from the plastic container, hoping his facial expression remained neutral. "Where did you hear that?"

"Bentley."

"Fuck Bentley."

"Thank you. I plan to. Often." She was a cold-hearted bitch.

"You want me to leave?"

"No. Look," her voice softened. "That's not why I'm here, at least not the main reason I'm here. Have you given any thought to what you're going to do next?"

"You mean since I can't play baseball again? That next?"

"Yes." She was getting frustrated with him now. Good.

"Nope."

She glanced around the room, a little nervously, he thought, but why would she be nervous? "Have you ever considered broadcasting?"

He rested his almost empty drink container on his thigh while he studied her. She was nervous. And serious. He thought back to the day a few months ago when Bentley invited him here for lunch then later, Ashley had suggested he move into the pool house. There had been some mention of a job opportunity then, but they'd gotten side tracked. "Maybe."

"Remember the position I talked to you about earlier this summer? The anchor spot on *Around the League*? Well, it's still open. Actually, we've held it open, hoping…well, not hoping, but thinking perhaps if things didn't work out for you…."

"Huh." She was looking at him again. She was fidgety, but she was fuckin' gorgeous. A man didn't have to be hetero to notice. "So…you've been hoping I would have a career-ending injury so you could offer me a job?"

"No! Of course not. It's just, there aren't many players out there who have the on-screen presence you do, who also happen to live in the Dallas area. I admit, we're on the brink of approaching someone else, but when you had your accident, I convinced them to wait a while. We have to make a decision soon, Sean. If there's any chance you might be back on the field, then I understand if you turn me down. But please, won't you give it some thought?"

If he didn't know the job had been up for grabs months ago, he would have sworn the offer was made out of pity. "If I say no?"

She shrugged. "It wouldn't change anything between you and me."

"You want me out of Bent's house."

"Actually…no, I don't." Her fingers were busy, picking at the hem of her stylish business skirt. "But that's another subject." She squared her shoulders, fixing her gaze squarely on him. "So…what's your answer? Do you want a chance at the job or not?"

"Tell me about it," he said, settling back in the sofa. He stared at his feet propped on the ottoman while she talked. The salary she named wasn't extravagant, but it was more than he thought it would be for sitting behind a desk a few hours a week, talking about something he loved. Nothing she described sounded like anything he would have trouble doing.

"It's a chance for you to spout off without management censuring you. You can interview whoever you want, ask them anything, within reason, voice your opinions on the players, the teams, and the league. The level of controversy is up to you, but we'd prefer you don't alienate every viewer in the lower fifty states."

"I've seen the show." According to her viewer stats, it was more popular than he'd thought.

"Then you know the format."

"I do." He dropped his feet to the floor then leaned forward, bracing his elbows on his knees. A few weeks ago, sitting in such a position would have been impossible. "Can I have some time to think about it?"

She dug in her purse then tossed a business card on the coffee table. "Can you let me know by the end of the week? I'm serious about our time line. We need to name a replacement soon in order to have time to get the new person up to snuff. If you think you're interested, we'll need you to come in, do a test run, let everyone see how you look on camera, meet the staff, the people who do the legwork—booking interviews, helping write questions, and polishing editorials. It's harder than it looks, Sean. You might not want to do it once you see what's involved."

"I appreciate the offer, I promise to think about it and let you know." He stood, but she remained in her seat.

"Now that our business is done, I have something else I want to talk about."

CHAPTER NINETEEN

Hell.

"Will you sit back down?"

He sat. She was back to trying to unravel the hem of her skirt. He had a sinking feeling in his stomach he wasn't going to like whatever else she had to say.

"Bentley doesn't know anything about this. He'd have a fit if he knew I was bringing the subject up with you right now."

Shit. This just gets better and better.

"He wants you to be his best man at our wedding."

"What the fuck?" He stood so fast a sharp pain in his hip almost sliced him in two. He winced, pacing to the other side of the room. Any closer and he might try throwing her out of the house. She looked fit, but he might be able to manhandle her out the door without putting himself in a wheelchair for the rest of his life.

"He said to wait, you weren't ready to hear it yet, but I disagree. I think you need to know where we both stand."

"Well, I damn sure won't be standing at the altar watching him get married."

"Please, Sean. Won't you listen to what I have to say?"

"Not if you're going to tell me you want me to be in your wedding, because you aren't going to convince me. Not in this lifetime, sweetheart."

"I have to admit, when Bentley told me about ya'll, I was shocked. I felt betrayed. As much as I wanted to hate him for what he'd done, I was curious, intrigued by it. I'd noticed a change in him weeks before he told me. I chalked it up to the stress of the season plus the wedding plans. But then when he told me, it all started to make sense. He proposed to me the same day you came to the house—the day I let you in."

He remembered. Hell, he'd wanted to fuck Bent so bad, but all he'd done was touch. Walking away had almost killed him.

"When I thought back, I realized that's when he began to change. He was different when he was with me, more aggressive, more forceful. Not mean or anything remotely similar, just more sure of himself, I guess. I didn't say anything to him, but I liked the new Bentley. You don't need all the details, but he did tell me what had been going on between ya'll. I reacted as you can imagine any woman would when she finds out her fiancé has a lover on the side. Except Bentley's lover was you—a man. That, for lack of a better term, blew my mind. I didn't know what to think. I was hurt, mad as hell, and shamed."

Goddamn. He did not want to feel sorry for her, but he did. "What we did was wrong. I'm sorry we hurt you."

She shook her head. "Don't be, please. I didn't come here to berate you. I came to tell you I understand. We have something fundamental in common—we both love Bentley Randolph, and he loves both of us."

"Yet, he's marrying *you*."

"Yes, he is. I get how you could be bitter about the situation. I'm a big girl. I can admit if the shoe were on the other foot, I'd feel the same way."

"Then you'll forgive me if I decline to dance at your wedding."

"No, I won't. I'm going to marry Bentley for two reasons. First—"

"I don't give a rat's ass why you're marrying him. This conversation is over." He pushed away from the wall he'd been holding up. He headed to the door with every intention of throwing her out, bodily, if necessary.

"First," she continued as if his wishes didn't concern her. "I love him, and he loves me."

"We covered that." He held the door open for her though she

hadn't moved from her seat.

"Second—to protect him."

"Protect him?" He slammed the door closed. "What the fuck are you talking about? Why does he need protecting?"

"He's going to need it once you move in with us."

She was speaking a language he didn't understand. "Huh?"

"Bentley and I have discussed this—at great length. We want you to move in with us. Officially, you'll live here, in the pool house, but in reality, you'll live with us."

"With you," he repeated, sure he'd lost his hearing and his brain was filling in random sounds to match the movement of her lips.

"*With us.*" She stood, facing him. Her breasts rose and fell as took a deep breath then let it out. "In our bedroom. In our bed."

After a long moment of tense silence, he reached for the doorknob, turned it then opened the portal. "Get out. Now." She'd fucking lost her mind. If Bentley was part of her hair-brained scheme, he'd lost his as well. For now, he wanted her out of his living quarters, the sooner the better.

She took a step toward the door then stopped. "The job opportunity is real, Sean, no matter what else happens between us. As for the other, anytime you want to give it a try, you know…to see if it would work for us, just come to the house. You know Bentley's schedule. It would be best if he's there."

Fucking insane.

He closed the door behind her then stood there, processing what had just happened.

Unbelievable. Fucking unbelievable.

He sank into the chair Ashley vacated and stared at the big, rusty Texas star on the opposite wall. Maybe it was some kind of joke. If it was, the woman had balls. Her face hadn't given anything away. In fact, she'd been as earnest about the moving in thing as she had been about the job, and he had no reason to believe the job wasn't real. Bent had mentioned it to him months ago.

No matter how hard he pushed himself at his PT session later, Ashley's invitation continued to ring in his head.

"Hey, easy. Not so fast." His personal Pixy of torture put a hand on his shoulder, breaking him out of his thoughts. "What's up? You know better than to push the limits."

Scrubbing one palm across his face, he let the weights settle back then slid his leg out of the resistance machine. "Sorry. I wasn't paying attention."

"Yeah, well not paying attention to your surroundings is how you ended up here in the first place. If you ever want to get out of here, you'd better focus on what you're doing. If you strain a muscle now, you could end up back at the beginning. Unless you've developed a weakness for aluminum walkers?"

He smiled, as she'd intended with her absurd question. "No, I have no intention of using one again for the rest of my life. Even when I'm an old, crippled up codger in the nursing home, I'm going to have me a custom made, souped up model—chrome with flames painted on the cross bars, maybe a horn."

"Then get out of here now. You've done more than enough for one day. As a matter of fact, and I can't believe I'm saying this, take tomorrow off. Swim if you want, but take it slow, half your usual distance. Not a foot more, understand?"

"Yes, ma'am." He saluted her then bent to place a kiss on her forehead. "I love to hate you, you know that, don't you?"

"I know. All my patients feel the same way about me."

"I *am* sorry. I didn't mean to sabotage all your hard work."

"It's your hard work you were sabotaging, not mine. My fault though. I should have been keeping a closer eye on you, but I thought you knew better."

"I do, I swear. I'll do as you say. I'll take tomorrow off. I have something I need to do anyway, so the extra time will work out well for me." He decided then and there to take a look at the job Ashley dangled in front of him earlier. Admitting he was done as a ball player was a bitter pill to swallow, but it was fact—which meant he was in need of a job. He'd always imagined he would coach, maybe work up to managing after his playing days were over, but he'd also imagined he'd be a lot older, too.

His agent had been calling, wanting updates on his condition, and Sean had lied through his teeth. But if Bentley knew he was done, then others knew. It was just a matter of time before his agent got wind of it. Walking to his car, he vowed to call the man tomorrow, after he'd talked to Ashley about the job. If he decided to make a career change, he would do it on his own.

❦

Ashley met him in the lobby of the downtown high-rise housing the network's offices. She looked every inch the executive she was in her smart suit and silk blouse. As he trailed behind her, he wondered if she knew the elaborate gravity-defying twist containing her mane of chestnut hair was an challenge to every male, hetero or not. Anything that uptight would explode with passion once it was released from its restraints. He'd bet his new hip Bentley lived for the times he could unravel her, one hairpin at a time.

She took him on a short tour of the building, beginning with the set he would soon occupy for a screen test then ending in her office. Waving him to a chair in front of her desk, she perched on the nearest corner, crossing her arms over her breasts, and stared at him.

"What?" he asked.

"Nothing." She uncrossed her arms then braced her hands on the edge of the desk on either side of her hips. "Just checking you out. Tit for tat, I think."

He raised one eyebrow.

"You were checking me out, so I'm returning the favor. Nice suit."

Heat crept up his neck. "I can appreciate beauty when I see it."

Smiling, she leaned close to whisper in his ear. "Bentley loves it when he gets to undress me after work." Straightening, she added, "Unfortunately, our schedules don't mesh very often."

"Sucks for him," he said, meaning it.

She took a deep breath then let it out. He could tell by the expression on her face, playtime was over.

"So, what did you think of the place?"

"It's big."

"True. We're going to redo the set when we introduce the new anchor." She handed him a stack of drawings off her desk. "This is the new set. More modern, lots of Lucite with brighter colors. Lighting we can change to match the colors of the team you're talking about, better graphics, state of the art touch screen technology. Are you up to learning how to use all the new equipment?"

"I'll have some time to practice with it?"

"A couple of weeks. We'll make sure there's someone to teach you how to use it. We'll do some mock broadcasts, so you can get comfortable with the camera changes and pacing."

"Sounds like a plan I can live with."

She looked down at her shoes, her lips doing a twisting thing while she thought out her next words. Sean fought the urge to run. When she turned her gaze on him, he knew what she was going to say, and he wished to hell he'd ran when he'd had the chance.

"Are you sure, Sean? Sure you aren't going back to the game."

He had longer than anyone knew to get used to the idea of not playing again. He'd known it deep down inside when he first woke up in the hospital, the pain all but unbearable. His doctors confirmed it not long after, but he'd convinced them to keep the information to themselves for a while. He'd just recently discussed his options or lack thereof, with the Mustangs.

He nodded. "I'm sure. I might be able to DH, but a Designated Hitter who can't run isn't much good. I'd love to coach or manage, but the truth is, I don't want to leave Dallas. I'd have to, *if* I was able to land a position. I don't have to tell you how big an if we're talking about. You know how scarce those jobs are. Broadcasting is my best option."

"Okay." Her smile was back. When she relaxed her shoulders, he realized how tense she had been. "Are you ready to give it a try today? We'll put you behind the desk with some copy to read then turn the cameras on. It will give you a sense of how it feels to do the job, as well as let the powers-that-be see you in action."

He broke out in a cold sweat the second his ass hit the anchor seat.

"You've done press conferences and dozens of interviews, Sean. Relax. Read the copy over a few times while we get everything set up."

It didn't take long to set up, then Ashley was showing him how to tell which camera was on, and where to look while he spoke.

"The camera is your audience. Speak to it. Don't rush, normal conversational tone will do."

A few minutes later, he was sitting in near darkness as the clusters of hot lights turned off, one at a time.

Ashley approached the desk, a smile on her face. "That was fantastic, Sean. Seriously, fantastic. I knew you would be a natural the first time I saw you answering questions during a post-game news conference."

He willed his legs to quit shaking before he stood. "You think so? I deviated from the script some. Hope it was all right."

"I'm glad you did. The script was written for Walters, not for you. You made it yours, which is exactly what we want. No one can take Walters place. We need a fresh voice, someone who can win over his fans plus draw in new ones, too. I'll pitch your tape to my bosses, but I don't think there's any doubt they'll love it."

His legs stopped shaking, and the knot between his shoulder blades eased. "You think so? I have to admit, I was terrified."

"You did a good job hiding it. It will get easier, I promise."

"What now?"

"Go home. Do what you do. I'll call you when I have news."

"How long?" As intimidating as the screen test had been, he wanted the job. He could stay in Dallas and afford to live, even put some into his 401K. His savings, along with the League pension that would kick in when he turned sixty-two would make his later years comfortable.

"Maybe as soon as this afternoon if I can get everyone to look at it."

Holy shit.

He couldn't ignore the ache in his chest at the thought of leaving the game he loved, but if he couldn't play any longer, talking about the teams and players—plus getting paid to do it—was the next best thing. As he drove back to Bentley's house in the suburbs, the odd mix of grief and excitement made his stomach churn.

With the day off from physical therapy he had time on his hands. He called his sister.

"Hey, what's up?" she asked.

"Not much." He wasn't about to tell her about the job until it was more than a possibility. "No PT today. Are you busy?"

"I'm writing, but I can take a break."

Ashley was at her office. The Mustangs were flying home from Seattle today, so it was safe to visit the main house. "Good, I'll be over in a minute."

Why Siobhan was still hanging around, he didn't know. She'd been a big help those first weeks when he couldn't do much for himself, but he was doing for himself again, she didn't need to stay.

She met him at the door to the kitchen, glasses of iced tea in her hands. *You'd think she owned the place.*

"Sis, why are you still here?"

"You mean, why am I still living in your friend's house, drinking his iced tea, and accepting visitors as if I have the right?" She smiled then sipped her tea.

"Why are you? I'm fine now. I appreciate what you did for me, but you should go home. Back to your life."

"I like it here. I'm getting tons of work done, and…I get to see you."

Why did he get the feeling she was going to say something else? "You haven't seen me in days," he said, calling her bluff.

"Well, I know you're just on the other side of the pool. I feel better knowing I'm close in case you need me."

"I could use a dinner partner this evening." He hadn't been out to any place that didn't serve food in a paper wrapper since his accident. For some reason he felt like celebrating tonight. "You game?"

She made a pouty face. "I can't, Sean. I have…plans."

His big brother senses went on high alert. "What kind of plans?"

"If you must know, I have a date."

Her staying when she was no longer needed was beginning to make sense. "When did you have time to meet a guy?"

She took a long drink from her glass. Delay tactics. He was not going to like her answer. He knew it.

"Bentley introduced us…after a game."

Oh no. She was *not* dating a baseball player. "To who?"

"Jake Tulleson."

His blood ran cold then, as if he'd walked into a blast furnace, his anger turned red-hot. "What the fuck? He's old enough to be your—"

She slammed her glass on the table. "Don't say it, Sean," she warned. "He's just fifteen years older than me."

Old enough to be her father. Hell, the Mustangs hitting coach probably had a string of bastards older than Siobhan. He ran through women faster than rain through a leaky roof.

"Like I was saying, he's old enough to be your father. What the hell was Bentley thinking, introducing you to that reprobate?"

"He's not a reprobate. He's nice."

"Nice, my ass. Go home, Siobhan. Find some nice guy to date but do me a favor and don't tell me about him until he puts a ring on your finger." She was an adult, but he still didn't like the idea of her with a guy, especially one whose questionable morals had been discussed in the locker room. He was better off not knowing. Once a guy came up to snuff with a proposal, he'd deal with it. Until then…. "Stay the hell away from Tulleson."

"You aren't the boss of me, Sean Flannery. I choose who I date."

He almost smiled at the childish reprimand, but it reminded him how young she was. "Those books of yours are fiction, Siobhan. They're nothing like the real world. Tulley is not a happily ever after kind of guy."

"What do you know about anything?"

Her face flushed—a sure sign he'd pushed her too far. It was too late to backpedal now. Besides, he wouldn't take back a single thing he'd said. Every word was true. In true big brother fashion, he couldn't seem to keep his mouth shut. "I know a hell of lot more than you do. I haven't been living with my nose to a computer screen. I know ballplayers. It wasn't long ago Tulleson was wearing a uniform. From what I hear, he wasn't fit to wear it. Still isn't."

"Mind your own business, Sean." She snatched her glass of the table then poured the remaining liquid down the sink. "When you figure out your own screwed up love life, maybe I'll listen to what you have to say about mine, but until then, fuck off."

She stormed out of the kitchen, the sound of her feet hitting the stair treads rang after her, followed by a door slamming upstairs.

Fuck. Siobhan wasn't supposed to know words like that, much less use them. The silence in the kitchen eventually drove him out of Bentley's house. His urge to celebrate was gone, replaced with a bit of remorse for making his sister mad, and a lot of worry. She'd been writing those sappy love stories so long she believed they were real.

Not in the real world, little bit. It was easy to write about happy endings, not so easy to have one. Just look at the divorce rate. Happily ever after was fiction. Jake Tulleson was a real life bastard.

He stormed back to the pool house as fast as his half-crippled legs would take him. He wished to hell he could contact another family member to talk sense into Siobhan, but he couldn't think of a single one who would take his call. She was it. The only one who knew his secret and still loved him. The thought of a lowlife like Tulleson touching her made him sick. But she was right, his own love life was a fucked up mess, so he had no right giving her advice on the subject. He'd keep a close eye on the situation so when Jake tired of her, Sean would be there with a shoulder to cry on. It was the least he could do for the sister who was always there for him—no matter what.

Brooding over his sister's situation, he'd forgotten all about his screen test earlier in the day until his cell phone rang. He hadn't programmed Ashley's number in, but he recognized it from dialing it earlier. It rang a few times before he got up the nerve to answer.

"Put your suit back on," she said.

"Huh?"

"Sean." She enunciated his name as if he was hard of hearing. "Put your suit back on then meet me at the house in an hour. Don't be late."

The phone beeped its end of call signal. He stared at the dark screen for a second.

"Why the hell do I have to put my suit on?"

CHAPTER TWENTY

She was taking a big chance. She knew it, but she was sick and tired of watching Bentley watch Sean. Having him so close, yet farther away than ever, was taking its toll on her fiancé. Up until today, she hadn't had a clue what to do about the rift between the two men.

There were any number of ways her plan could go wrong—any of which could cause permanent damage to the various relationships involved. But as she drove home with Sean's contract on the seat beside her, she refused to think bad thoughts. It was clear neither of the men were going to do anything to fix the situation between them, so resolving the matter was up to her.

Well, so be it.

The butterflies in her stomach turned to chattering mockingbirds the minute she saw Sean crossing the distance between the two houses.

"You're an idiot, Ashley," the birds said.

"Forget your plan before it's too late."

"Give him the contract then send him back to the pool house."

But damn, he looked fine, except for the frown on his face. She ignored the warnings coming from her stomach and smiled at the man approaching.

"Sean," she said, opening the French doors. "Thanks for coming."

He entered, glancing around as if he expected a horde of crazed clowns to jump out at him, or maybe he was afraid of encountering someone else.

"He's not here," she said.

His shoulders relaxed some, but he still looked like he was ready to bolt. "My sister?"

"She called earlier, said she was going shopping, then meeting her date somewhere later."

The cords in his neck tightened, and he balled his hands in to fists at his side.

"Is there a problem?" she asked.

"Did she say who she was meeting?"

"No, but she's been seeing Jake Tulleson, I believe. I assumed that's who she meant."

He nodded, but remained a block of brittle ice. He needed to be much more relaxed for what she had in mind. Time to change the subject.

"Well, I have good news," she said, forcing cheer into her voice. "Congratulations, Sean. You're the new anchor for *Around the League.*"

Surprise lit his eyes. "Really?"

"Yep. I brought your contract home with me." She ushered him into the living room where she'd left the document. "Come in, have a seat so we can go over it."

He looked a little lost—her fault for shifting gears on him so fast she supposed. She joined him on the sofa then slid the papers from their folder.

"It's pretty straightforward," she said. "Let me point out a few things in particular, then I'll give you some time to look it over. If you have any questions, I'll be happy to answer them."

After she'd explained the clauses she wanted to make sure he understood, she handed him the document then stood. "I'll get us something to drink while you look it over. What's your poison, beer, wine, champagne?"

"Water or a soda, if you have it," he said.

So much for smoothing out his rough edges. "I'll see what's in the fridge."

As soon as she was out of sight, she pulled out her cell phone and texted Bentley.

How was your flight?

Fine. I'll be home soon. Miss U.

Miss U 2.

Now she just had to keep Sean in the house until Bentley arrived. The flock of birds in her stomach took flight again, making her hands shake when she pulled two diet sodas from the fridge.

Play it cool, Ashley. All business so he doesn't suspect anything.

On impulse, she opened the cabinet where she stashed the junk food.

Just one, she promised herself, biting into a chocolate cookie. She closed her eyes to savor the dark flavor enhanced by the creamy filling. Cookies were her weakness, chocolate ones being pure decadence in her opinion. She kept a stash on hand, but rationed them to times of complete stress or celebration. Resisting the urge to down the rest of the package, she returned it to the cabinet then picked up the sodas. She had a sneaking suspicion she would be finishing off the cookies later anyway. The night ahead would either be cause for celebration or a complete disaster. She couldn't see any in between.

Sean was just where she'd left him, contract in hand. He didn't acknowledge her as she rejoined him on the sofa, setting their soft drinks on the coffee table.

She had to give him credit, he apparently was reading the whole thing, word for word. He was so much more than just a ball player. In the short time she'd been around him, she'd seen a bit of the man inside. Sean Flannery was intelligent and insightful. The way he'd taken the script written for someone else and turned it into his own was nothing short of genius. He'd be an asset to any sports news department. They'd be lucky to get him if he signed the contract.

Sitting silently by, she ticked off the minutes in her head. Bentley would be home any time. She took a sip of her soda just as Sean finished reading then flipped the last stapled page over.

"Done?"

"Done. It looks good to me, but what do I know? Mind if I let my lawyer look it over?"

"No. I think having your lawyer read it is an excellent idea."

"I know you want an answer soon, so I'll ask him to make it a priority."

"Thanks. I can't tell you how happy I am to have you onboard."

Cocking his head to one side, he smiled. "You're sure I'm going to sign?"

"Positive." She smiled back at him. "You'd be insane not to. The terms are excellent, the pay and benefits package are above the industry standard. What more could you want?"

"I admit, not much. I appreciate the opportunity, Ashley. Unless my lawyer finds a trap door, it appears I have a new job."

"Excellent," she said.

The door to the garage slammed. Her heart shot into overdrive. Bentley was home. Lord, getting through the next few minutes was going to be harder than she'd thought.

Sean stood, too fast by the look on his face. He glared at her. "I have to go."

Grabbing his hand, she held on tight. "Please, don't leave."

He was going to murder her. "You set me up."

She stood, latching onto his arm so the only way he was moving was if he dragged her along with him.

"Please," she said, her eyes begging him to trust her. "No matter what happens the rest of the night, just remember it won't affect your contract in any way."

"Ashley? Honey? I'm home!"

Bentley's voice sent Sean's libido racing, triggering his fight or flight response. He tried to pry Ashley's fingers loose from his coat sleeve.

"Don't do this," he implored, making no headway in removing her from his body. He had no idea what she thought was going to happen, but he wagered it wouldn't be pretty.

Bentley rounded the corner then stopped in his tracks, eyeing the two of them standing there, his fiancée wrapped around another man. His gaze darted from one to the other, finally landing on Ashley. "What's going on here?"

He'd heard that tone before. It seemed Ashley had, too. She tensed, gripping his arm tight enough he winced.

"Hey, ease up," he hissed.

"Sorry." Loosening her grip on his arm—but not by much— she glanced up at him before returning her gaze to her irate fiancé.

"We're in the mood to celebrate," she said. "Sean is going to be the new host of *Around the League*. I brought his contract home tonight. He was just taking a look at it."

Bentley advanced into the room. His gaze darted to the document on the coffee table then back at them.

"Is that so? Congratulations, Sean." He stared at him, those blue eyes showing genuine happiness at the news…and more.

Desire, simmering low ever since he'd heard the man's voice, began to burn out of control. His dick went hard in the blink of an eye. He shifted his feet to ease the discomfort.

Shit. "Thanks," he said, once again trying to extricate himself from Bent's fiancée. "I should be going."

"Stay."

He froze at the command in Ashley's voice.

"Babe. What's going on?" Her fiancé moved closer, one cautious step at a time.

God, he looked good. It had been a long time since he'd been this close to the man he loved. It was hard to take his eyes off him. His suit was rumpled from traveling, his tie loose around his neck, the first two buttons of his dress shirt open revealing a patch of tanned skin. Sean would tear his new contract up for a chance to kiss that triangle of skin.

"Like I said, we should celebrate." Her voice was low, seductive. She wiggled next to him, sort of like a pole dancer and he was the pole.

What the fuck?

"What did you have in mind?" Bentley was no more than an arm's length away. Nothing but the coffee table stood between them.

"I know how much you like it when I wear a suit," she said. "I thought perhaps you might like *two* suits."

Bent's eyes sparkled with mischief. His lips curled up on both ends, his focus entirely on his fiancée. "I like to strip you *out* of your suit," he corrected her. Then he turned his gaze on him. It was all Sean could do to remain upright under Bent's heated perusal. "I haven't got a problem with removing his suit, either."

Someone tugged on his arm. He looked down. Ashley. "What do you say, Sean? Will you stay with us tonight?"

Holy fuckin' shit. This is what he and Bent had talked about, lying naked together after making love, but he'd never once believed it would happen. He tore his gaze away from her to see what the other man might be thinking. His dick screamed, "Hell, yes!" while brakes screeched in his brain.

"Bent?" he asked.

"Up to you," he said. "If you stay, I'm going to fuck both of you all night long."

He looked back at the woman clinging to him.

"Stay, Sean," she said. "Bentley needs you in his life."

"What about you? Why are you doing this?"

"For him. But also because the more I think about ya'll together, the more I want to be a part of it. Let's let him have his fun, then I'll race you to see which one of us can make him beg first."

The man in question groaned. "It fuckin' won't take much. I'm dying here."

This is crazy. "I…." He couldn't think straight. The war between his dick and his brain was escalating, and if it was a matter of the one with most blood wins, his lower appendage was way out in front. "What if…?"

"One night at a time," she coaxed. "We'll never know if we don't give it a try."

"You want to be with us?" he asked her.

"I do. One night, Sean. We'll worry about tomorrow when the sun comes up."

Bentley had walked into an alternate universe. There was no other explanation for what he was experiencing. His cock felt like it might explode. His balls were on fire. Hell, even his fingertips tingled, and his mouth watered. Ashley looked like the object of every hot office fantasy he'd ever had. Her hair was up in one of those tight bitch do's that screamed, "Take me if you think you can"—a challenge he never could resist. The severity of her office attire was relieved by a sexy, silk blouse peeking out from her lapels, hinting at a repressed feminine side longing to be set free. He'd kiss her into oblivion while his hands liberated her breasts. Then he'd turn her around, bend her over the back of the sofa, hike her form-hugging skirt to her waist. He'd fuck her until her hair and her morals shook loose.

But maybe it was too late for the morals part. It seemed those had already sprung free. They'd talked about a threesome with Sean, but as much as he longed for it to be a reality, he'd never expected it to come about. Leave it to his fiancée to surprise him—yet again. She had a way of doing that. His heart swelled with love for her as she tried to convince Sean to stay. For him.

Sean looked amazing in his dark blue suit and red, power tie.

God, he'd missed him. Missed his body. Missed holding him. Memories of the last time they'd been together flickered like a fireworks show through his brain. He'd taken him the same way he had just fantasized about taking Ashley—with his suit disheveled but still on, from behind.

Shit.

"I'm a sucker for a suit, it seems." He directed his comment at his former lover, willing him to remember.

The man's gaze snapped to him, held for what felt like a lifetime before his lips twitched upward on one corner. "You owe me for dry cleaning."

So…he remembered.

"Fuck your dry cleaning."

Damn. He could hear his own heart beating—the silence in the room was so complete as the veiled challenge hung in the still air. He was having a hard time focusing on anything but his need to fuck these two people. Yet, when Sean looked at him, all smug and knowing, he felt an unnerving need to surrender to the man—to lie beneath him—to know, in giving himself, he was loved and cherished.

"You guys are steaming up the windows," his fiancé said, slicing the sexual tension in the room with her wit. "Bentley."

He cut his gaze to her.

"Are you going to undress us here, or should we go to the bedroom?"

It took him two tries to get a word out of his mouth. "Sean?"

"My sister?"

"Could come back," she said, "though she didn't seem to think she would."

"Upstairs," Sean said. "I'm not taking any chances." He turned toward the stairs.

"Wait!"

He stopped at Bentley's sharp command. He crossed the room to his fiancée. She glanced up at him. The love and understanding in her eyes almost brought him to his knees.

He cupped her face in his hands. "I love you," he whispered against her lips before he kissed her. He poured all the passion he felt for her into the kiss. When he broke from her, she smiled up at him.

He turned to his lover who stood statue still, having watched the entire kiss. He couldn't read a thing on the man's face. Was he turned on, repulsed, indifferent? He'd force a response from him. Toe-to-toe with him, he cupped the other man's face, kissing him with the same passion he had lavished on his fiancée. Where she had caressed his forearms, showing him her tender acquiescence, Sean wrapped his hands around his head and crushed their mouths together in a war of dominance.

Their bodies collided below the belt. The answer to his question came in the hard ridge of the erection dueling with his own. They kissed until they were out of breath before breaking apart. The drop of sweat trickling from his temple to his jaw was mirrored on his lover's face.

"Let's take this upstairs," Ashley said, her voice husky. She was aroused. Well, that made three of them.

In silence, she lead the way up the staircase, followed by Sean. He trailed behind, mesmerized by the two people ahead of him. Inside their bedroom, he closed the door. They stood facing him, Ashley looking so damned prim and proper. Her lips were red from their kiss downstairs; her face flushed with desire. She shifted on her feet, a clue to the nerves skittering below her calm exterior—a reminder she'd never been in a sexual situation with more than one person at a time. He had no idea if his lover had, but he didn't give a fuck. He needed to make the first time good for his fiancée or the first would also be the last.

Taking a moment to compose himself, he crossed the room. He emptied his pockets, tossing his wallet on top of the dresser. Another landed beside it. Sean's. In all their hotel room encounters, they'd never emptied their pockets before sex. He stared at the leather rectangles, stunned by the intimacy of the simple act of coming home—the implied permanence of it. They'd sleep together. Wake up together. Dress and go out into their normal world together.

Sean slipped his feet from his shoes then went back to stand beside Ashley. Bentley toed off his shoes, leaving them on the floor next to his. He turned to his lovers.

He approached her first. Locking gazes with her, he slipped his hands beneath her suit jacket to bracket her waist. The silk of her blouse was cool to his fingers as he inched it loose from the waistband of her skirt.

His thumbs brushed bare skin. She sucked in a sharp breath,

her eyelids dropping. He switched his focus to her parted lips as he continued to explore her body with slow but thorough hands. He inhaled her intoxicating scent, a sweet musk that called to him, captivating him in a sensual web of desire and need so acute it made his knees weak.

Her breathing became erratic, tuned to the exploratory whims of his fingers. He palmed one lace-covered breast. Her head fell back, allowing his lips access to a long column of alabaster skin. Kissing his way from her chin to the sweet swell of her breasts, he encountered the first in a line of obstacles—a pearl button. He began to work it loose with his teeth. Something moved in his line of vision. Sean moved behind her, easing her back to rest against his chest, his long fingers massaging her shoulders.

The sight of his strong hands on her sent a bolt of pure lust ricocheting through his system. He wanted them both. Wanted to lay them out side-by-side and make love to them until none of them were able to move.

Determined not to rush, he worked each tiny pearl loose, savoring every inch of skin as he peeled the thin layer of fabric away. When the last one popped free, he pressed his lips to her stomach. She brought her hands up, spearing her fingers through his hair, urging him upward toward her breasts. He leaned back, one hundred percent onboard with granting her wish. Sean's hands slid along the length of her arms, captured her wrists, guiding her to clasp the back of his neck, elongating her torso and forcing her back to arch. He watched as masculine hands released the center clasp on her bra, pushed the lace cups aside then cupped her cream and rose-tipped mounds in his palms—offering her to him.

It was the most erotic thing he'd ever seen. He locked gazes with his male lover for a second, acknowledging how much his participation meant to him. Then he dipped his head to suck one perfect nipple into his mouth.

She gasped. He switched to the other side. Sucking and tugging, he let the soft cries coming from her lips guide his actions. Loathe to leave one breast unattended, he reached for the lonely one, cupped Sean's hand with his, commanding him to tease her tight nub. Either he'd done it before or he was a quick learner. Either way, he left the other man in charge of her breasts. Kneeling, he wrapped his hands around the back of her knees.

With infinite care not to miss a single inch of her firm thighs, he inched his hands up, her black pencil skirt piling atop his wrists like accordion bellows. He continued, up and over the sweet globes of her ass, the skirt dipping low in the front to hide her delicate mound. Before he could move his hands to fix the situation, Sean reached down, gathered the fabric in his long fingers, lifting it to her waist.

She didn't have a scrap of fabric on under her skirt. Her bare pussy, concealed between clenched thighs, beckoned him.

Bentley swallowed hard. He'd never imagined another man taking an active part in his love making with Ashley, but damn, it was sexy as hell and driving him mad with the need to have them both. As much as he enjoyed the sight of her soft skin exposed to him by callused hands, he was on a mission to end the raging hunger inside him.

He grasped her legs, urging them to part. Once again, another came to his aid, using his sock-clad feet to force hers apart, holding them wide, exposing all her tender, pink secrets to him. He tilted his face up—met Sean's gaze head-on. A fire burned in the blue depths of his lover's eyes as he held Bent's fiancée in his embrace—one hand beneath her chin, immobilizing her—one fist clenched against her belly, exposing her. For him.

In that heated moment, he knew Sean wasn't jealous of his love for Ashley. If the banked fires in his gaze were any indication, he was turned on watching him with the woman he loved.

You're next, my love. You're next.

He reached between her legs, grabbed the man's balls through his trousers and squeezed hard.

"Fuck!"

Smiling, he buried his face in his fiancée's pussy.

She dug her fingernails into the back of Sean's neck and held on to him as if he were the single thing preventing her from slipping off the top of Reunion Tower.

She'd expected Bentley to take charge, but not for his male lover to become her anchor. Oh, holy hell, it was erotic being held by him while her fiancé tormented her body, one tender kiss at a time.

This was nothing like what she'd imagined when they'd talked about the three of them together. She'd imagined…something less…overwhelming. Sean on one side of the bed, watching, then her returning the favor while they took turns loving each other.

But, oh dear God, this was…mind blowing.

She'd been prepared for him watching—thought it would add an edge of naughty to their lovemaking, but….

Bentley's tongue teased her clit then swept through her folds, flattening out to lap at her as if she were one of those swirly lollipops from the candy shop at the stadium. The stubble on his cheeks scraped against her skin, adding to the complete feeling of possession that took hold of her the minute the two of them teamed up on her.

If she could just touch him, see him as he drove her closer to the point where she'd lose her grip and free fall into pleasure. But a callused hand on her chin and the one at her waist, held her pinned. His feet were immovable objects spreading her open. Vulnerable. Loved. Cherished. Possessed.

She couldn't bear it to go on another minute, never wanted it to end. Bentley's mouth was the sweetest torture, driving her close to the brink then backing off again. Each time, she thrust her hips toward him, begging while frustrated moans whispered past her lips. Each time, Sean's words, meant just for her, brought tears to her eyes.

"Shh, sweetheart," he crooned. "Let the pain take you higher. You're going to fly when he lets you come."

He knew the sharp edge of pleasure, knew how it sliced yet hurt so damned good. Yes, she wanted to fly. Wanted to spin off into oblivion….

"Relax," he whispered once when she thought the frustration might take her away. His rough fingers stroked her neck, soothing and arousing. His hot breath on the shell of her ear was more erotic than the words he spoke.

"Feel his tongue, tasting, feasting on you. He can't get enough, sweetheart. You bring him to his knees. He worships at your feet. He loves you so."

Her heart wept, knowing the words were true. Bentley loved her, would do anything for her, even give up the love of another to make her happy.

"Come for him, sweetheart. Give yourself to him."

As if they'd choreographed their moves, her fiancé chose that moment to flick his tongue over her clit. He bit the throbbing nub, tugging and sucking as he speared her with his fingers. It was too much. It would never be enough. She lost her tenuous grip on reality. As the man holding her predicted, she flew—not the graceful flight of a dove, but the ungainly flight of a mechanical bird tumbling wing over wing in a downward spiral. She plummeted to earth at the speed of light, convulsing and weeping with the frightening beauty of it.

When she crashed, her men were there to catch her. Reduced to a boneless rag doll, she leaned against one then the other while they removed her clothes then laid her on the bed. Clothed, they lay beside her, touching and stroking. She should have felt self-conscious, naked in bed with two fully clothed men, but she didn't. Bentley had seen her countless times. After the way Sean held her, seemed to read her mind with his whispered words, his dedication to her pleasure, she felt as if he'd already seen inside her, and that was more important than seeing the outside.

"You okay?" Bentley peered down at her, one hand bracing him over her, the other resting low on her stomach, swirling, sending sparks of desire through her once again. The words were casually spoken, but he was asking about more than her physical status and they all knew it.

"Perfect," she replied, smiling weakly. "Never better."

"Ready for round two?"

She nodded. "Thank you."

His brows knit together in a frown. "For what?"

"For…everything." She felt too much to explain it. Maybe later, but for now, she wanted to return the favor. She turned her head to look at the new addition to their bed. He was lying on his good side, his cheek resting on his arm stretched above his head. The fingers of his other hand played with a lock of her hair.

"Your turn," she said.

He, too, rose up to look down on her. "Are you sure?" he asked.

She smiled. "I'm sure." She sat up, forcing the two men to scoot out of her way. With a symbolic shove to the chest, she pushed Sean out of the bed. "Come on, Bentley. I'll help you have your way with him."

The look on the newcomer's face was priceless—shock, fear, and lust. Her fiancé shuffled to his feet in front of his lover. She moved behind Sean. Standing on her tiptoes, she reached over his shoulder to loosen his tie. Bentley watched her slip the knot then free the top two buttons on his dress shirt. His eyes never left her hands.

"What now?" she asked her fiancé.

"Pull his shirttails out then unbutton his shirt from the bottom up."

Sean held his arms out wide. She wrapped hers around his waist, tugging the starched fabric from his waistband. When it hung loose all around, still behind him, she worked the fasteners free. With her cheek pressed against his back, she was aware of every ragged breath he took. She could only imagine what it felt like to have a woman prepare him to receive his lover.

She smiled to herself. It was fun, feeling the trembles wracking this powerful man when she parted his shirt.

Peeking around his broad shoulders, she glanced at Bentley for further instructions. His fists hung at his sides, his jaw looked carved of granite. She could practically see heat radiating off him as his chest rose and fell rapidly. He was holding it together by sheer willpower, much like Sean. When they came together, the collision would be explosive.

"His pants. Undo them."

Again, from behind, she freed his belt buckle. After that, the waistband fasteners and zipper were easy.

"Push them down, underwear, too. But not all the way. He can hold them up." His lips turned up on one side. "It'll give him something to do with his hands."

His fragile hold on sanity was slipping fast. Impulse or instinct or some such shit had propelled him into action when Bentley was undressing Ashley. Goddamn, but that had turned out to be about the hottest sexual encounter he'd ever experienced. The expression on his lover's face when he recognized what he was doing was priceless. Shock first, followed by lust and approval. He'd do damn near anything to see that look directed at him again.

Now, here he stood, small, feminine hands all over him, doing Bentley's bidding. The man had a thing about suits, no doubt about it. He was pretty damn sure he had another cleaning bill in his future, but he couldn't bring himself to care as long as the man gazed at him like a lion biding his time while his lioness prepared his prey. He was about to be eaten alive, and he couldn't be happier about it.

But when he expected Bentley to suck him off, the man instead beckoned the woman to him.

"Unzip me," he commanded. "Just the zipper, then take my

cock out."

He couldn't see what she was doing, but from the look on his lover's face, she was following instructions to the letter. Having completed the task, she stepped back.

"On your knees," he commanded her. "Take me in your mouth."

Oh, damn. His gaze followed her head as she dropped to her knees. He was able to catch a glimpse of Bentley's engorged cock before his fiancée opened her mouth to take him in.

With one hand on the top of her head, the other fisted at his waist, Bent kept his gaze locked on Sean's while she worked his cock over with long strokes and noisy, slurping sucking. Sean kept a death grip on his slacks, grateful for something to hold onto when what he wanted was to wrap his hand around his dick to find some relief.

Fuck you, Randolph.

As if he'd heard him, or read his mind, Bentley stayed his woman's attentions. "Enough." He pointed to the nightstand an arm's reach away. "Get a condom and put it on me."

As she stepped to the side, he got a good look at his lover's cock. It stood proud, wet. The color had deepened to purple from being sucked. It was all he could do not to fall to his knees and beg for a taste. It had been so long.

Sheathed, Bentley took his fiancée by the hand, leading her to stand behind Sean. Like a tender lover, he worked Sean's tie free of his collar then swung the tails over his shoulder. "Grab the ends," he said to his woman. "Pull on it so he doesn't look down."

She tugged on his tie. Bentley adjusted it so the loop rested just below his chin, forcing his face toward the ceiling. Her naked form pressed against his good side then a hot, wet mouth slid down the length of his cock, swallowing him whole and wrenching a string of curses from his lips.

"Fuck it—that feels good." His knees were jelly. His injured hip began to ache from holding himself under tight control for so long. He was dying to look—knew he'd see the top of Bentley's head, the hollows of his cheeks as he worked his cock in and out of his mouth.

A small, warm hand flattened over his heart, steeling the breath from his lungs. Then she began to talk to him.

"He looks so beautiful, loving you this way. It almost takes my breath away."

God, he knew the feeling, but he was still alive, more alive than he'd been in months. He supposed he must be breathing.

A hand between his legs forced him to let his pants slide a little farther down. Heat cradled his balls, rolled them around then tugged. *Ashley.* When had she moved her hand from his chest?

This must be heaven. Nothing on earth could feel this good. He'd give anything to see the two of them, loving him, taking and giving at the same time.

"You're beautiful." She must have stood on tiptoe to mumble the affirmation in his ear. A shiver skittered across his skin when she sucked his earlobe into her mouth to nibble on it.

Fuck. He bucked his hips, almost shoving his cock down Bent's throat, earning a sharp reprimand from the man. Wrapping one hand around the base of Sean's dick, he dug the other into his ass cheek and began an all-out assault on his sanity.

He was two heartbeats away from coming when the man stopped. Sean's knees buckled. He collapsed forward into his lover's arms. Bent eased him to his knees then pressed his face to the floor.

He put his hands out to brace himself. His belt buckle *thunked* against the carpet. Kneeling between his thighs, Bent tossed his suit coat and shirttails over the small of his back.

"Lube," he said to his female accomplice. A drawer opened and closed. Strong hands parted him. He hissed at the cold liquid dribbled between his cheeks.

Bentley entered him fast and hard. He closed his eyes in order to concentrate on breathing as the big cock demanded his submission. The first penetration, after so long, stung like a motherfucker, but after, he was able to focus on the beauty of giving himself fully to the man he loved.

Yes, Bent, yes. I'm yours. Fuck me. Yes, just like that.

A hand slipped beneath the clothes on his back, startling him out of his blissful revelry. Bent had managed to make him forget all about the other person in the room, but he was certain it was her, stroking along his spine, rubbing circles at the small of his back then up to his shoulder blades.

Heated breath caressed his cheek. He opened his eyes. Ashley was curled up on the floor beside him, almost nose to nose with him, one soft hand still on the small of his back.

"He possesses you, doesn't he? Just like he possesses me."

He sensed she wasn't expecting a response, which was good because he had none. He stared into her eyes, and felt a soul deep connection with her take root and blossom.

Good God, it had been too long since he'd seen Sean on his knees, but he was there, his ass in the air for the taking. Bent stripped off his clothing in record time then knelt between the man's thighs. It was tempting to take what he wanted without any preparation as punishment for his rejection. Seeing him, open and trusting was all the apology he needed. He wiggled his fingers, palm up at Ashley, requesting the lube.

Sean's hips jerked when the cold liquid hit his heated skin. He almost smiled, but the sight of his glistening asshole was no laughing matter. He looked into his fiancée's eyes. Smiling, she leaned in to kiss him on the mouth. With her beside him, her arm around his waist, he drove his cock deep inside his lover's ass.

Gritting his teeth, he threw his head back. It took every ounce of control he had to keep from coming right then. Ashley stood, wrapped herself around him, his back to her front. Her arms were bands of unconditional love binding his heart to her. "Love him, Bent. Love him the way he needs to be loved."

His chest felt so full he was sure it was going to explode any minute. He pulled almost all the way out then glided back in, smooth yet hard enough his balls slapped against Sean's. The contact reverberated throughout his body. It felt so damn good he did it again, and again. The man's submission humbled him. His fiancé's acceptance and love elevated him to a plane he never knew existed. Caught between his lovers, he was a king.

When she knelt beside him, reaching out to touch Sean's back with such tenderness, he almost drowned under the tsunami of emotions washing over him. He didn't deserve either one of them, but he'd be damned if he'd let either of them go. She lay down on the floor and spoke to his lover. He couldn't hear what she said over the blood rushing past his ears, but whatever it was, it seemed the man accepted it as truth.

A few moments later, she stroked her palm along Sean's jaw, causing him to open his eyes. Her lips moved as she spoke into his lover's ear. He'd give anything to hear the secret she shared with him. When she rose to her knees, a change came over his teammate's face. Before she leaned in to whisper in his ear, he knew what she wanted.

He'd been content to let Bentley have his release, knowing he could find his own later, but there was someone else to consider. Ashley wanted to see it all. Fucking Bentley would be no problem. He'd been aching hard for him since he'd walked into the house and announced his presence. The man had a voice that matched his body, sexy and powerful. His body responded to it without fail. It had caused him no shortage of problems since his arrival in Dallas.

Bent's fiancée was a remarkable woman. He'd had enough doubts to fill a stadium, but so far, she'd dispelled every one of them. There was only one left. How would she react to seeing her macho baseball playing man being fucked by another man?

He was about to see. Nerves skittered like a horde of crazed elves dancing with spiked cleats down his spine. As soon as his lover slipped out of him, he pushed to his knees. Ashley was there, offering her hand to help him stand, her other clasped in her fiancé's.

"I think the bed, this time," she said, pulling them both along with her. She laid back, her head on the pillows, her legs splayed. Bent stripped off the condom, tossing it in the wastebasket near the nightstand.

"Lube's there." He pointed to a plastic bottle with a flip-top cap sitting on the floor. Sean leaned down to pick it up. When he straightened, Bent was between her legs, sliding into her.

He watched for a few minutes, taking his dick in hand, stroking to match the rhythm of the couple on the bed. Desperation clawed at his gut, but he understood women took longer to peak than men. He'd give the guy a little more time, because *he* sure as hell wasn't going to last long. He'd probably erupt like Mt. Vesuvius as soon as he was inside Bent's tight channel. It had been too long a wait. He was so fucking horny it was a wonder he hadn't actually sprouted a few.

Damn, she was something. He'd been with a few women, back in his denial days. None of them had looked like she did during sex. Bent was good with her, gentle, but his technique was firm, leaving no doubt as to who was in charge. He seemed to know just how to move to coax helpless little moans of pleasure from her. She was writhing beneath him, her head thrown back, her eyes closed when Bent nodded at him.

He took the hint, moving behind him on the bed. He smiled at his lover's hissed curse when the cold lube hit his ass. *Payback's a bitch.*

Waiting was a bitch, too. At last, Bent growled out, "Now!"

Positioning the head of his cock, Sean rode the wave of Bent's hips once before thrusting deep just as the other man sank into his fiancée. Pleasure blinded him for the span of a heartbeat then he realized the two people beneath him were both moaning. Her with frustration at having been close, the momentum interrupted. Him at the intrusion of Sean's cock.

"Fuck. I forgot how goddamn big you are," he said over his shoulder. Braced on his hands over his fiancée, Bent's head dropped between his shoulder blades. It felt to fuckin' good to be inside him. He wasn't in the mood to hear any complaints. The asshole could fucking whine when they were through.

"Shut the fuck up," he said, retreating then slamming back in as hard as he dared with the woman on the bottom.

"Bent." Her voice was soft, laced with concern. One arm was raised over her head in surrender, the other extended toward him, her hand caressing his cheek. "Are you okay?"

"Fine." The word sounded like it had been dragged over ground glass before it made it past his lips. "I'm okay," he said, breathless this time. "It feels good. Really good. Both of you."

Sean took the words as his cue to continue. *Fuckin' right it feels good.*

Conversation ended there. Bent found Sean's rhythm, and Ashley found Bent's. It wasn't long before feminine gasps and groans, signaled her release, followed by a hissed curse from the man in the middle. He'd heard that a time or two—hoped he'd hear it a few thousand more. He gave in to his own raging need. Thrusting hard several more times, he came, filling his lover's ass with hot cum.

They toppled onto the bed like a domino tower with the foundation knocked out from under it. He landed on one side of Ashley, Bent on the other. He closed his eyes in order to focus on breathing. His hip hurt like a bitch, but he wasn't worried about the pain. He was just using the muscles in a way they hadn't been used in months. It would get better—with practice.

It was the practice that worried him. He'd had great sex before—with Bent. But today? Fucking mind-blowing. Over the top. He couldn't say it would always be this good for them, but he damn sure wanted to find out. It might take years of research, but he was up for it. The question was, were Bent, and especially, Ashley, on the same page? He didn't dare ask.

He was pretty sure he wouldn't pass out from lack of oxygen

to his brain if he sat up.

With a sigh, she lifted both her arms over her head. "I never knew how beautiful making love could be." She rolled his direction. He turned his head to look at her.

"You do love him, don't you?" she asked.

No words came. He simply couldn't respond. Bentley owned him, body and soul.

"Yeah, that's the way I feel sometimes, too." She sighed again then rolled to her back. "No words, except, when can we do it again?"

ABOUT THE AUTHOR

USA Today Best-Selling author Roz Lee is the author of over thirty romances. The first, The Lust Boat, was born of an idea acquired while on a Caribbean cruise with her family, and soon blossomed into a five-book series originally published by Red Sage. Following her love of baseball, Roz turned her attention to sexy athletes in tight pants, writing the critically acclaimed Mustangs Baseball series.

Roz has been married to her best friend, and high school sweetheart, for over four decades. They have two daughters and are the proud grandparents of three adorable grandkids. Roz and her husband live in the wilds of New Jersey with their Labrador Retriever, Bud which is code for Big Unruly Dog.

Even though Roz has lived on both coasts, her heart lies in between, in Texas. A Texan by birth, she can trace her family back to the Republic of Texas. With roots that deep, she says, "You can't ever really leave."

When Roz isn't writing, she's reading or traipsing around the country on one adventure or another. No trip is too small, no tourist trap too cheesy, and no road unworthy of travel.

www.RozLee.net